EMMA SPARROW

'Do you enjoy your job here, Emma?' He could at least ask that.

'It's a job, sir.' Emma sat down in front of the circular machine and picked up a jacket.

'But that's all?'

She took a length of silk braid, her head lowered as she fed it into the machine.

'It brings in quite good money.'

'And that is all-important?'

'As a matter of fact, it is, sir.'

'But what about job satisfaction?' He was making a fool of himself. He could feel the other machinists watching them carefully. 'Surely these days . . .?'

'If you will watch me now, sir.'

Emma Sparrow was deliberately ignoring him, and Simon stepped back as smartly as if she had slapped him across the face.

Also in Arrow by Marie Joseph

MAGGIE CRAIG
A LEAF IN THE WIND
FOOTSTEPS IN THE PARK
GEMINI GIRLS

Non-fiction
ONE STEP AT A TIME

Emma Sparrow

MARIE JOSEPH

This book
belongs to

....

Arrow Books Limited
17-21 Conway Street, London W1P 6JD

An imprint of the Hutchinson Publishing Group

London Melbourne Sydney Auckland
Johannesburg and agencies
throughout the world

First published by Hutchinson 1981
Arrow edition 1982
Reprinted 1982 (twice) and 1983

Made and printed in Great Britain by
Anchor Brendon Ltd, Tiptree, Essex

ISBN 0 09 928310 7

One

It was blouses that week, so the buttonholes were being made on the machine, not bound as they were for the dresses and jackets. Emma Sparrow manoeuvred the satin-look material into position beneath the foot, guided it carefully and swiftly round the pencilled outline, then moved onto the next.

She knew she was going to cop it for being late for work that morning, so when the summons came to take the long walk to the office, past the rows of electric sewing machines, past the cutting tables and the ironing boards set in a long row, one behind the other, she showed no surprise.

Harry Gordon, manager of Delta Dresses Limited, was a stickler for punctuality, and being late two mornings together was a crime he would never overlook. Excuses cut no ice with him either, so it was no use Emma telling him that both her stepbrothers were sick and sorry for themselves with mumps, or that Sharon, her stepsister, had refused to get out of bed. Or that her father had gone grumbling out of the house because his breakfast hadn't been ready on time.

'My heart bleeds for you, lass.' That was all Mr Gordon would say if she was daft enough to tout for sympathy.

'This happens to be a clothing factory, not the bloody Civil Service,' he had said last time. Then just for a minute, but only for a minute, his expression had softened. 'I've heard as how you are up against it at home, love, but rules is rules. Time means money. That is why we have that clocking-in machine up on the wall, and as you rightly know, clocking-in time is eight-fifteen, not eight-thirty.' He had wagged a fat forefinger at Emma. 'Don't you go forgetting it now. I could have another lass with her behind on your stool quicker than

5

skinning a black pudding.'

Emma opened the door of the glass-fronted office and went inside. Mrs Kelly, the clerk-typist, nudging sixty but admitting only to forty-five, stopped typing to wink kindly, but over by the window, behind his own large and cluttered desk, Mr Harry Gordon did not even bother to look up. Emma stared at the top of his head where a bald patch showed as round and pink as a baby's bottom. Harry Gordon was a fair-minded man, but with eighty girls in his employ he had developed an immunity to hard-luck stories. 'Soft soaping' he called them. So Emma stood before him, head bowed, waiting philosophically for what must be.

It had been one o'clock that morning before Sharon had come in, glowing rosily from riding home on the back of her boyfriend's motorcycle. Emma tried to smother a yawn. Being a substitute mother to a sixteen-year-old rebel was a waste of time; Sharon took no notice of anybody.

Some days, like today, Emma had a desperate longing to run away from everything. Out of the little house in Litchfield Avenue, running as fast as she could away from the responsibility that was at times too much to bear. A longing to tell the lot of them – Alan, Joe, Sharon and her father – that it was time they tried to fend for themselves and stopped leaning on her. That at twenty she was unequal to the task of taking the place of her stepmother, killed two years ago crossing the street in the dark on her way home from work by a driver who hadn't even bothered to stop.

Life being what it was, Emma guessed that most of the girls in the factory were up against it in some way or other. A third of the workforce was Pakistani, part of the twenty per cent making up the population of the Lancashire cotton town. Not that there was any racial discrimination. Emma had to admit that Mr Gordon treated all his girls with scrupulous fairness.

'Religion, colour, politics, creed, makes no difference to Harry Gordon,' he was fond of saying. 'What matters is getting the stuff out on time, nowt else. So there's no need for bloody chips on bloody shoulders here. There's more prejudice in the bloody United Nations than what there is here!'

'Ah. Emma Sparrow,' he said at last, shifting a slim cigar from one side of his mouth to the other. 'Aye, well, what have you to say for yourself this time?' He turned his head to a strange man sitting silently at the corner of the desk. 'Won't be a minute, Mr Martin, though I'm not exactly deviating from what we were talking about. Punctuality is all part of the set-up, and what I have to say won't take long.'

Emma glanced briefly at the man, then as quickly away. Mr Martin. Mr Bernard Martin. Managing director of Delta Dresses. So this must be – this was almost sure to be his son. Managerial type anyway, sitting there in his dark suit, with a striped tie neatly knotted over a shirt of a spanking brilliant white. About thirty or a bit more, and when he spoke Emma placed him immediately as coming from down south. London. From Head Office maybe, or from their sister factory on the outskirts of Acton. Not top drawer, but certainly from the middle, with money behind him and the privileges that came with it. Not cockney, but not public school either. Confident and sure of himself, and amused, if the twinkle in his eyes was anything to go by.

Emma did not realize that her quick ear for a tune and her accurate ear for the geographical placing of an accent were synonymous. What she did realize was that the presence of this man was causing Mr Gordon to show off, to parade his authority, and to hide his usual benevolence.

'I'm not a hard man, Emma.' Mr Gordon was speaking at her but not to her. 'Never say that. Nobody could say this place was run like one of them sweat shops in Victorian days. You all get proper tea-breaks and a good bonus at Christmas, plus the two paid weeks in July.' He threw a ball-point pen down on the desk with a sudden show of impatience. 'But getting in late I won't stand for. Dammit, lass, you're nowt but a young whippersnapper! Why, at your age I'd done a paper round and cleaned my father's car before breakfast. At younger than what you are. How old *are* you, Emma?'

'Twenty, Mr Gordon.' Emma stared down at the floor. 'I am really sorry. It won't happen again, I promise.'

She liked Mr Harry Gordon, and if he wanted to show this London bloke how he ruled his employees with an iron fist then she was prepared to sound as penitent as possible. What she wasn't prepared for was the way he suddenly stubbed out the cigar, jumped to his feet and leaned over the desk, pointing an angry finger at her, jabbing the air to emphasize his words.

'Once more, lass. Just one more late card, and that's it! Finished! Out! With a reference that won't get you a job sweeping the street. Is that clear? Is that perfectly clear, Emma Sparrow?'

He was shouting so loudly that Emma backed away, nodding her head before escaping from the office and running back to her machine.

In a right state he was, she muttered as she switched on. An' all because of the dark bloke with the lazy twinkle in his eyes sitting there in judgement. Emma reached for another blouse and slid the right-hand button trim underneath the foot, the tip of her tongue protruding slightly as she guided the trim into position.

So the rumours going round about the Lancashire branch of the firm doing badly could be right. She shot a quick glance at the rows of heads bent in concentration over the sewing machines ranked either side of the long table. At the busy fingers pulling the material backwards and forwards, twisting, stopping, breaking off threads and starting again.

What would happen to all these girls if the factory were to close?

Her own father had been a small boy at the time of the Depression, but he was for ever telling how his parents used to describe the early days of *their* marriage.

'They lived not one week ahead, but one *meal* ahead,' he would say when Sharon grumbled at having to hand over six pounds a week. 'Raw onions many a time for their dinner. Just an onion dipped in salt, and lucky to get that at times. So don't talk to me about being hard up. Nay, being hard up means being hungry, not sitting watching colour telly and spending money on frozen stuff tipped out of packets and shoved under a grill. Nourishing soups they had, made from marrow bones stewed till the stock set like jelly, and rice puddings that gave you a layer to your stomach, aye, and ox-tail stew so thick you could have made a poultice out of it. . . .'

Emma pushed a strand of brown hair away from her face. One thing about this job – it did mean she could let her thoughts wander. She could switch on, switch off, press the pedal, release the pedal, all with the same automatic rhythm as if she were an extension of the machine. Leaving her mind free. It was no use making excuses to a man, to any man. If things went wrong, they always found a woman in the background to blame somehow. Blaming women boosted men's flagging egos. It would never occur to her father that his daughter didn't have the time to stew marrow bones till they set to flamin' jelly. Emma tried to blow the wayward piece of hair out of her eyes. An' it was a good job she wasn't martyr material either. Not for her the injured silences, the hurt withdrawals, the quivering lips. She smiled to herself. Aye, life was what it was, flamin' awful at times, and there was nothing to do but just get on with it and hope that some fine day the scales balanced in your favour. *If* you were lucky. . . .

Mrs Arkwright, the supervisor, a neat woman who just missed being pretty, dumped a pile of blouses on to Emma's table. Automatically Emma reached for the top one, her thoughts still far away. She frowned. Take Ben Bamford now, her boyfriend. He was just as bad. *Blaming* her because she wouldn't go out with him every night. Men were all the same.

'Why don't you just let them get on with it?' Ben would grumble. 'Tell them you have your own life to lead. It's not your fault your dad married an ailing woman. She'd never have got run over if she'd been a bit nippier on her feet.'

'That's cruel!' Emma had been horrified. 'She had rheumatism bad, yet she used to go to work when she could hardly crawl. You're not blaming her for getting herself killed, Ben Bamford. Surely?'

There it was again. Blaming, always blaming.

Ben blamed his sister Patty for the mess she'd made of her life, but he still lived with her, and her man of the moment. Waited on hand and foot, Emma told herself, by Patty who, because she was a woman, had got the wrong end of the stick again.

She reached for yet another blouse, pushed her hair back behind an ear, then guided the material into the exact position, her face as pale as the ivory satin-look material slipping through her fingers.

Emma Sparrow of Litchfield Avenue. . . . A bonny girl, of average height, with long, silky, brown hair tied back during the day with a narrow velvet ribbon, or even with a rubber-

9

band at times. A bonny girl with brown eyes amber-flecked, and bright with an untutored intelligence.

If she had not believed that the soul could transcend its environment, she would have given up long ago. She knew that most people were victims of circumstance and, clinging to this, she accepted the drabness of her life and the boredom of her job, not with resignation, but with the optimistic surety that some day, somehow, things would get better.

At exactly twelve o'clock she switched off her machine and got down stiffly from her stool to join the rest of the girls on their way down to the canteen.

Delta Dresses took up the whole of the top floor of the tall Victorian red-brick building. The packing and dispatching department was down in the basement, and it was there Ben Bamford worked at the moment, using the job, Emma knew, as a temporary stopgap before moving on to something else.

He was waiting for her at their usual table, drinking coffee, eating a meat-pie, calling out to the men at the next table, laughing, throwing his head back when he laughed as if he were coming apart at the seams. A carefree young man of twenty-two, popular and admired, followed around by the more reserved types who basked in the aura of gaiety that surrounded him.

'Two!' he called after Emma as she joined the queue for coffee, and she nodded and smiled and did exactly as he asked. It was no good coming women's lib with Ben. She had tried that more than once, and he had thought she was joking.

When she set the two coffees down on the table he jerked his head in the direction of the tall windows.

'Seen the gaffer's son from London? Group accountant he's supposed to be – at least that's his title, but I know better.' He lit a cigarette. 'A snooper, that's what he is. He's come up here to check that Big Daddy down there is getting his money's worth out of us peasants. Have us lot down the salt mines if they had any round here, he would.'

'Oh, Ben. . . .' Emma opened a packet of biscuits and passed it over. 'I didn't have time to bring sandwiches this morning. I was late again, and Mr Gordon threatened me with the sack if I didn't pull my socks up, an' he meant it too.'

Ben pulled a face as the scalding hot coffee stung his mouth.

'Get one of your mates to clock-in for you, Em. There's always a way if you know how.' He tapped the side of his forehead. 'We're the bosses now, girl. Not them. One more threat like that from old Gordon, and you complain to your union. Then if they called the lot out, where would old Duck's Arse be?' He turned round. 'Just look at the two of them, queueing up for a meat-pie and coffee, trying to make out they are just like us. They'll never be like us, Em, you know that.'

'That's stupid, Ben.' Emma curled her hands round the thick white cup. 'Mrs Kelly told me once that old Mr Martin started with a stall in a street market after the war.' She glanced over to where the two men were carrying trays to a vacant table. 'An' if Mr Martin is an accountant, then he's worked hard to get his qualifications. Anyway, he was on my side when Mr Gordon was ticking me off. He didn't say anything, but I could tell. He's worked his way from the bottom up, he has.'

'And bottoms up to you, Em.' Ben grinned, lifting his cup and toasting her. 'Pick you up at seven tonight. Okay?'

'No.' Emma shook her head so that the skewered pony-tail did a little dance. 'Not tonight. The boys are really poorly, and there's a pile of ironing as high as the ceiling. No, I can't come out tonight.'

'Bloody hell!' Ben pushed the cup aside. 'Get your Sharon to do the bloody ironing. She's not exactly run off her feet working behind the sweets counter at bloody Woolworth's. Tell *her* to stay in for once. Force her to pull her weight, Em.'

'Me? Force *Sharon* to do anything she doesn't want to? That would be the day.' Emma sighed. 'It wouldn't be so bad if our dad backed me up, but all he does is sleep in front of the telly after he's had his tea. His chest's that bad he has to sleep sitting up now, but will he see a doctor? Ben . . . I can't keep on at them all the time, can I?'

Simon Martin, drinking his canteen coffee, found himself stealing glances at the girl Emma Sparrow, sitting with the curly-headed fair boy. He had decided earlier on in the office that here was a girl who was not merely pretty, but almost beautiful. Her brown eyes were the eyes of a trusting child, and there was a touching vulnerability about her, a delicate awareness.

11

'Never spoilt a garment yet,' Mr Gordon had told him. 'And she's not cheeky with it like some of them.' Then he had seemed to remember his position of authority. 'But you can't let them get away with lateness. Give them an inch and they'll take a yard.'

The fair boy was leaning across the table now, taking Emma's hand in his own, running his finger round the inside of her wrist and whispering. There was a sensual intimacy in the gesture, and Simon looked quickly away, but out of the corner of his eye he saw how Emma snatched her hand away and how the fair boy was no longer laughing.

'I've got it bad for you,' Ben was saying. 'But let's get one thing straight. I'm not used to birds who play the hard-to-get game. If you won't come out with me tonight, then there's plenty who will.' He jerked his head towards a table where a group of young machinists giggled together. 'Young carrot-top there. She won't say no. Not to anything she won't say no.'

'Oh, Ben.' Emma kept her voice low. 'You *know* I'm not as free as they are. On top of the hours I work here I've got everything to do at home. I couldn't come out every night, even if I wanted to.'

'Hah!' Ben's good-looking face set into sulky annoyance. 'Look, Em, we're not a couple of kids playing at courting. A cuddle in a doorway doesn't do a thing for me.' His face flushed pink. 'I got over that lark when I was fourteen. Are you my girl, or aren't you?' He stubbed out his cigarette. 'You're not a kid, Emma Sparrow. I won't let you come to no harm. Bloody hell, our Patty was on the pill when she was fifteen! If that's what you're frightened of, why don't you go down the clinic? They don't ask questions. They just think you're being a responsible citizen, they do.'

'Hush!' Emma's face was red with embarrassment. 'Stop talking about that here, Ben Bamford! Suppose somebody heard?'

'Come out with me tonight. *Sleep* with me tonight,' Ben said clearly, narrowing his blue eyes and reaching for her hand again. 'You know what you are, don't you? There are two words for what you are.'

'Don't say them!' Emma pushed back her chair and stood

12

up. 'You've called me that before, an' it's not true. It's a terrible thing to say!'

Ben, looking like an angel with his golden curls and his round blue eyes, stared straight at her and said it. Slowly and deliberately, not too loud but loud enough to be heard by his mates at the next table.

With their laughter ringing in her ears, Emma turned and almost ran from the canteen, tears of humiliation and shame pricking behind her eyes.

And watching her go, wondering what the fair boy could have said to distress her so, Simon Martin felt an illogical urge to leap to his feet and seize Ben by the scruff of his neck, lifting him till his feet swung clear of the floor.

'You were saying, Mr Gordon?' He composed his face into a listening expression. 'I have a feeling the discrepancies may lie in the distribution. Could you give me the name of the local transport firm you use, once again? I think I'll call at their offices this afternoon.'

Simon Martin was a typical product of the now almost defunct grammar school. Captain of rugger, sixth form prefect, he had left with three A levels, bummed it around Europe for a year, then gone straight into his father's firm. His accountancy examinations had been taken through a concentrated correspondence course, and the paper qualifications had pleased his father, a self-made man who had started a market stall with his gratuity after serving six years in the army, mostly in the Middle East.

Not exactly a whizz kid, Simon Martin had an inborn air of assurance, of confidence, of knowing what to say at the right time and exactly how to say it. Not good-looking in a stereotyped kind of way – his eyes were too deep-set and his nose too hawk-like for that. He had married at twenty-six, been divorced at twenty-eight, and was now sharing a one-bedroomed flat in Maida Vale with a girl called Chloe.

He had never said in so many words that he would not marry again, but when he did, and *if* he did, it would have to be right. And for the time being anyway, Chloe seemed to be quite happy with the way things were.

The first thing he did when he got back to the hotel that evening was to pick up the telephone by the side of his bed and dial the number of the London flat. He was wrenching off his tie as he listened to the ringing tone, unfastening the top button of his white shirt, dying for a cigarette, and wishing for the hundredth time that he hadn't been so firm about stopping smoking six months before.

He heard the ringing tone, and saw in his mind's eye the two-toned telephone on the low coffee table in front of the leather chair by the bookshelves. He knew that Chloe would be in from her job as bilingual secretary to the financial director of an export firm in the City. The flat was so tiny that with all the doors open it was possible to see into the cupboard-cum-kitchen and the bedroom leading into the windowless bathroom with its avocado tiles and shower unit.

'Come on, love,' he muttered. 'Where are you?'

He sat down on the edge of the bed and stared at the bible on the lower shelf of the bedside locker. He wondered if any of the hotel's guests ever got around to reading it, and tried to remember the last time he had even held one in his hands.

Some day he would tell Chloe how he sang in a church choir as a soprano with a white ruffle round his neck, he told himself, then shifted the handset to his other hand as the ringing tone went on and on.

There was no telephone in the house where Emma lived. Once, when her father had been in regular employment for a few years, they had one installed, but it was hardly used, and when the bills stayed unpaid the telephone company sent an engineer to take it away.

The house was on an estate, built in the fifties from the debris of rows of terraced houses, an identical twin to its semi-detached neighbour, an echo of each pair in the long winding avenue.

When Emma got in from work that evening, John Sparrow was sitting in his usual chair by the electric fire, with all three bars full on, coughing through his twentieth cigarette of the day, staring gloomily at the television. The announcer's face was a vivid orange shade, his shirt a bright yellow, and he

14

appeared to be sitting in a snowstorm, but it had been like that for so long that nobody seemed to notice anything was amiss.

At right angles to his chair the two boys, Alan and Joe, both in the acute stage of mumps, sat close together on a settee with a faded moquette cover, their faces and necks swollen to such proportions that their heads seemed to grow straight from their shoulders. They were gazing at the screen through eyes sunk into feverish slits.

Emma went through into the kitchen and saw without surprise that the stainless-steel sink was piled high with plates and cups. She stood in the doorway and addressed the backs of three unresponsive heads.

'Where's Sharon?'

'Upstairs getting ready.' Her father said this without moving his head a fraction, the only movement about him being the spiral of smoke ascending from his cigarette.

'She might have put the kettle on.' Emma went back into the kitchen, pushed the sleeves of her green sweater up to her elbows and turned on the hot tap. The frustrated rage that sometimes caught her unawares rose up, revealing itself by the way she clattered the cups on to the draining-board. Then her natural sense of the ridiculous asserted itself. 'Learn to co-operate with the inevitable.' Where had she read that? She couldn't remember, but if fitted. Oh, yes, it fitted all right.

Women's suffrage had been supposed to put a stop to inequality. Chinese women no longer had their feet wrapped up, but because she was the only woman in the family, apart from Sharon dolling herself up upstairs, it was taken for granted that *she* would see to the house. Alan was ten and Joe was eight, but already they were accepting the roles they considered life had fitted them for. Emma remembered her stepmother shuffling round the kitchen on swollen feet, handing her husband his pot of tea.

'Sugar in, love?' he would say. 'Stirred?'

Emma opened a large-sized packet of beefburgers, laid them in rows underneath the grill, set a tray of 'oven-ready' chips into the cooker, then shook frozen peas into a pan of boiling water. So much for marrow bones stewed till they set into jelly, and rice puddings cooked slowly with the nutmeg settling into a brown toffee crust on top.

15

'Do you think you can manage to eat anything?' she asked the silent viewing pair on the settee, and two thick necks inclined slightly forward in the affirmative.

After checking that everything was boiling, grilling and heating up at the same time, Emma ran lightly upstairs.

'You might at least have tidied the kitchen, our Sharon.'

The small fair girl applying eye make-up in front of the dressing-table mirror winced as the mascara brush caught the corner of an eye. At sixteen, Sharon had the delicate prettiness of a cameo, with a figure that belied the stodge she was forced to eat.

'There's a ladder in your tights,' Emma told her, and she whirled round to see.

'Shit!' she said, and the word exploding from the rosebud mouth sounded so incongruous that Emma burst out laughing.

'Well, that makes a change from "flaminenry", but love, do you *have* to go out tonight? Alan's been sick in bed, so there are his sheets to do, then there's the ironing, and I promised myself I would at least try to tidy the bedrooms.'

Emma pulled at the ribbon holding her hair back, then pushed the long fall of brown hair behind her ears. 'I don't mean to nag, love, but I can't . . . I can't do it all. And Dad's been drinking again. I can smell it on him, and where does he get the stuff from, for Pete's sake? And what time did he come home from work? He looks as if he's been sitting in that chair all day.'

Sharon was examining her young face critically in the mirror again.

'Oh, why do I always get a flamin' spot on my chin when I'm going somewhere special? I look awful, and don't tell me I don't because I do.' She unscrewed a tube of cream and dabbed at the almost invisible spot. 'It's not with eating the sweets at work because I never do.' She applied more cream, rubbing it in with her little finger. 'A woman came in today and bought three pounds of caramels. Just imagine! Three flamin' pounds of caramels, an' she wasn't spotty. Fat, but not spotty.'

'Where *are* you going, Sharon?'

Emma sat down on the edge of the double bed, pushing

aside a tangled collection of tights, bras and tiny briefs. 'How old is he, this Ricky? Does he know you are only sixteen? Why don't you bring him in and let us have a look at him?'

'We're going out Bolton way to a sporting club. We're soon there on the bike.'

Sharon turned round, as pretty as a Victorian doll in a lace-trimmed box, her small breasts straining against the ribbed pattern of the too-tight sweater dress.

'Oh, for crying out loud, don't look like that, our Emma. I always wear a helmet. Ricky's got one specially. He's nice, honest he is.' She pouted. 'Oh, flaminenry, I know I am mean. I can *feel* myself being mean. I don't like myself all that much.' She came and pressed her lips against Emma's cheek, leaving the imprint of a perfect cupid's bow. 'An' I know I look like a punk or a tart, but Ricky *likes* me this way. I just want to have *fun*, can't you see? Soon I'll be getting married, then I'll be like Mam was, slopping around in slippers with kids yelling, and nappies soaking in a bucket.'

'Married!' Emma got up quickly and backed towards the door. 'You have to be joking! You've got years and years before you need to think about getting *married*. I haven't given up hope myself yet!'

Downstairs, she served the silent trio round the television, eating her own meal with Sharon at the kitchen table, a table that was no more than a flap let down from the wall. She saw the way Sharon kept turning her head, obviously listening for the sound of a motorbike in the road outside, and the way her hand holding her fork trembled a little as she raised the food to her mouth.

Emma tried to remember the way she had been at sixteen, but it seemed a lifetime ago, not four short years. She had been a *child* at that age, surely? A thin child in a navy-blue skirt and blue blouse, walking home through the park with her books in a plastic bag, that being the only acceptable way to carry them that year.

Boys? Oh, they had been around of course, but her attitude to them had been one of disgust, especially when they whistled at her. She had taught herself to walk stiffly without wiggling her behind, and she had grown her hair long so that it covered her face.

But even then the boys had always seemed to win. With monster bikes bought on their dads' credit cards, tearing round the roads as if to show that the whole world belonged to them. And they didn't have the curse either. Emma rubbed the small of her back and, as the front door slammed behind Sharon's flying figure, got on with the washing-up.

Next time round she was going to be a fella, she told herself. Definitely.

Simon Martin rang his Chloe again after dinner, getting no reply, then worked steadily on the papers brought from the factory until ten o'clock. Then he went downstairs to the bar and ordered a whisky and soda from a barmaid who looked as if she had materialized from a strip cartoon – high-piled hair tortured into intricate swirls, scarlet jersey-top showing rounded breasts in imminent danger of popping out of the neckline, and eyelashes sticky and beaded with navy-blue mascara. Simon warmed to her at once.

The lounge bar was fairly crowded, but as nobody was buying rounds at that moment, Simon went into what Chloe would have called his 'chatting-up routine'.

'A bit on the quiet side tonight?'

The barmaid leaned across the counter, causing Simon to draw in his breath sharply. 'Yes, sir. This is allus a slack night. Must be summat good on the telly.' She smiled, showing teeth like ivory piano keys. 'There's nowt keeps them out quicker than a serial on about royalty. Specially if it rakes a bit of muck up. If somebody wrote one about Prince Andrew's sex life it would clear this place out quicker than what a dose of salts would.' She jerked her head in the direction of a table in the corner. 'And that lot's not drinking bitter lemons either, and I should know because one of them's my brother. That one snogging with the girl with red hair.' She sniffed. 'Find the money to spend like it grows on trees our Ben can, but ask him to give me his money of a Friday, and it's like trying to get it from a Jew with no arms.'

She glanced at Simon's black hair and aquiline features and clapped a hand to her mouth. 'Trust me, sir. I hope I haven't put my big foot in it.'

18

Simon laughed, turned and recognized the fair boy he had seen arguing with the girl Emma Sparrow in the factory canteen at lunchtime. Ben was nuzzling his chin into the neck of the red-haired girl, pretending to be unfastening the buttons of her blouse.

'That your brother, then?' Simon turned back to the bar.

'For my sins. He lives with me, and oh, he's all right, really.' She wiped invisible spillage from the counter. 'You don't come from these parts, do you, sir?'

Simon shook his head. 'Another whisky please, and get one for yourself.'

'Ta very much.' Patty Bamford, unmarried mother of a mongol girl of four, now living with a man who knocked her about when he drank too much, went reluctantly to serve a customer at the far end of the bar.

Her face, washed once a day, with blusher rubbed into the cheek bones almost every hour, was as clear and unblemished as if she spent a small fortune keeping it so. Her eyes were bright blue, bold eyes, but lowered now as she poured herself a ginger ale.

'There goes a real gentleman,' she was telling herself, stealing a sideways glance at Simon as he sipped his drink. Not like her brother or the fella she was living with. Posh, not too posh, but with a twinkle in his eye all the same.

Patty reached for a cigarette, the blue eyes suddenly bleak. An' if she thought she stood half a chance she'd be twinkling right back at him. She would that an' all.

When Simon finally got to bed there was still no reply from the flat down in Maida Vale. And when he rang first thing in the morning, there was still no reply.

So Chloe had stayed out all night. . . . Well, he had no hold over her, and it was a free country.

Simon was waiting for the lift to take him up to Delta Dresses when Emma Sparrow came round the corner, cheeks flushed and brown eyes anguished above a long white knitted scarf wound twice round her throat.

'Have you got the time, sir? Please?' She held a hand to her side. 'Got a stitch with running. The bus went past full and

19

I've run all the way.'

'Ten past eight.' Simon pressed the bell and waited for the sign to operate, but nothing happened. He pressed it again.

'Oh, no! It sticks sometimes if somebody at the top doesn't shut the doors properly.' Her words came out in breathless ragged jerks. 'Excuse me, sir, but I'll have to run up the stairs.'

'Stay where you are!' Simon demanded over a disappearing shoulder. 'You can't run up four flights of stairs in that state. Stay right there!'

The stairs were steep and uncarpeted, but he took them two at a time, and as she had said the lift was there on the top floor with the doors open. He stepped quickly inside, and as it reached the ground floor and the doors opened, he almost pulled Emma inside.

'Pipped at least ten people on the way up,' he told her. 'Must be all that running I've been doing in Regent's Park.'

Emma smiled briefly. She was still as taut as a violin string, standing there with her eyes raised as if she would will the lift to go faster.

'Thank you, sir.' She spoke without looking at him. 'That was a very kind thing to do, sir.'

For a startled moment Simon thought she was going to cry. He couldn't take his eyes from her. He rubbed his chin thoughtfully. There was something about this factory girl that reached right out to his emotions. Vulnerable, that was the word. Vulnerable and yet somehow fierce. Determination was in the line of her lifted chin, and he wanted to tell her that even if she had been a minute or two late he would have seen that it didn't matter.

He found himself wanting to stretch out a hand to her, to tell her that nothing in the world was worth the terrible anxiety he could almost feel emanating from her tense little body.

'It's not just the fear of being late, is it, Emma Sparrow?' he wanted to say. 'Why don't you tell me what's wrong?'

And if he had, how foolish he would have been. He had never been on a management course but the first thing his father had taught him was that the gulf between management and staff can on occasions be narrowed, but never crossed.

'Thank you, sir.' Emma rushed forward as the lift doors

20

opened, one hand already extended to the clocking-in machine on the wall outside the glass-fronted office.

Not one of them had got up that morning. Not the boys, still sick and sorry for themselves, but not too sick to eat the toast she had carried upstairs. Not Sharon, who lay humped over to her side of the double bed refusing to budge, nor her father, leaning on one elbow and coughing through the inevitable cigarette.

'You'll lose your job, Dad.'

Emma felt a twinge of shame now for the way she had stood there, bullying, shouting, hearing her voice shouting and not being able to stop herself. 'You've had so much time off, they'll sack you, and then where will you go?'

'There's other firms wanting drivers.' John Sparrow drew smoke down into his lungs, then coughed till his eyes ran tears. 'Besides, I got the sack anyroad. Sent me home yesterday.' He held the cigarette neatly between finger and thumb, staring down at it morosely as if regretting the loss of the inch he had smoked.

'Dad!' Emma had dug her nails into the palms of her hands to stop them snatching the burning cigarette from him and stubbing it out in the big glass ashtray by the side of his bed. 'You can't have lost that job! Not already! Not after them taking you on knowing you had a record? And why do you smoke when you must know it's killing you? Why?'

She had closed her mind against the pathetic, drooping, gasping little man, with his pyjama jacket buttoned up to his chin, and his brown hair sticking up at the back in an untidy tuft. How could she possibly love this weak, snivelling little man who lost one job after another? A father who spent money that should have gone on food and clothes on cigarettes and drink? How could she retain the slightest feeling for him, let alone experience this abiding love that sometimes ached through her body like a physical pain?

'*Why* did they give you the sack, Dad? You've not been pinching again? You wouldn't be such a fool, *would* you?'

With one eye on the alarm clock ticking away, she still had to ask that.

His glance shifted away from her. 'Too long a story now, love. I'll tell you about it tonight, eh?' His eyes followed hers to the clock. 'You'll have to buck up if you don't want to be late. That clock's a good five minutes slow, and you know what the buses are like this time of a morning. Come when they feel like it. They have card schools down at the depot, that's why there's two come together with long waits in between.'

'Oh, Dad. . . .'

Emma pushed the wayward strand of hair behind an ear and reached for another blouse. He really thought he was being kind and considerate reminding her it was time to get off to work. He took it for granted that when he opted out, *she* would be the breadwinner.

And *why* had he lost another job? There had been something in his face . . . shame she would have called it if she hadn't known him better. The usual reason was that the job was too demanding, too hard, too shut in, too heavy. But this time he had not been asked to do long-distance trucking. This time, because of the letter from the Welfare, the work had been local, light and reasonably well paid. So why? With one fine, and one suspended sentence behind him. Surely? No! He'd promised, with tears in his eyes.

'We do the blouses on the machine, and with dresses and suits we use the stripping machine for edgings and finish the bound buttonholes off by hand.'

Harry Gordon's voice startled her so that her fingers were stilled for a moment.

'Emma. Show Mr Martin how the new stripping machine works.'

Turning her head, Emma stared straight into the dark eyes of the man directly behind her. And for a moment Simon saw that she was struggling to make the transition from some far away place. He saw the intelligence in the amber-flecked eyes, and felt again the illogical urge to stretch out a hand towards her.

'If you will come over here, sir.' Emma led the way to the first of the round machines, and began to explain how it worked.

'Do you enjoy your job here, Emma?' He could at least ask that.

'It's a job, sir.' Emma sat down in front of the circular machine and picked up a jacket.

22

'But that's all?'

She took a length of silk braid, her head lowered as she fed it into the machine.

'It brings in quite good money.'

'And that is all-important?'

'As a matter of fact, it is, sir.'

'But what about job satisfaction?' He was making a fool of himself. He could feel the other machinists watching them carefully. 'Surely these days . . .?'

'If you will watch me now, sir.'

Emma Sparrow was deliberately ignoring him, and Simon stepped back as smartly as if she had slapped him across the face.

Two

'You'll have to tell me some time, Dad, so why not now?'

Emma had sent a pair of grumbling boys off to bed, stood at the bottom of the stairs as they fought a rearguard action on every step, shouted in vain through a locked bathroom door at Sharon who had been ensconced inside for almost an hour, and washed the tea things before giving the kitchen floor a swift wipe over.

'I'll tell you summat, our Emma. You go more like your mother every day.' John Sparrow shifted in his chair, got up and turned the television sound up as if to show that what his daughter had to say would fall on deaf ears.

Goaded beyond endurance Emma immediately switched off the set and stood with her back to it.

'It's no good, Dad. I'm the one who balances the budget, so I have a right to know. An' saying what you've said won't help. I know all about my mother. You've told me often enough.' She sat down in the chair at the other side of the glowing electric fire. 'She left you when I was not much more than a baby. But why did she do that? Why did she go off with somebody else? You forget to say you had more or less moved Mam in with you. An' the man my mother went off with didn't want to start married life with a baby, and Mam, being the way she was, didn't mind taking me on. I wish you would tell me something good about my mother for a change.'

'Her own flesh and blood.' John Sparrow pulled at this lower lip, then lit a cigarette. 'What woman could leave a babby scarcely out of nappies? An' *why* did I take up with someone else? Because I couldn't stand her nagging, that's why. Like a bloody gramophone she was, an' now it seems we've come full circle.' He drew deeply on the cigarette and started to cough, a deep cough that brought tears to his eyes. 'I'll tell you something, lass. That lad of yours won't be hanging around here much longer if you keep on. There are some women who can't help it, you know. Nag, nag, nag. Just for the sake of it. It's enough to drive any man to drink.'

'That's why you lost your job, isn't it?' Emma tried to keep careful control of her voice, knowing that if she once gave in to her feelings she would scream at him, ranting and raving like the woman next door. 'You got the sack because you had been drinking. Even though you know that drinking on a driving job means instant dismissal. You knew that, and yet you did it. Why?'

Her father leaned over in a paroxysm of coughing, clutching at his chest, the veins on his forehead standing out. 'A little nip,' he muttered, when he had found some semblance of control. 'Just a little nip to keep out the cold. We had to hang about the depot waiting for some stuff to come in, and I felt me chest coming on again, so all I did was warm meself up a bit.' He thumped the front of his much-washed sweater. 'It was that so-called supervisor copped me. Had it in for me right from the beginning, he had. Walking about with his clipboard and acting like God Almighty. What does he know about driving on icy roads, and being booked for bloody parking? All he does is sit on his backside in his bloody office with a fan heater blowing out warm air to keep him snug. He'd wipe the manager's arse for him if he was asked to. That's the sort of man he is.'

'Did they give you a reference, Dad?' Emma heard Sharon clattering her way down the stairs on her too-high heels, and her voice rose higher. 'Dad! We've got to get this family in some sort of order, an' we can only do that if you *try*. Did you get a reference, this time? Well?'

Ignoring them, Sharon walked straight through the living-room into the kitchen, the collar of her black coat pulled up high so that only the made-up eyes and the tip of her nose showed above. Emma followed, and heard the television blare into instant ear-shattering sound. She rubbed at her eyes like a child. 'Sharon? This is three nights now on the trot. Sharon! This is a family house, not a boarding house. I've just been trying to talk to Dad, but it's hopeless.' She watched as Sharon took a final peep at herself in the round shaving mirror over the sink. 'Did you know that he lost his job through drinking? Do you even know how much the rent is now?' To her dismay Emma heard her voice break on the verge of lost control. 'Alan's gone through his shoes again, and the last pair was twelve pounds! Twelve pounds for a pair of shoes for a boy of ten. And I don't know what the electric bill will be next time. Dad keeps all three bars on all day when he's at home.'

Sharon turned from the mirror, her small face anxious above the ridiculous highwayman's collar. 'Emma? You're not going to cry?' She rummaged in the small plastic shoulder-bag and took out a crumpled five pound note. 'See, I don't need much spending money, not when I'm going out with Ricky. Take this and I'll give you extra when I give you my whack on Friday.' She came close so that Emma was engulfed in a wave of cheap scent. 'It's not fair on you, our Emma. I know that, but things will work out; they always do.'

She gave Emma's arm a little shake. 'Why don't you go out a bit more? What about that Ben who was always round? He never looked as if much bothered him. You don't get enough laughs, that's what's wrong.' She lifted her head in a listening gesture. 'Did you hear a horn just then? I'd better be outside when Ricky comes. He's like one of them heroes in a love story. Must be the boss, or else.'

Planting a quick kiss on Emma's cheek, she rushed out through the living-room, round the back of her father's chair, into the square of a hall, banging the door behind her. As Emma walked back slowly into the living-room she heard the roar of an engine, fading away until everything was still once again.

'I'm going to wash my hair, Dad.'

Through a haze of cigarette smoke John Sparrow nodded without slewing his eyes a fraction to either side. Emma walked slowly upstairs, heard laughter and ominous thumps coming from behind the boys' bedroom door, and resolutely turned her back on it.

She stared round the bathroom in dismay. It was a mess; highly-coloured bath salts littered the vinyl floor like scented crumbs left from a cake, Sharon's work sweater and skirt drooped over the plastic dirty-linen tub, an unsqueezed flannel had wedged itself into the plug-hole of the bath, and a tube of tooth-paste without its cap lay in the washbowl next to a pair of eyebrow tweezers.

Emma picked up a damp towel, wiped the mirror with it, and saw her face. It was shiny, pink and devoid of make-up. Her eyes looked enormous and were ringed with strain. Even her nose looked pinched, and her mouth was set into a grim line. That was her face. She was twenty years old, and she was turning into a pasty-faced shrew, a nagger, like her father had said. A spoiler of joy, a penny-pincher, a tired drab. And what was it that Mr Martin had said that morning? 'But what about job satisfaction?'

She pulled the restraining ribbon from her hair with a fierce tug. Oh, Mr Boss's son Martin. What did *he* know about job satisfaction? Standing behind her in his dark suit and his oh so white shirt. She had thought he was nice, kind even, but Ben was right. Oh yes, Ben was sometimes right. They saw you, the bosses, looked straight at you even, but they weren't really seeing you. To Mr Martin she was just a number, a bottom on the seat of a buttonhole machine. Emma ran the taps and bent her head over the washbowl.

'But, please God, don't let me natter too much. I do it, I know. I can hear my voice going on in my own head over and over.' She poured some of Sharon's yellow lemon-smelling shampoo on to her head and began to lather it in. But perhaps if someone *listened* to her, she would not need to nag. The boys, well they were just ordinary boys, telly-mad, scruffy, fighting and rolling over the floor when their energy had to be expended inside the house. Sharon . . . she was just all out for a good time and honest about it. There was no real harm in Sharon.

Emma rinsed, then applied more shampoo.

And her dad . . . she could never decide whether it was his weak chest and constant bronchial setbacks that made him so helpless, or whether he had been born dead lazy. She groped with tightly shut eyes for the attachment for the taps. It never had fitted properly. Her mother, her *own* mother, must have been goaded beyond endurance to make her leave the house and the town with a man who flatly refused to take a small

27

daughter. What kind of woman was *she*, for heaven's sake? Emma tried to imagine herself deserting a child of her own – tried and failed.

She brushed and dried her long hair into a drape of brown silk turning slightly up at the ends and swinging towards her face. If she tried the same reasoning powers on the family that she used on herself, instead of trying to force them into co-operating, maybe they would all benefit.

This time the mirror showed her a smooth face with shining hair framing it. Even her mouth seemed to be a better shape. Emma smiled and wrinkled her nose at herself.

'Positive thoughts,' she said aloud. 'Sweet reasoning, and no more yelling. Okay?' then she went downstairs to put up the ironing board in the living-room so that she could watch television with her father as she worked.

'Good play, Dad?' Her voice was determinedly cheerful as she tried to live up to her resolution right away.

'Rubbish. Nowt but bloody rubbish. Don't know who writes the things, nor who puts them on. I can tell now that it's going to be one that finishes when you think it's only halfway through. Nowt solved, nowt decided. Rubbish!'

'Then why watch it?' Emma laid a shirt over the board and did the lap, giving the iron a chance to hot up. 'Switch it off and talk to me.'

'What about?' John Sparrow turned in his chair and regarded her with suspicion. 'I've told you, it was through me having the smell of drink on me, that was all.'

For a brief second Emma's hand was still as she forgot she was holding an iron. Then she snatched it away from the shirt and laid it down on the asbestos mat at the side of the board. She had heard that whining note in her father's voice before and always, always when he was in some sort of trouble.

Closing her eyes she reminded herself of the conversation she had held with herself upstairs. Because of circumstances the papers would have said were beyond her control, she was never able to be really herself. It wasn't in her nature to be constantly suspicious of her own family. From the look on her dad's face right now it would seem that he was almost afraid of her, and sometimes when she yelled at the boys upstairs they would exchange glances as if to say 'here she goes again'.

And yet there was this pricking at the back of her neck, a warning prickle telling her that her dad was keeping something from her, something he was willing himself to tell.

'There's a can of beer in the fridge, I think. Shall I go and get it for you?' She smiled. 'And I'll have a drop of it myself. Ironing's thirsty work.'

'It wasn't just the drink,' John said, turning away so that his voice came from the back of his head. 'I'd got some bits of things in the back of the van, and with that mealy-mouthed bloke sending me straight off there wasn't the chance to put them back.'

'Put them back where?' Emma put a hand over her mouth in a childish gesture.

'In the stores.'

'What were they, Dad?'

'Boxes of spare parts. Small bits, but worth a bob or two, being hard to come by.' Her father started to cough, beating his chest and gasping for breath.

Patiently Emma waited until he had finished. 'You mean you'd pinched them, Dad? Pinched them to sell again? Oh, dear God! And they're bound to be found?'

'Unless one of me mates gets there first, but knowing what I know they'll be found all right.' He blew a cloud of smoke which rose like ectoplasm above his head. 'I did it for you, lass. I know what it's like trying to feed and dress them two upstairs decent, and Sharon hardly pays for what she eats. I was going to save the money I got and not tell you, then maybe this summer we could have gone away for a few days.' He started to cough again. 'It was no skin off their nose. There's more stuff wasted than what I nicked. I was only taking the same as what the bosses take.' He turned round in his chair. 'What about them with their company cars and their business lunches? We don't get no perks, not my sort. Bleed you dry, they will, then give you the sack as easily as brushing a fly off their rice pudding.'

'Dad!' In spite of her resolution Emma's voice came out like a bark from a sergeant-major. 'I'm not your judge and jury, so stop trying to justify what you've done.' She bent down and pulled the plug from the skirting board. 'Where will that van be now? Right now? It's prison this time, Dad, you know that.'

29

John Sparrow blinked twice. 'Why? What's that got to do with it?'

'Where will it be?'

'At the depot, of course. In the sheds with all the rest.'

'And will there be anyone there now? Anyone working nights? Any of the maintenance staff? Any of the mechanics?'

He rubbed his chin. 'There could be, but I doubt it. Since they had to cut costs there's not much night work done . . . nay, I doubt it. Why? Why, lass?'

But Emma was already running upstairs for her coat, tying a headscarf round her newly-washed hair, calling out to her father that she would be back, that if she were lucky there might still be time. . . .

The bus was just trundling away from the stop, but the Pakistani driver, with a grin to match his ebullient nature, stopped and opened the doors to let her in.

'You training for the Olympics, ma'am?' he took Emma's fare, then waited to start the bus until he saw she had found a seat, quite unperturbed when she returned his smile with a vacant stare that dismissed him as if he were not there.

'Takes all sorts,' he told himself in a Lancashire accent at variance with his dark skin. 'But that face was meant to smile, weren't it?'

'It was all locked up and in darkness,' Emma told Sharon, who came in at just after midnight, glowing and happy with her lipstick smeared and her hair mussed. 'He's gone to bed, but he says it will mean the police.' She followed Sharon through into the kitchen. 'He doesn't seem to realize that it could mean prison. He seems to think he was only taking what was his due.'

'The stupid bugger!' Sharon lit the gas and put the kettle on. 'The stupid ignorant bugger. Course he'll get prison this time. Oh, God, and Ricky and me talked about getting engaged tonight.' She dropped a tea bag into a mug. 'Now you know why I wouldn't bring him in. Ricky's father's strict Chapel, so how could I bring him in to meet our dad sitting there coughing and spitting? Oh, God! Fancy having a gaol bird for a dad.' She poured a stream of boiling water on to the tea bag and stirred it round with a spoon. 'I expect we'll have to go and see him and talk to him through a grille like they do on the telly. Well, if he thinks I'll go he's got another think coming.'

'But you can't get engaged. Not at sixteen.' Emma was so tired, so overwrought, so filled with despair, that she was totally unable to get even the priorities right. Her dad going to prison, her stepsister getting engaged to a boy they had never met – what was the difference? 'I thought you said you just wanted to have fun?' She rescued the tea bag, dropped it into a mug and poured hot water on it without waiting to boil up the kettle again. 'What brought this on?'

'I love him, Emma.' Sharon sat down at the table and curled both hands round the steaming mug. 'He's nice, really nice. He has a good job too.'

'What?' Emma sat down opposite to her, her exhausted face as milky pale as the weak tea.

Sharon's blue eyes filled suddenly with unexpected tears. 'He goes round houses putting them PVC doors and windows in. Everybody's having them now to save on fuel bills.' Her pretty face crumpled. 'Oh, our Emma. Will our dad really have to go to prison?' The tears overflowed and ran down her cheeks, leaving a trail of navy-blue mascara. 'How can they put him in a cell with his bad chest? What will he be like if he catches cold? How will they know that he has to have the steam kettle going when he's bad?' Pushing the mug of tea aside, she spread her arms wide on the table and lowered her head on to them, sobs shaking her slim shoulders. 'I didn't mean it, what I said, I'm not ashamed of him really. Not really.' She lifted a blotched face. 'I leave you with it all, our Emma. I go out and leave you with all the work. An' I'm not really crying now because of . . . because of our dad. Inside me I'm so happy I could burst. What's wrong with me? It's like being glad and sad all at the same time, with me the important one all the time. Perhaps I should start going to church again. I've never been since I was confirmed, and I felt proper holy then.'

'Holiness never lasts, love.' Emma got up and rinsed out the two mugs, then gave Sharon's shoulder a little squeeze. 'Come on, chuck. Let's go to bed. Maybe it won't look so bad in the morning. Maybe now they've got rid of Dad they won't report it. Some folks are kind. . . .'

When they were in bed, curled up together like spoons in a box, Emma stared up into the darkness. Sharon engaged to be married. Little Sharon, who a short while ago was at school, a reluctant student, giggling with the boys and walking home with the girlfriend of the moment. Sharon, who could recite the Top of the Pops backwards, and who believed the confession stories she read. Married. Emma sighed and gently shifted her position.

Where would they live? Certainly not here, there just wasn't the room. How could they possibly afford to rent even the smallest flat? And this boy who was just a barely glimpsed face beneath a crash helmet. Hardly husband material. . . .

It had been a stupid thing to do, rushing out like that, hoping and praying that somehow she could have got one of the fitters to remove the stolen parts from the van. If anyone had seen her there in the darkness, beating on the big doors with her fists, she could have got into trouble. And now all she could possibly do was sit tight and pray that a miracle would take place.

'Some folks are kind,' she had told Sharon, 'but that sort of kindness didn't come often. Like Mr Gordon, angry with her for being late – business came first. Profits, accounts that balanced, they were what mattered, and a workman on the make had to be made an example of. She knew that.

Through the thin wall dividing the two back rooms Emma could hear her father coughing. She heard the springs of his bed creak, and imagined she heard the click of his cigarette lighter.

'Nothing's happened yet,' she told Ben the next night. 'And with every day that passes we can feel safer. That's right, isn't it?'

They had been to the Sporting Club and Ben had played snooker whilst she drank Coke and gossiped in the lounge bar with the girls. Now they were sitting in his shabby car, parked on the spare land earmarked for more council houses before the enforced cuts in council spending. They had moved to the back seat to be more comfortable.

'I blame your dad for leaving himself wide open,' Ben told

her, nuzzling his curly head into her neck. 'He should have worked it in a pair so that his mate could have covered for him. Anything knocked off should have a double chance. Anybody knows that.'

Emma sat up straight. 'You seem to know a lot about it. Ben? You wouldn't – you wouldn't get involved in anything like that? *Would* you?'

A light from a street lamp showed her his face, his eyes with their stubbly eyelashes glinting with laughter, his wide mouth parted over small even teeth.

'Oh, Em.' He shook his head from side to side. 'Course I wouldn't.' He pulled her close and tangled his fingers in the soft weight of her hair. 'I wouldn't get caught, if that's what you mean, but everybody's on the fiddle. Your dad's too old, that's his problem.' He slid a hand inside her coat. 'The defence will say it was what they call a desperation offence, him being sick and trying to keep his family together. You're acting as if he was one of them bank robbers carrying a gun. What he's done's nothing, Em. Oh, forget it and relax.'

'*Have* you take anything from work, Ben?' Emma took hold of his wandering hand and pushed it firmly away. 'Because if you have, you'll get caught.' She wriggled free. 'That's why Mr Martin is up from London. It's all over the factory. Ben! Those dresses, the skirts and jackets, they cost seventy pounds to buy in the shops. Do you know that? They're high-quality stuff, Ben, not trash. And the satin blouses, they're seventeen pounds each. Mrs Kelly told me. A girl singed one when she was pressing it, and Mr Gordon had her in tears. Ben! You're not even listening to me!'

She could feel his heart thudding, and his mouth searched sweetly for her own. He was clean-smelling, and even as she tried to push him away there was a part of her not wanting to. After the glum atmosphere in the house, with her father sitting chain-smoking, the television blaring, and the boys fighting and pushing at each other on the settee, it had been heaven to get away from it all. To laugh and be accepted as Ben's girl, to share in his obvious popularity, to feel young and carefree, and now to respond to his kisses.

'Please, Em, let me . . . oh, please.' He was moaning now, his hand underneath her skirt, persistent, moving.

'Bloody tights,' he said, then groaned as she moved and pushed him away.

'What's wrong with you? You're not normal, do you know that? I wouldn't harm you, Em. I've got some rubbers. I know what I'm doing. Why won't you trust me? Why have you to be different? An' you're not one of them frigid birds, so don't pretend different.'

He was sulking now, searching his pocket for cigarettes as Emma straightened her skirt and pulled her sweater down, trying to tuck it back into the waistband. She could feel her heart beating wildly and felt a sudden urge to pull his head down to her breasts and hold him there as she stroked his thick hair.

That was all she wanted really – to hold and be held. To assuage the hopelessness she felt for the way things were. But that was naïve, even she knew that, and maybe Ben was right, maybe she was abnormal.

'Perhaps you're one of them that only fancies other women,' Ben said, and she laughed, then immediately was serious.

'I couldn't. Not here.' She tried to explain. 'Not in the back of the car with folks walking past over the road.' She buttoned her coat. 'I'm not a prude, Ben. I feel what you feel.' She sought for the right words. 'Maybe not as bad, but I . . . oh, *if* I decided to do that, I would have to have thought it through. I would want to feel that there was something real between us.'

'You mean like me asking you to marry me?'

'Not even that. But *more*, well, more of a relationship.' She rubbed at the steamed-up window, turning her face away from him. 'I don't mind, but I know you go out with other girls when I have to stay in. An' if ever we made love proper, then it would have to be just you and me. For as long as it lasted, anyway.' She reached for the door handle, despising herself for the next question, but asking it just the same. 'Do you . . . with the other girls you go out with? I mean . . . do they?'

'Every man Jack of 'em,' Ben said, coming to join her in the front of the car, his good humour completely restored, his blue eyes sparkling with mischief.

'Oh, Ben . . . .' Emma shook her head in mock despair. 'I never know when to believe you. Not about what you've just said, nor about . . . well, about what goes on at work. Some-

34

times I think it's just big talk, then I'm not sure.'

'Then you've nowt to worry about, have you?' Ben said, as he let in the clutch.

'You come to a stage,' Emma told herself, 'when you just can't worry any more. It's there, the worry, but somehow it has got pushed to a numb part of your mind. Another week, say, and if nothing happens, then Dad has got away with it.'

She was at a stripping machine, carefully guiding the braid trim round the collarless neck of a jacket, the tip of her tongue protruding slightly and the unruly strand of hair falling forward over her face. 'Maybe, just maybe, at Dad's place there is a kind man with a Father Christmas mentality, who has decided to overlook the spare parts in the back of the van.' It was tricky work, but long practice still left her active mind free to wander. 'And Ben. It would be just like him to let me think he was on the fiddle, just as he tries to make me believe he's God's gift to women. And you can't love him or you would be gnashing your teeth with jealousy at the very thought. No, you don't love him, but if you stopped seeing him, how dreary life would be. He's generous and fun, such fun to be with, and maybe he really likes you fighting him off all the time. If what he says is true about the other girls he goes out with, then at least you're a change. And they say a change is as good as a rest.'

Simon Martin, wandering round the big workroom, saw her bending over the circular machine, and had to restrain himself from walking over to stand by her chair. He was leaving early that day to drive down to London for the weekend, but he felt again the illogical desire to speak to Emma Sparrow and offer help where he was not even sure that help was needed. He said her name quietly to himself, and thought how it suited her. Brown and small, with that soft wing of hair partly concealing her lovely face. She stuck out from the rest of the girls like a flower on a muck midden.

'On Monday we'll have the invoices out, going back for the past two years,' he told Mr Gordon. 'But I don't see how we can cut staff yet. Not with the new set of orders in.' He grinned. 'The country is supposed to be in the doldrums, but it seems that women can still find the money for high-quality clothes.'

'They say that northern women don't know how to dress, but I know better.' Harry Gordon's smile was like that on a wicked grinning gargoyle. 'Make some of your London lot look as if they're dressed by Oxfam. Aye, Lancashire women know a bit o' good when they sees it right enough. Mind how you go. There was fog forecast on the motorway, but not till you get past Birmingham.' He pushed a heavy pair of horn-rimmed spectacles back up the bridge of his nose. 'That's another thing you London lot have wrong. Weather. It might be a bit windier up 'ere, but at least we can breathe. Like living in a sauna down yonder. No wonder tha's all pasty-faced.'

Simon pressed his foot down on the accelerator, keeping the car at a steady seventy down the M6 and on to the M1. He had telephoned Chloe to say he would be back about eight, but when he let himself into the flat in Maida Vale he thought at first it was empty.

'In here, Simon.'

Chloe's voice came from the bedroom, and when Simon walked through from the living-room she was sitting up at the side of the bed, reaching down for her shoes with the guilty expression of a housewife who has been caught resting when she thought she should have been rushing around with duster and polish.

'No meal for your lord and master?' Simon waited until he had kissed her with lingering thoroughness before he asked the question. 'I drove straight down without stopping, and I only had a cheese butty at lunch time. I'm starving.'

There was no need for Chloe to apologize, but she started explaining in a rather breathy voice that she had been kept late at the office, that the tube was so crowded she let one go and waited for the next. That she had been too tired to do the weekend shopping, that she had thought maybe they could do it together in the morning and go out to eat that evening. . . .

'But of course we'll go out, love.' Simon took off his jacket. 'Just let me get out of this suit and into something a bit more casual and we'll go right away.' He went into the avocado bathroom, leaving the door ajar so that he could talk through the opening. 'Okay, are you, love?'

'Why do you ask that?'

He moved back from the washbowl to see Chloe sitting on the dressing-table stool, doing nothing. Staring at herself and doing absolutely nothing. He frowned. 'You've never asked me how it went yet.'

'How what went?' Her voice sounded flat and unlike her.

Simon ran the hot water in the green bowl and began to lather his hands. 'My trip to the land of tripe and onions.'

'How did it go?'

'Pretty good. I like the friendliness, and the warmth. The lack of reserve and the sincerity.' He slipped easily into dialect. 'When they call a spade a spade up there they don't mean it's a bloody shovel.'

No reply from Chloe. No laugh. No nothing. Just the back of a head viewed from the half-open door as she sat still before the dressing-table mirror.

'Now, come on, love. What's it all about?' Simon waited until they were sitting opposite each other at a corner table in the Greek restaurant, just a few minutes' walk away from the flat.

'What's all what about?'

Chloe was breaking Greek bread into small pieces, tearing at it with fingers trembling. Simon felt a sinking feeling beneath his ribs. He waved the wine waiter away telling him to come back later, then, reaching across the cutlery and the red candle in a brandy glass, he took Chloe's hand in his own.

His Chloe was a big, smiling girl, easy to know and easy to live with. The daughter of an English father and an American mother, she had a slow, attractive drawl in her voice and a disconcerting way of voicing what she considered to be unpalatable truths about herself. 'Look at me, honey,' she had once said to Simon. 'Practically boobless, and with freckles on my back as big as saucepan lids. Hair like a frizzed-out Jesus freak, and teeth as big as tombstones.'

'Fishing for compliments again?' Simon always said when she was in that self-disparaging mood.

But now her distress was genuine. The green of her silky polo jumper, worn beneath a smock-like brown and green

37

dress, accentuated the pallor of her face, and her eyes when she raised them were shadowed and ringed with dark lines that owed nothing to her eyebrow pencil.

'You're pregnant.' Simon nodded and smiled. 'So it wasn't the dose of 'flu you had three weeks ago making you miss.' He squeezed her hand lying listless in his own. 'So – we'll get married. Come on, love. Don't look like that. You knew it was just a matter of time. Chloe? You didn't think I would throw you out and send you back to your momma, surely? I'll go and see about a special licence or whatever you do, and we'll be married next weekend. You don't want a big do with your parents flying over from the States and two friends from the office in primrose yellow, do you? You always said that when we got round to it we'd have a quiet trip to a Register Office. Suits me, love. You know that.'

The waiter brought two small plates of fried whitebait and arranged the fish knives and forks before moving away. Simon picked up his fork and motioned to Chloe to do the same.

'Come on, sweetie. You have to eat for two now. Okay?'

He wasn't sure how he felt. One part of him was excited, exuberant almost. The thought of being a father tickled his male ego, even though he was already accepting the fact that a lot of adjustments would have to be made. The flat with its one bedroom and no hall to park a pram in was far too small. With the money he was still paying to Ellen, his first wife, and the difficulty of getting a mortgage when there was nothing to sell, he'd be hard pushed. He trickled lemon juice over the tiny silver fishes. Still, they'd manage, and maybe his old man would help out a bit. Simon imagined the look on his father's face when he told him he was going to be a grandfather and smiled, suddenly excited again.

He was totally unaware of the fact that Chloe was sitting quite still, making no move to pick up her fork, just sitting there watching him, with an unfathomable expression in her eyes.

'Aren't you supposed to jump up and kiss me, or even call for a bottle of champagne or something? Or are you too busy totting up a balance sheet in that computer mind of yours?'

Chloe's tone was light; she was smiling, but the smile was at variance with the despair showing on her face. She leaned forward a little. 'I've read books where the expectant father goes white with shock, then gets down on the carpet and buries his head in the expectant mother's lap. I've even read them where he slaps the little woman around the face, calls her a stupid, careless bitch, then goes out and gets drunk.' Her smile was brilliant. 'But I don't recall ever reading one where the father-to-be does private sums in his head, then trickles lemon juice over his supper whilst telling her that things will work out, at the same time as urging her to do that crazy thing and eat for two.' The smile vanished. 'My God, Simon. If ever I'd had any doubts whether what I did was the right thing – not that I had – they'd have disappeared right now.' To her dismay, the tears she had not shed welled up in her eyes and ran slowly down her cheeks.

'What did you do, Chloe?' Simon knew the answer before he asked the question.

'I had an abortion, Simon.'

Her chin was held high as she made no attempt to wipe away the tears.

'That was why you could not reach me by telephone at the beginning of the week. Because that is where I was. I stayed over one night, and came home the next day. The second day mooching round the flat, then back to work. Oh, yes, it's as simple as that.'

Simon suddenly knew he did not want to look at her, so instead he stared down at his plate, and it seemed as if all the shiny, crisp little fishes were watching him. He wanted to sweep them down on to the red carpeted floor, followed by everything else on the table. He ran a finger round his collar as if it were strangling the breath out of him. He was so angry that he wanted to lift Chloe bodily from her chair and shake her until her teeth rattled. For a moment he sat there without moving, bewildered by the discovery that he possessed a rage of such passion.

Crumpling the scarlet linen table napkin, he threw it down on the table.

'We can't talk here. Come on!'

Chloe opened her mouth to remonstrate with him, saw his face and obeyed.

'I'll catch you up,' he muttered, so she saw nothing of the

way he made placatory noises to the head waiter, ignoring the stares of the fascinated diners. She did as she was told and waited for him on the pavement outside the restaurant, pulling the long knitted scarf closer round her throat and shivering a little in the evening's sudden chill.

Chloe was a little afraid of the scene she knew must surely follow. A little, but not much. She had realized many years ago that her mother had kept her parents' marriage alive by being the boss and never once admitting it, maybe not even to herself. 'Women are cleverer than men. Men are so *obvious*, honey,' she had often said, and now Chloe was very much her mother's daughter. She stepped back into the doorway. What she had had done, she had had done to her own body. That was true, wasn't it?

'Now you can perhaps try to tell me why?'

Simon had almost frog-marched her back to the flat. Stood beside her in the lift, walked beside her down the silent, beige-carpeted corridor flanked at intervals by storage heaters. Like a corridor in *Doctor Who* he had often thought, but now all he wanted was to get Chloe into the privacy of the flat, to drag the truth from her, to make her tell him why she had done this monstrous thing to him. Because that was exactly how he felt, as if his own body had been violated.

'Why?' he demanded. 'Why, in God's name, why? Without even telling me, or giving us a chance to talk it through.' He flung his jacket on to a chair and faced her, his eyes narrowed.

Chloe switched on the electric fire and rubbed her arms. She was almost as tall as he, and at that moment her dignity and the way she seemed to be in full control of her feelings made her seem even taller.

'I did it because I knew we were not ready.' She sighed. 'And your first reaction back there in the restaurant told me I had been right.'

'I said *nothing*. Absolutely nothing you could have objected to.' Simon held his hands out palms upwards. 'If you had given me a chance I might have told you how pleased I was. How *happy*.' He walked over to the window, staring out over the lights of London, with the Post Office Tower standing like an illuminated phallic symbol in the distance. 'Just because we'd decided no babies for a while didn't mean I would have

40

wanted you to do a thing like that.' He turned round. 'Do you realize what damage you could have caused to yourself? Women who do that sometimes become sterile. Didn't you know that?' He ran his hand through his hair. 'And what about the psychological damage? That was *our* baby, Chloe. Didn't I have a say in whether you murdered it?'

'Honey. . . .' She came towards him, but he knocked her hand away with a downward motion. 'Honey . . .' she said again. 'I have not been to some dirty crone in a back street. I went to a private clinic. First I saw this man in Harley Street, then I took the letter to a nursing home, then I was booked in, then I stayed one night. For Pete's sake, Simon, it's only like having a D and C, a *scrape*. I wasn't even sore.'

Simon looked as if he was going to be sick. 'How much?' he asked coldly, reaching into his pocket for his cheque book. 'At least let me pay for my own mistakes. That's common justice, isn't it? A man must always pay for his own mistakes.'

It was hard to keep calm after that, but Chloe managed. She was a little white round the mouth, but outwardly she managed to hang on to her usual serenity.

'Listen to me. Simon, honey . . . you know as well as I do that this box of a place isn't right for a baby. And, no, *listen*. Since you became group accountant and keep moving around it isn't even a practical idea to put a down payment on a house. Do you realize how much we would have to find as first-time buyers? And we decided we weren't going to let your father or my parents help. Simon! We're not *children*. I'm twenty-five and you're seven years older. We're not teenagers having to get married and moving in with Mum and Dad. We are intelligent beings, able in this day and age to extricate ourselves from whatever mess we get into. And besides,' her head drooped forward, 'since your divorce you've told me over and over that the next time has to be right. That there must be no doubt, not the slightest doubt. "The next time has to be for ever." You've said that. Over and over.'

'I would never have agreed to it. Never!' Simon left her and walked through into the bedroom, and Chloe followed him.

He was sitting on the edge of the double bed, his hands held loosely between his knees — like a little boy determined to sulk, she thought, with a sudden pang of tenderness so acute that she had to sit beside him and risk being pushed away.

'If I had discussed it with you, honey, I would have put you on the spot.' She took one of his listless hands in her own and caressed it gently. 'I won't need to go to a shrink, honey, to sort out any possible hang-ups. I am more practically minded than you . . women are in the main.'

'Well, if I'm not practically minded, then I'm in the wrong job, love.' There was almost a chuckle in his voice, and Chloe knew that the worst was over. Then she recoiled from the look in his dark eyes as he turned to face her. It was a look she had never seen before, a look that weighed her up and found her wanting.

'I did it for you,' she whispered later when they went exhausted and hungry to bed. 'I did not want to *force* you into marrying me.' She buried her face in his bare chest. 'I guess I'm not a very maternal person either. I felt no surge of joy when I realized what had happened. My momma wasn't maternal either. She told me once she hated me till I grew old enough to hold a decent conversation. "Shitty nappies were never my thing, honey," she told me.'

Simon smiled into her hair. 'I like your momma. She is maybe the only really honest person I know.'

'And I'm not honest?'

Gently Simon stroked her hair. 'You deceived me, Chloe. You took something that was half mine and destroyed it. And it's going to take some getting used to. . . .'

From the living-room the telephone rang, and Simon groaned. 'That will be my father. I expect he'll have been waiting in all evening for me to ring, and I forgot. I never gave the business a bloody thought.'

Chloe lay there on her back, half listening to the conversation, a one-sided conversation telling of profit margins, loss leaders, depleted stock, staff problems, missing invoices and promising new lines. She noticed that the defeated tone in Simon's voice had vanished as he slid easily into his man's world and became brisk and professional once again.

' "Love is of men's life a thing apart . . ." ' she murmured sleepily, then jerked half awake as Simon got into bed beside her and settled her into their sleeping position with her bottom snuggled comfortably into his lap. 'I never got to hear how it went up north. Did you meet anyone interesting up there, honey?' She was unconscious almost before the words had left her lips, worn out with the emotion of the week and the violence of Simon's reaction. Now all she wanted was to forget . . . to get on, to get back to the way things had been and forget. Her leg jerked against his as she dropped into sleep, leaving Simon staring up into the darkness.

There was a weight in his chest like an undigested meal, and even as he tightened his hold on Chloe's soft warm body he felt a sudden urge to push her away from him. She was wearing panties beneath her nightdress and somehow that little thing, that little feminine necessity, brought the thing she had done sharply into focus again.

'Did I meet anyone interesting?' Simon addressed her unresponsive back. 'Well, I don't know. They're a warm nice lot, the Lancastrians. No side to them, no side at all. And yes. Actually there was a girl, a strange tormented girl called Emma Sparrow. . . .'

Three

'There's nowt here, I'm telling you. You can search the place, but you'll be wasting your time, because you'll find nowt!'

Emma had gone straight from work to the supermarket, arriving home laden like a pack-horse. She was putting the groceries away when she heard her father's voice, but she had been listening ever since the knock at the door, followed by John Sparrow's shuffling steps as he answered it.

'Right then, Mr Sparrow. We'll do that. Thanks.'

'Detective Constable Stewart.' The tallest of the two police-men showed his identification card and nodded at Emma. 'Sorry to trouble you, love, but this won't take long.' He turned to the shorter man. 'Upstairs first, Ray? Right. Let's get on with it.'

A cowboy with an orange complexion and a purple neck-tie galloped across the television screen in a thunder of hooves, firing into a lurid shaded middle distance. Alan and Joe, their faces deathly pale, but their features restored to normality, watched with fierce concentration.

Emma clutched the back of a chair and stared disbelieving at their impassive expressions. Did they understand what was happening? There, in their living-room? Or was the television drama more real to them as they sat there, side by side on the settee, chewing gum with rhythmic attention?

'Switch that thing off!'

As if they were Siamese twins, joined down the middle, both heads swivelled round to regard her with amazement. Emma started to tremble. She could feel her heart thudding, and as she turned to her father, her young face was the face of a woman of forty, lined with a terrible despair.

'Oh, leave it then.' Her shoulders sagged as the two heads resumed their viewing positions. John Sparrow's fingers shook as he groped for, then lit the inevitable cigarette.

'Come through into the kitchen, Dad.' Emma winced at the sound of drawers opening and shutting upstairs, then she closed the kitchen door.

Her father sat down in a chair and buried his face in his hands, still holding the cigarette between his fingers. His voice came muffled.

'Our Sharon's in the bathroom, having a bath. They'll scare the living daylights out of her if they go barging in.' He raised his head. 'There's nowt in the bathroom, anyroad.'

'And in *your* room, Dad?' Emma stared up at the ceiling. 'Because that is where they are. They've gone straight in there by the sound of things.'

She stared at the boys' duffle coats hanging behind the door. They were hanging there limp, like her hopes, it seemed; like prayers of the past days. Prayers she knew now that were not going to be answered.

Her father drew deeply on the cigarette, then coughed as the smoke caught his throat. The cough deepened, and he began to thump his chest as if he would force oxygen through to his lungs. Tears filled his eyes and his face flushed to a fiery red.

'And in *your* room, Dad?'

He refused to look at her. 'A few odds and bobs, mebbe. Nowt much. Nowt amounting to much.'

'Where?' Emma picked up a large packet of cornflakes, cradling it to her as if she needed the comfort of something to cling to. 'Where have you hidden it? *Where*, Dad?'

'On top of the wardrobe. In boxes. Just some stuff I couldn't pass on.' He studied the vinyl flooring, tracing the pattern with his foot. 'I was going to dump it, but what with me chest being bad, and the weather being bad, I never got the chance. Nay, you could buy what I've got up there in a car accessory shop, that's why I got meself stuck with it. Not worth the nicking, that lot weren't.'

Emma steeled herself against the grey look of his face. Now that he had stopped coughing he looked desperately ill, with mottled patches on his cheek bones, and eyes sunk into hollow sockets. She tightened her hold on the cornflake packet.

'Oh, Dad. . . .' She spoke in a whisper. 'This time they won't listen to excuses. You know they've clamped down on stealing.'

'Pilfering, lass. Pilfering.' He flicked ash on to the floor. 'I thought we might have a holiday this year. Just a week at Blackpool or Morecambe – with all the meals made and everything – I was going to try to put a bit by. . . .'

He was getting maudlin, and as Emma went to put a hand on his shoulder she smelt the whisky on him and stepped back in despair.

'So we would like you to accompany us down to the station . . . . We think you may be able to assist us. . . . A few questions. . . .'

The policeman's words were drowned in the sudden and terrifying fit of gasping and wheezing as John Sparrow clutched his throat, rolled his eyes back and tore at his collar. Fighting for every breath, and escaping temporarily, as he had done so often before when life got too difficult and circumstances were more than he could cope with.

'Get his coat, love.'

It was said quietly, but Emma nodded at once. Behind the policeman standing in the doorway, the second one hovered, carrying four square cardboard boxes in his arms.

'*Now*, love.'

She took a worn leather jacket down from behind the door, replacing the boys' duffle coats before handing it over.

'It's cold out. He'd best have his scarf.' She handed that over too, and wound it slowly and gently round her father's neck. 'And his cigarettes.' She patted his pocket to make sure they were there.

Then she stood back and watched them take him away.

Through the living-room, past the settee with two tousled heads just showing above the back, then down the path to where the car waited at the kerb.

How little he was, she thought, as dwarfed between the two detectives her father bent his head and climbed into the back of the car. It was funny how she had never noticed particularly just how small he was before.

Emma closed the door, still with the strange calmness on her, and walked back into the kitchen. There were still some of the groceries to put away, and the fish fingers to set in rows beneath the grill. It was a Friday after all, and even though they weren't Catholics – heaven forbid, as John Sparrow always said – they always had fish on a Friday. She tore at the packet. She supposed that fish fingers counted as proper fish, in a religious way, that was?

'Has our dad got nicked, our Emma?'

Joe stood behind her, slightly worried, but not apparently overmuch. He scratched his head, and as he took his hand away Emma saw the dirt down his nails. There was yellow sleep in his eyes as if he had stayed unwashed all day.

'Have you had a wash today?' She laid the fish fingers in a row like bread-crumbed dominoes, lining them up carefully. 'As soon as you've finished your teas you can have a bath. Both of you. Okay?'

'Will he be coming back soon?'

'Oh, yes, quite soon.' There was a light feeling in her head as if part of her floated away, leaving the rest of her to talk normally and even smile. 'Don't say you've left the television, Joe. You might be missing something.'

'It's only the adverts,' he explained kindly. 'Our Alan likes them, but I think they're rubbish.' He turned away, undersized like his father, socks falling over the tops of his scuffed shoes, shirt hanging out of his trousers. But not before Emma had seen the uncertainty in his eyes.

'Joe!' She called his name so fiercely that he whipped round, his whole stance a question mark, a needing to know. 'Oh, Joe. . . .' The cry came from Emma's heart, not from her lips. In one more moment she knew she would have to run to him, kneel down on the floor and sob into his unbrushed hair.

But he was eight years old, that was all.

'I'll soon have your tea ready.' She indicated the fish fingers. 'And there's a new bottle of tomato sauce. Okay?'

Joe's bottom lip quivered. 'Our Alan says our dad's gone to be grilled. He's not, has he?'

Hysteria bubbled in Emma's throat. 'Like the fish fingers? Oh, love, I've told you. He'll be back soon.' Then she did get down on her knees and put her arms round him, smelling the little boy smell of him, and feeling him grow stiff as a plank in her embrace.

'What's up?'

47

Sharon stood behind her, every hair on her head wound into pink rollers, a small transistor radio belting out pop music clutched to her, as much a part of her as if it were a second skin.

'You mean you haven't heard anything?'

Emma pushed Sharon into the kitchen and closed the door, but not before she had seen Joe take his place on the settee once again.

'You mean you didn't hear them upstairs? You mean you sat in the bath with all that going on right upstairs?'

'All what going on upstairs?'

'Two bloody policemen searching the bedrooms, that's all. And switch that bloody thing off! This house is so bloody noisy you can't hear yourself think!'

'Stop swearing, our Emma. You *don't* swear!' Sharon, forgetting she had turned off the radio, shouted at the top of her voice. 'And where's our dad?' She looked feverishly round the kitchen as if expecting to see him hidden behind the cooker. 'Don't tell me they've arrested him! Oh, my God! Not tonight! Not with Ricky coming for me, and me asking him in and everything!'

'You selfish little bugger!'

Emma heard her voice shout the words, but there was no holding back now. The calmness had evaporated, and all she was conscious of was this yelling, shouting, raucous voice saying things she hardly meant, even though the fact she was saying them at all meant they must have been festering inside her for a long time.

'God knows what he'll be going through down there at the station, and all you can think about is your flamin' precious Ricky coming! You've known I've been worried sick, and you've slept all night. I've *felt* you sleeping right beside me. You've seen him sitting there in the chair, going to pieces, bit by bit, because he knew what was coming to him, and you've never said as much as a single word.' She suddenly snatched the grill pan from the cooker and stared in horror at the blackened row of burnt fish fingers. 'An' now the flamin' tea's ruined, an' I'll have to find something else.' She glanced wildly round the kitchen. 'An' if your flamin' Ricky pokes his head round that door this minute I'll chuck this lot at him. So you know.'

Sharon was very dignified in her rollers and the faded quilted dressing-gown that had been too small for her for three years now. She stared at Emma with shock. It was like seeing the Pope tear his hair and shout swear-words from the balcony in Rome, as she told Ricky later. Emma *never* shouted. Sometimes she raised her voice a bit, or her mouth went tight, but she never yelled like somebody common. Sometimes her eyes were longing eyes, as if she was imagining herself in another place, and there was a time, before Mam had been killed, when Emma had teased her and called her a butterhead. Now Emma's own brown hair was scragged back from her face like one of the toffee-nosed models in magazines, just scragged back showing her rounded shiny forehead, and her eyes all glittery as if she was going to cry.

'You've changed, our Emma.' Sharon said this with sadness tinged with regret. 'It's not my fault the tea's burnt. Anyway, I'm going to Ricky's mother's for my tea, so you don't have to bother about me.'

She was watching Emma's face wrench itself out of shape when the door-bell rang. Two piercing rings, followed by two knocks, rapidly, one after the other.

Sharon's eyes and mouth flew wide. 'Oh, flaminenry, it's him! It's Ricky! Oh, no, he can't come in and see me like this!' She tore at the rollers, rasping strands of hair with them, clattering them down on the table. 'Emma . . . oh, *you* let him in. I'll run upstairs, then. . . .' She turned briefly. 'You won't tell him where Dad's gone, our Emma? Please?'

When Emma let the boy in the white crash helmet into the house, Sharon's flight upstairs must have been quite visible to him through the round glass inset in the door, but he just nodded as if to himself and followed Emma through into the living-room.

'You're Ricky.' She motioned to her father's chair. 'Sit down. Sharon won't be long.' She tried to smile, but her face felt stiff, and the same stiffness seemed to be affecting her whole body. The face beneath the crash helmet was foxy sharp, and the dark eyes shifted restlessly without settling on anything particular.

Emma nodded towards the silent viewing figures on the settee. 'Sorry about them. I'd switch it off but it won't make any difference. They'll just sit there waiting for it to come on again.'

'Yes.'

Emma backed towards the kitchen door. 'She'll not be long,' she said again, and closed the door. Then she crossed her arms and rocked herself backwards and forwards. Oh, that boy! That *little* boy with the spots, and the almost nothing of a chin! That thin, undersized, paralysed with shyness kid. Keeping Sharon out late night after night, and wanting to be engaged to her! Kissing her with those thin red lips – and had that been a suspicion of a moustache? He couldn't be more than seventeen . . . he *couldn't*. Emma felt the hysteria rise thick in her throat, then she crossed to the pedal bin and shook the burned fish straight into it from the grill pan. She clenched her hands and fought so hard for control that she felt sick.

There were the boys to feed and chivvy into the bath, and there was her father to wait for. And when he came back it would be all right. He would be up in court like the last time, and they would give him another fine, with time to pay, and he would go out and get another job, and life would go on just the same.

But even as she tried to convince herself, she knew it wasn't true.

By Monday morning she was back on her stool in the factory, a fresh pile of blouses in front of her, her hands busy and her mind wandering into dark places, her usual optimism gone completely.

'Are there any other offences you would like us to take into consideration?'

They had asked John Sparrow that down at the station, and he had said there were. Shrunk into his chair he had told her that he would have to report at the local court, maybe in two to three weeks' time. And this time he accepted the fact that it might mean prison.

The boys would come home from school to an empty house, but they were used to that. Sharon would go out nightly with her fiancé; and she, Emma, would carry on with running the house.

And how would it be for her father in prison? Emma, with only television documentaries to fall back on, saw him emerging from a cell, slop bucket in his hands, clad in loose-fitting prison jacket and trousers, coughing, always coughing.

She turned the slippery material too quickly, pressed the switch, and the needle went straight through her finger.

'You're sure you feel okay?'

Simon Martin's face hovered above her, seen as through a veil. There was a drumming in her head, and when she tried to stand up her knees buckled beneath her.

There was no sick bay in the factory, just a first aid box in the office, with Mrs Kelly pulling the needle out and dabbing the place with antiseptic, and handing her a glass of water laced with soluble aspirin.

'I'm taking her home.' Simon held her firmly by the elbow and guided her out of the office. Someone brought Emma's coat, helped her on with it and draped the long woollen scarf round her throat.

This was more, he told himself as he almost pushed her into the passenger seat of his car before going round and getting behind the wheel, this was more than the shock of getting a needle through a finger. Emma Sparrow was so white that her skin appeared to be almost transparent. And what made it worse was that she was trying to smile, assuring him over and over that it wasn't necessary, that she would be quite all right.

'You'll have to tell me which way to go.' He followed her instructions, given in a voice so low he had to turn his head to catch what she was saying. 'You mean to tell me you ran all this way the day you missed the bus?'

'Yes,' she told him. No, her finger didn't hurt all that much, it was just that her father had been ill the day before, stopping in bed and frightening the life out of her when she had thought he was going to stop breathing. Bit by bit, as they drove through the centre of town towards to the newly-built houses fringing the outskirts, Emma answered his questions, very conscious of the fact that she was sitting beside the boss's son, being driven home in one of the works' cars on a Monday morning when she ought to have been busy at her machine.

'There's no need for you to come in.' She fumbled with her bandaged hand for her key, and when she found it at last in the depths of her brown shoulder-bag, Simon took it from her and opened the door.

'There's no need for you to come in, sir,' she said again, but even as she said it he was already in, standing by the settee in his dark suit, fingering his striped tie, staring round with open curiosity.

'I'll just nip upstairs and tell my father. He'll be wondering who it is coming in in the middle of the morning.' Emma left him abruptly, seeing through his eyes the shabby room with Sharon's magazines slipping in an untidy heap from the low table, the moquette covers on the settee cushions with their springs bulging like molehills, and the television screen, blank now the boys were at school, filmy with a layer of dust.

When she came back downstairs he was in the kitchen with the kettle going on top of the cooker. 'I found the tea bags,' he announced cheerfully, dropping two into the brown teapot, 'but I can't find the cups and saucers. Or do you use mugs most of the time, like us?'

'The cups and saucers are in the top cupboard, but they might need washing.' Emma felt shame spread over her like a warm wave. 'We only use them when we have company, and we haven't had much of that lately.'

He turned and smiled at her. 'It's okay, Emma. You go and sit down. I'm used to this. I've had long periods of living alone, so I don't stand on ceremony.' He grinned. 'I remember when I was young my mother would have died rather than serve a visitor without a lace-edged cloth on a tray and the silver teapot and the sugar tongs at the ready.' He took a bottle of milk from the fridge. 'At least, when I say silver I mean silver-plate – we didn't rise to such heights as solid.'

Emma went to sit down as she was told, but first she bent down and switched on one bar of the electric fire. Her finger throbbed and ached, and there was an alum-tasting bitterness in her mouth.

Why couldn't he leave her alone? Talking about his mother and her flamin' silver teapot, then trying to make amends by saying it wasn't real. *Patronizing* her. Playing at being kind, and oh, dear God, surely he wasn't washing-up? Emma sat on the edge of her chair, nursing her injured finger, cursing herself for her stupidity in letting it happen. Even the new girls on the sewing machines hardly ever got the needle through.

'Here we are, then.' He came into the room carrying two mugs of steaming tea, handed one over, then sat down facing her. Emma narrowed her eyes. He was so sure of himself, this son of the boss down in London. So confident, she wouldn't have put it past him to run upstairs with a mug for her father. All without a by-your-leave.

And if he did that, if he saw her father propped up on his pillows, unshaven, wearing his vest underneath his pyjamas, smelling of whisky, coughing through a cigarette butt, then Mr Simon Martin would have a fine tale to tell his wife when he got back to London.

'Why don't you tell me what's wrong, Emma?'

She was drinking when he said that, and the question surprised her so much that she blinked at him over the rim of the thick pottery mug.

'How do you mean, what's wrong, sir?'

Simon gave up. For days the white face of this girl had come between him and his ordered thinking. He had watched her, shoulders hunched over that devilish buttonhole machine, stopping now and again to push her hair back behind her ears, then reaching out for another blouse. Like an extension of the machine herself.

He had asked himself why. Why should the sight of this one girl doing what she was paid to do affect him so? It wasn't as if he hadn't seen it all before. The factory in North London was three, almost four times the size of this one, and he had walked daily up and down past the long tables without giving the machinists more than a passing glance. He had even mentioned to Chloe at the weekend that he had a niggling worry about one of the girls in the Lancashire place.

'If I used the expression "a soul in torment", then I would say she's got one,' he had said, and Chloe had stopped chopping onions for a risotto and shot him a glance from streaming eyes.

'Probably pregnant,' she had said without thinking, then blushed and, as Simon turned away, called after him, 'Oh,

'Oh, don't be a hypocrite, honey. Do you really think it was the time to start a family with the world the way it is? You *know* I was right, but you're just too scared to admit it. You've got cosmic ideas, did you know that? You try to equate realism with emotion, and you can't. They don't add up, not even in your book.'

'That's too profound for me,' Simon had answered untruthfully, and walked away.

'Your mother, Emma?' Simon persisted, knowing he had no right to persist, almost feeling his father standing behind him telling him not to be such a bloody fool. 'Does she go out to work?'

Emma tilted her chin, showing the long line of her throat and reminding him of a young Audrey Hepburn. 'My own mother left me with my father when I was very young and got a divorce so that she could marry another man.'

'And you see her sometimes?'

'Never! She lives down near Birmingham somewhere and he, my father, won't hear her name mentioned.'

The man sitting quietly opposite to her sipped his drink thoughtfully. 'And your father married again?'

Emma wondered what would happen if she asked him to go, then as quickly reminded herself that she couldn't afford pride, not with her job at stake. She spoke so softly that Simon had to lean forward to concentrate on her reply.

'Yes, he married again and had three children. I have two stepbrothers and a stepsister. My stepmother was killed two years ago.'

'Killed?'

'Crossing the street. She was a good mam to us.'

'So you do everything?'

'The best way I can.'

He ignored the dignified resentment in her voice. 'Things can't be easy for you, Emma'

'We manage.'

'And your father? Is he out of work at the moment?'

The pain in Emma's finger was spreading up her arm. It had been chaos getting the boys off to school that morning after being away so long. Alan had lost his dinner money, even after she had handed it to him personally; Joe had broken a shoelace; and Sharon was still in bed when Emma had left the house, running for the bus, not missing her breakfast because she had forgotten she had not had any. And now this man was quizzing her as if she were a candidate on *Mastermind*, snapping out the questions and expecting her to give with the immediate answers. One more question and she'd say 'Pass'. She would. As Sharon would say, 'Flaminenry, who did he think he was?'

'Yes, he's out of work at the moment.' Well, that was true, anyway. She waited, the tension mounting in her, for the next question.

But instead Simon Martin stood up and looked down at her. He seemed to be struggling with his thoughts, fighting a private battle in his mind; then he came and sat down on the settee beside her.

'Emma. Emma Sparrow. If we . . . if I found your father a job, say in the packing department, a light job, do you think he would take it?'

His eyes were kind, so filled with kindness that Emma was dismayed to feel her own eyes grow moist. For a full minute she stared at him, not knowing what to say. Kindness was a funny thing. Just a minute before she had been conscious of a growing anger. Now, faced with the obvious compassion in his expression she wanted to put her head down and weep. Instead she told him the truth.

'My father has been charged with stealing from the firm he worked for as a driver. It isn't the first time, and when he comes up at the . . . before the magistrates in two to three weeks' time, they will most likely send him to prison.'

Simon was very businesslike. There was no shock on his face, nothing but an earnest desire to help. Almost without volition his hand crept to his pocket. It was his way – had always been his way. If help was needed and it was in his power to do so, then he gave it. When Chloe needed more money she asked and it was immediately handed over. For an accountant, she often told him, he managed the domestic finances with the expertise of an inefficient housewife.

But before he could open his wallet Emma was on her feet.

'No! We don't need that kind of help, sir! We're hard pressed, but we're not starving. I get me wages of a Friday, and that's all I'm accepting.' She wagged a bandaged finger at him. 'An' if you don't mind, sir, I'll go upstairs to see to my father, an' I'll come back to work tomorrow. This afternoon likely.' The tears in her eyes were tears of humiliation and anger now. 'I won't be the first one going straight back to work when the needle's been pulled out of a finger.'

'Sit down, Emma.' Simon replaced the wallet in his pocket and patted the seat beside him. It was all wrong. The whole situation was out of control. He was getting in too deep, and he knew it. It was breaking the unwritten code sitting down in this house with one of his girl machinists, even though her father was upstairs coughing his heart out by the sound of it. And another thing. This unusual girl, losing her temper, was talking to him as an equal. He shook his head, contradicting himself. She *was* his equal, blast it. In his father's day the employees were expected to be subservient, but not now. And anyway, this Emma Sparrow seemed to have a knowledge, an awareness that even he, with his superior education, lacked. With this girl his rationality was reduced to emotion, and if his father found out he would be appalled.

'Never get familiar with the workroom girls, son. Never! Not even if you fancy one like hell. Spit where you like, but *never* on the factory's doorstep. Message taken?'

But it wasn't like that. How could it be? Chloe was his girl. He would marry her some day. She had been carrying his baby up to a short while ago. Would Emma Sparrow have done what Chloe did? Simon rubbed a hand over his forehead and was surprised to find that it came away dry. This girl with her gentle brown eyes and her soft creamy skin, with the trick she had of tilting her head when she was angry or upset – unusual wasn't the word for her.

'Look,' he said gently. 'Look, I'm sorry I was tactless, and Emma, try not to anticipate the worst about your father. It's not certain that he'll be sent to prison. They take a lot of things into consideration, you know, at the courts. When they go into it and find he is a widower with a young family. . . . His voice tailed off as he saw the expression in her eyes.

'He was warned last time, but it made no difference.' Emma lowered her head. 'I think it's ever since my mother left him. He's not got a chip on his shoulder – what he's got is a whole

56

forest of trees.' She raised her head and looked directly at him. 'But he isn't all bad. He's the sort of man who would pinch your last penny, then make you a pot of tea and hold your hand till you felt better.'

'You're very fond of him.'

'He's my dad! I love him.'

Simon swallowed hard and stood up abruptly. 'I'll be getting along. If that finger is still painful tomorrow I'd see the doctor, but don't come in this afternoon.' He smiled. 'I dare say Mr Gordon can bring in fresh troops to man the button-hole machine temporarily.'

Had he really said that? He knew she had thanked him for bringing her home, remembered she had stood at the door, the bandaged hand laid across her chest like Nelson at the top of his column. Then he sat at the wheel of his car, combing his hair with his fingers in a new and nervous way before he drove away.

'It's nothing. Honest. Anyone would think the needle had gone through my head, not my finger, and anyway, who told you?'

Emma had answered the knock at the front door at ten o'clock that night to see Ben Bamford standing there, his fair hair like a halo round his head, his jeans so tight-fitting they could almost have been a second skin. Beneath his brown leather jacket he wore a polo-necked sweater she couldn't remember having seen before, exactly matching the vivid blue of his eyes.

'You look gorgeous,' she told him as she let him in. 'An' you smell nice too.' She wrinkled her nose. 'You make me feel like a little brown mouse.'

'Aye, and you look like one too.' Ben went to stand on the hearthrug, doing a little shufflle with his feet as if the thought of standing still was bothering him. 'Why don't you go and get tarted up and we'll go somewhere? I've got the car.'

'At this time?' Emma raised her eyes ceilingwards. 'You know about the police coming and finding the stuff?'

'Sure I know. Our Patty's fella knows the bloke who shopped him. He'll get three months, I reckon.'

'Even when he's not fit?'

Ben pulled her close up to him, sliding a hand down her back. 'He can walk and talk, can't he? Then he's fit to do time. If he stops breathing for long enough when he's inside, then they'll shove him into the prison hospital till he comes to.' He squeezed her thigh and grinned. 'Anyroad, what's this I hear about the gaffer's bonny lad fetching you home, eh? I reckon he fancies you!'

'Oh, Ben. . . .' Emma pulled away and sat down, moving a pile of ironing to one side first. 'Mr Martin's okay. An' you know something? I think he is really quite shy. No, honest. I told him about my dad and he tried to make light of it, just to make me feel better. He said that the police couldn't possibly put away everyone they caught, there's too many doing it. He said when they find out we're a one-parent family they might just take that into consideration.'

Ben prissed his mouth up into a mocking pout. 'One-parent family! Oh, lah-de-dah, are we? A fat lot he knows about the rozzers. You could have seventeen kids and a bedridden wife, and they wouldn't make no allowances. The stupid git.' He sat down and drew Emma into his arms. 'Everybody tucked up in bed, eh? How about a bit of that there then, eh?' His blue eyes glinted with laughter. 'Okay then, Em. If you're scared your dad will come down and catch us at it, let's go out.' He jumped up and snapped his fingers. 'Okay? Five minutes to get ready and we'll go and loosen up a bit at a place I know. C'mon. That finger can't stop you dancing. The needle went through your hand, not your bloody big toe!'

He was so alive it seemed as if sparks flew from him, and as she ran upstairs Emma realized why she liked him so much. He was sunshine in a dark room, life where none existed, joy where there was none. And if he heard her say that, he would just die laughing. She pulled on a pair of blue sateen trousers, struggled into a paler blue overblouse, the bandaged finger making her movements clumsy and slow. Then, with Sharon's blusher shaded over her cheekbones and her hair loosened from its restricting ribbon, she was ready.

'Sharon's got her key,' she called through the open door of her father's bedroom. 'I'm going out with Ben.'

The coughing started as if her words had pressed a switch,

58

but it wasn't until she was sitting beside Ben in his car that the habitual feeling of guilt crept into her voice.

'I ought to have stopped in. What if my dad wants a drink? What if he . . .?'

'Oh, shit,' said Ben, and pressed his foot hard down on the accelerator. 'Let him get his own bloody drink for once.'

The place was a converted barn, a stone's throw from a pub, and when they went inside Emma had the feeling she had stepped into a dark cave, lit by flashing coloured lights, with music pounding out so fiercely it seemed as if the roof would lift with the noise. As if she had no will of her own, she was sucked into it, excited by the deafening beat, seeing Ben move as if he were part of the music, then joining in, the throbbing pain in her finger forgotten.

Co-ordinated to the strong rhythm, the strings of coloured lights ran round the huge amplifiers. In front of the disc jockey's table massive round beams of red, blue, green and yellow crossed and recrossed. When the lights dimmed for a moment, huge spotlights glared, blinding, piercing the gloom, whilst the couples danced, swaying, twisting, jerking with grinding movements like prehistoric figures in an animated frieze.

Closing her eyes Emma allowed herself to become a part of it all. Here there was no chance to think. It was so loud she couldn't have *heard* herself think, she told herself. And Ben was like the music ripping across the crowded room, tearing at her senses, so that she was almost convinced that what she felt for him was love.

Emma shook her head until her long hair covered her face, and when he suddenly pulled her to him, she felt his body, his hips moving against her as if they were making love right there on the dance floor. When the white spotlight came on she saw his face, shiny with sweat, his lips parted over his even teeth, and his bright hair lit to sudden glory.

'Love yah, love yah, love yah!' The repetitive lyric hammered in her brain. Totally uninhibited now, Emma danced like a firecracker. She was *young*. Flaminenry, she was only twenty years old! She was no longer Emma Sparrow, trying to be a mother to two young lads who cared for nothing as long as their food was put before them, and the telly was working. And her dad . . . if he went to prison then it was his own fault. She couldn't be responsible; no longer could she be responsible for Sharon either. Let her stay out all night with the foxy-faced spotty boy if she wanted to. Tonight was for dancing, for forgetting, for remembering that she was young. Young!

Tossing the hair from her eyes she saw that now she was dancing opposite to a boy as dark as Ben was fair, that somehow without noticing she had changed partners.

'Crazy!' he shouted, and swung her up into his arms so that her feet left the floor, whirling her round so that her limbs felt fluid and her body had no substance.

What happened next happened so quickly that even as Ben hit the strange boy she was still dancing. Then they were on the floor together, with Ben hammering the dark boy's head into the floorboards as if it were a nail. Showing no mercy, not even when blood spurted from the other's nose spattering his white tee-shirt with a pattern of scarlet.

Hands tore at Ben, dragged him off, frog-marched him from the room, whilst other hands pulled the dark boy to his feet, supporting him dazed, ashen-faced and half unconscious.

'You might have killed him.' Shivering now, the mood of exhilaration snuffed out like a candle flame, Emma followed a glowering Ben to the car. 'What got into you? Was it the music? Ben? You're lucky they didn't send for the police, do you know that? He was only *dancing* with me, for heaven's sake. I didn't know him from Adam, an' if I had known him I couldn't have recognized him in there.'

Without answering Ben started the car so quickly that she had to pull hard at the door to close it as they drove out of the car park at speed on to the main road.

'If I'd had a knife on me I'd have stuck it in him.'

Emma hunched herself lower in her seat as the car gathered speed, watched wide-eyed as the needle crept up to eighty, and clung to the sides of her seat as Ben took it round a corner on two wheels.

'You know what you are, don't you?' His face was set as he crouched over the steering wheel, wrestling with it as if it were alive. 'You're nothing but a whoring tease, Emma Sparrow. That's two fellas you've egged on today.' Ben jumped the lights, heedless of the blare of an outraged motorist behind him. 'First the gaffer's son, and now that black-headed devil back there.' He tore at seventy through a thirty-mile limit. 'You'd let anybody paw you but me. Anybody, bloody anybody!'

'You might have killed him,' Emma whispered again as the car shuddered to a halt outside her house. But before she could slam the door with her good hand it was snatched from her grasp and as she stood there on the pavement, shaking and bewildered, the tail lights of the car were disappearing over the brow of the hill.

All she wanted to do was to creep upstairs, to bury her head beneath the sheets and blot out the memory of the expression on Ben's face as he banged the dark boy's head into the floor. It had been sheer naked aggression, and she shuddered to think what might have happened if he hadn't been pulled away so quickly.

But there, crouched in his chair by the electric fire, her father sat huddled into his old brown dressing-gown, smoking and flicking the ash on to the tiled surround.

'What time do you call this? And where's our Sharon?' He was far from drunk, but by no means sober. His voice was petulant and his eyes sunk deep into bloodshot slits. 'Is this what's going to happen when they put me away? The both of you out till all hours, and them two lads left in the house alone? And Alan's been smoking, did you know that? Pinched the money out of your purse, the little bugger.' He inhaled deeply. 'Smoking at ten years old! What's the world coming to, I'd like to know?'

Emma sat down on the settee, clasping both hands together to stop their trembling. 'Don't worry about Sharon, Dad. I've met the boy she's going out with and he's harmless enough. It seems his parents are all for him having a steady girlfriend, and most nights Sharon goes round to their house. He's a little boy, Dad, honest. He doesn't look much older than Alan. Really.' She tried to smile. 'My guess is they're just playing at courting like a couple of kids. Sharon will have lots of boy-friends before she settles down, for all her talk of getting married. Stop *worrying*, Dad, and get back to bed. Come on.'

Pushing himself up by the wooden arms of the fireside chair, John Sparrow got to his feet, and shuffled towards the door.

With a hand on the knob he turned. 'Aye, well. You're a good lass, Emma. An' I know you'll see to things. Aye, you've allus had your two feet on the ground, right from a little lass.' He began to cough. 'But I've had me chips, love. If they put me away it will finish me off. I can feel it here.' He thumped his chest, and with the cigarette held loosely in his fingers began to climb the stairs, leaving Emma staring into the comfortless glow of the electric fire.

Four

On the day before John Sparrow faced the bench in the local magistrate's court in Lancashire, Simon Martin was facing his father in the office of the Acton branch of Delta Dresses, with a scheme he had in mind.

'Okay, so the Bolton factory is three times the size of this one; okay, so it's been taken over by an astute Ugandan Asian, but it's a challenge I would very much like to take up, Dad.' He walked over to the window and stared down into the car park. 'This mail order contract means big business, and I'd like to settle up there. Truly. If I bought a house part-way between Delta Dresses and the Bolton factory, I could easily commute between the two.' He grinned. 'They need a guy like me and, well, you know me when there's a challenge. You can manage without me down here, and the Bolton deal was that we supply the staff, so where's the problem?'

Bernard Martin, a big man with a florid complexion, with all his son's business acumen but a little less of his charm and finesse, was frankly puzzled.

'You amaze me, son. I thought when you had sorted out the problems at Delta Dresses you would have been all too ready to come back down here.' He reached for his pipe and busied himself with filling it. 'Now you tell me you want to *live* up there?'

He pressed the tobacco down with a practised thumb. 'You always said London was the only place to be for culture and what have you.' He struck a match. 'Besides, what does Chloe have to say about all this? Are you going to tell me now that you're going to get married again?' He went on without looking up. 'You're not going to make the same mistake twice, are you? I seem to remember that one of the things Ellen objected to was you putting the job first.'

'Chloe doesn't know about it yet. I haven't discussed it with her. I wanted to sound you out about it first.' Simon turned back to the window again, away from the calculating gleam in his father's eyes. It wasn't like his father to bring his private life into business discussions, or even mention such things at all. Simon knew that although his living with a girl was accepted with equanimity, the old man kept what he really thought strictly to himself.

'You *like* Chloe, don't you?'

The words were out before Simon realized he had said them. For the life of him he didn't know why he had said them. He bit his lip, annoyed with himself. What was he seeking, for God's sake? An assurance he didn't need?

Bernard Martin puffed thoughtfully at his pipe. This was where he trod warily; this was where he measured his words, if he had any sense. As if he were applying a slide-rule to each bloody letter.

This young man asking the loaded question was not his young son who had gathered sports trophies and A levels at school as if they were just there for the gleaning. This was not the determined lad who had eventually – when he'd put his mind to it – sailed through his accountancy exams as easily as if he had set the bloody papers himself.

This grown man staring moodily out of the window was not the fiercely independent eighteen-year-old rebel who had taken off for Europe with a knapsack on his back, either; sleeping rough in Yugoslavian mountains and tramping across Greece, living in caves, or so he had made out, then playing his guitar in seedy cafés for the price of a loaf of bread.

Nor was this the lad who had married too young a girl who was such a bad cook she could burn a bloody cup of tea. A girl with a face so covered with a fall of long hair he had only glimpsed her eyes once or twice.

No. This was a grown man facing some sort of crossroads, and not knowing which road to take.

Suddenly the love and the pride he felt for his only son caught at Bernard Martin's throat, so that he was glad of the pipe in his mouth, and the concealing cloud of smoke.

'Since you ask me then, yes, I do like Chloe,' he said carefully. 'She's a bright girl with a lot going for her, but I can't see her somehow giving up that well-paid job and her trips abroad to settle down in a semi-detached up north – because that's all you'll be able to afford at first – washing filthy nappies and peeling spuds.'

He failed to see the way his son's back had stiffened, as he warmed to his theme. 'That's what your mother and me have often talked about. Grandchildren.' He chuckled. 'I remember your mother rushing you to the doctor when you swallowed a milk-tooth, certain it would have pierced a lung or something. And I remember where the doctor told us to watch out for it, and where, sure enough, it appeared.' He puffed contentedly. 'Then, when you wanted to take off after you left school, how we worried you might end up in a Turkish gaol suspected of drug smuggling.'

He slapped the desk with the flat of his hand. 'And look at you now, standing there and asking for the chance to work so hard there'll hardly be time left to eat and sleep.'

Simon turned round, his eyes narrowed. 'Who said anything about grandchildren? Who said anything about even getting married? I thought we were talking about the possibility of me talking over the northern side of things, not my domestic set up!'

Bernard Martin got heavily to his feet.

'Let's go into the meeting, son,' he said.

'Can I see my father now, please?'

Emma Sparrow asked the question humbly. Policemen always made her feel humble, though she wasn't sure why. 'Will I be allowed to see him before . . . before he goes away?'

The policeman murmured his reply, one eye on the busy courtroom below the public gallery. 'Not till the court finishes, love. Then you'll be able to see your dad for a few minutes.' He inclined his head. 'They'll be looking to him, love. It wasn't a proper faint, not really. Lots of men, bigger than what your dad is, collapse when they are sentenced. You go back to your seat, till this lot's over and done with. Okay?'

Emma tiptoed quietly back to her seat and sat down. The

light-oak panelling and the high-backed benches reminded her of the Methodist chapel she had attended as a child. But the chairman of the bench hadn't ranted and raved about hell fire the way she remembered some of the lay preachers doing. He was a mild-spoken man, with a noble Jesus profile, and he had listened with great care to what the detective constable and the clerk of the court had told him about John Sparrow's case.

From where Emma sat she had only been able to see the back of her father's head, and the way his fingers had gripped the front of the dock. He had looked strangely bereft without his cigarettes.

'You and your kind are a disgrace to the community at large,' the chairman had said, leaning forward so that the light caught the sheen of his silver hair. 'You were warned and warned again about what would happen if you abused the trust placed in you by your employer, and this time I have no option but to sentence you to. . . .'

And when the morning's session was over and she was taken down to see him, he cried as if his heart would break. Great gulping sobs, with his mouth wide open and the tears dripping from his weak chin.

'All this has come about because of Mam getting herself killed. It started me off wrong, Emma. It was the shock. The drink and the shock.' He stared at her, pleading for understanding. 'It was being told like that, with a neighbour knocking at the door and telling me Mam was lying in the street. Nobody could be the same after that.'

He wobbled his lower lip, the thin whippet lines of his face dropping into the familiar violin-shaped mask of self-pity.

Emma gazed back at him, helpless, ashamed of her embarrassment, not knowing what to do.

'It will soon pass, Dad,' she said at last. 'Six months is nothing. You know what Mam always used to say: it will all be the same a hundred years from now.'

But at the mention of her stepmother, the tears spurted from John Sparrow's eyes like a shower, and Emma allowed herself to be led from the room.

The worst thing was telling Alan and Joe. Joe turned his little face away, his pointed features set into stiff indifference, but Alan perked up immediately, a shifty pride in his dad obvious.

At first Emma had considered telling them that their father had gone away for his health to a convalescent home for treatment of his cough. Then her natural common sense had asserted itself. If she lied, then there was nothing more certain than that they would hear an embroidered version of the truth from their friends at school.

So she explained carefully, as gently as she could, that their father had taken things from work, had been found out, and was now being punished.

'What was it he nicked? Cars?' Alan's brown eyes lit up.

Emma shook her head and swallowed hard. 'No, not cars. Just spare parts of car engines, parts hard to come by, so that he could sell them to bad men for money.' Torn between trying to help them to keep faith with their father and impressing on them that what he had done was wrong, she faltered. 'It wasn't exactly *what* he took. That doesn't come into it at all. What does matter was that the things weren't his to take. They belonged to his firm, to his employers, and he had no right to them.' She raised her voice. 'So the only way he can be shown how wrong it was is to send him away from us and shut him away for a while.'

There! She had done her best. Emma sighed. And nobody could do no more, as the woman at the sweet shop down the road was always saying.

'Spare parts!' Alan's hoarse little voice dripped scorn. 'Flamin' spare parts! Them's nowt, our Emma. Why didn't he tell them they was planted on him?' A surfeit of television cops and robbers serials lent weight to his theme. 'He could have said some bloke grassed on him.' The brown eyes screwed up into calculating slits. 'Or he could have said he didn't know how they got there. He could have said *we* nicked them, me and Joe. They don't send kids to prison. They just give kids a good telling off, don't they, Joe?'

Joe nodded, impressed as Alan elaborated his story. 'How big were them parts? Big enough to shove under the bed, or little enough to flush down the toilet?'

Emma could see his mind working feverishly. 'Dad could have got rid of them when the rozzers knocked at the door.

67

Chucked them through the window or something. He could have. He *could*!'

'That's not the point!'

Emma could not look away from Joe's averted face, but she knew that somehow she had to get through to him. 'It was taking parts in the first place that matters. Stealing is *wrong*.' She knelt down, and drew Joe to her, and felt him grow rigid in her lightly held grasp. 'You understand, don't you, chuck?'

'Will he have to break stones?' The small voice wobbled. 'There was this film on the telly and these men, they had to have chains fastened round their ankles. An' they could only walk with their legs apart, an' they went on lorries to chop great big rocks, an' they had to ask a rozzer before they could take their caps off to scratch their heads. An' if they were ill, they got kicked. . . .'

'They were in a *chain gang*!' Alan's voice oozed derision. 'There are no chain gangs round here. Are there, our Emma?'

To her surprise Emma detected a look of fear in Alan's eyes. Inadvertently she glanced towards the television screen, mercifully blank for the moment.

'Look,' she went on, nodding to Sharon who had just walked into the room. 'There'll be nothing like that. Your dad will be locked in a small cell, maybe with another man, and he will have work to do during the day, certainly. But it won't be chopping stones. Sewing sacks,' she said, searching her own inadequate imagination. 'Or maybe even working in the prison library when they see he's not well enough to do rough work. He'll have good food, and a doctor will come and see him if his chest gets bad, and in the evenings before he goes to bed he will be able to play ping-pong and watch television. 'Okay?'

'Television!' Alan's face settled into its normal mask of indifference once again. 'Jammy bugger!'

'I'll stop in tonight,' Sharon told Emma when the boys were seated in their viewing positions and the tea things had been cleared away. 'You look awful, our Emma, honest you do. Was it terrible down at the . . . you know . . . the court place?'

Emma emptied the washing-up water down the sink and

dried her hands on the roller towel behind the door. 'Well, it was, quite. Dad got a bit upset when they said he had to go to prison, but you know Dad. When he gets upset he coughs and when he coughs he gets more upset.' She started to put the plates away in the cupboard. 'I'm scared. I don't know why, but I am really scared inside. It's partly the boys and partly our Dad.'

She closed the cupboard door with a bang. 'What is he going to be like when he comes out? I mean, what if he comes out all bitter and twisted inside him? He'll be shut up with real criminals, Sharon, and you know how impressionable he is.' She rubbed at a mark on the door of the fridge. 'What if he comes home with a grudge against life? I mean, not *once* has he ever said he was sorry for what he did. He seems to think he only took what was owing to him; that he had done no more wrong than one of his bosses going on his holidays and using the firm's petrol.'

'Well, that's true, isn't it?' Sharon was studying her face in the mirror over the sink, touching a spot and worrying over it. 'It's one law for them and another for us, isn't it? I mean, take me and Ricky. What chance have we of getting a place when we get married? We'll have to live with Ricky's mum and dad, but *they*, the bosspots, *they* don't have to muck in, do they?'

She tried a lock of hair over her forehead and stood back a little to judge the effect. 'I mean, take that bloke who brought you home in his car when you got the needle through your finger. Now *he* wouldn't have to live with his mum and dad when he got married, would he? I know you're a bit stuck on him, but be honest, Emma. Even his secretary wouldn't get time if she wrote private letters on the firm's notepaper, or took a stapler home for her kids to play with. I reckon our dad had a rotten deal.'

'I am *not* stuck on him!' Emma felt her face flame. 'Anyway, he hasn't been in this week, so he's likely as not gone back to London and I'll never see him again.' She felt the need to change the subject quickly. 'Do you know, I think I will go out tonight. I know where Ben will be, and where Ben is there's always plenty of laughing going on. An' I feel my face needs a laugh tonight. Okay?'

'Suit yourself, our kid.'

Sharon leaned closer to the mirror and began to scrutinize her face once again.

When she walked into the lounge bar at eight o'clock Emma saw Ben sitting with the usual gang at the corner table. He was laughing at something one of them had said, and when he saw Emma he got up and with a mock bow waved her to a seat.

'Don't say you've been let off the hook for a night? What's happened then? Sharon decided to renounce her wicked ways and go into a nunnery or something?' He leaned across and touched Emma's knee. 'How did your dad get on? I knew when you didn't come into work today what day it was.'

'He got six months.'

Emma said the hated words straight out, not even bothering to keep her voice low. She had decided during the long wait at the bus stop that there was no point in even trying to be circumspect. People would know and people would talk, even if it didn't get into the paper on Friday. And besides, what was done was done.

She had prepared herself for that, but what she wasn't prepared for was the sudden silence, the immediate lull in the conversation as five faces, all expressing concern, turned towards her. Mandy and Jill, blue eyes and grey opened wide, and Mike and Jimmy, cheeky grins beneath curly-permed hair subdued as they stared at her. Even Ben watching her carefully as if he expected her to burst into tears.

For that single moment kindness, yes, and more than that, *love* embraced her, then Ben jumped up and walked with his usual jaunty stride over to the bar, where his sister Patty polished a glass with a glazed look in her eyes.

'A gin and tonic for old Em,' Ben said. 'An' make it a large one, okay?'

He pushed a pound note across the counter and Patty's fingers closed over it. Her face beneath the hectic blusher looked peaky and lined with strain. She spoke softly.

'I thought your girlfriend only drank lager and lime?'

'Not tonight she doesn't.'

'Then I'll keep the change towards what you owe me. Right?'

Patty moved to turn away, but not quickly enough. Like a snake latching on to its prey Ben's hand shot out and his finger and thumb caught the skin on his sister's forearm, nipping so fiercely that she only just stopped herself from crying out in pain.

'One of these fine days,' she whispered, blinking back tears of shock, 'one of these fine days your precious girlfriend is going to find out what you're really like, Ben Bamford. Then you won't see her for dust. She's far too good for you anyroad and one of these days I am going to have you chucked out of my house, if it's the last thing I do. So help me.'

Then, as Ben walked back to the corner table holding the drink aloft and smiling broadly, the change intact in the pocket of his jeans, Patty picked up the glass and the polishing cloth again.

There was a mark on her arm that she knew would blossom into a bruise, and as she twisted the cloth round and round in the glass she asked herself, not for the first time, how her brother came to be the way he was? How could a man have two completely different sides to his make-up? There was the Ben whom everybody liked, the Ben without a care in the world, who could laugh when there was nothing to laugh about. The brother who could lift his little mongol niece up in the air, tickling her until she cried for mercy, and who had once carried her home from a fairground with her socks and pants in his pocket because she had wet herself.

'I couldn't stand to see her uncomfortable,' he had explained.

Then there was the dark side. The violence ready to take him over, so that as his uncontrollable temper flared he lashed out with his tongue or his fists. Ben *enjoyed* inflicting pain, Patty was sure of it. It gave him a kick, she could tell.

'The usual, sir?'

She smiled her wide smile at the tall dark man who had come into the lounge bar from the residents' staircase. 'I've not seen you for a while, sir. Been away?'

Simon nodded and eased himself on to a stool. He had driven up from London in the fastest time yet, going over and over in his mind the details of his new assignment, trying to forget the scene with Chloe when he had told her about the job

71

up north.

'It's not the fact that you decided to move *before* you told me.
. . .' Chloe had got out of bed and pulled her thin dressing-
gown round her. 'It's the *assumption* that I would just agree.'

She had run her fingers through her hair until her fringe
stuck out in spikes. I like *my* job, okay? So surely you could
have just asked me whether I was prepared to give it up and
follow you. Like some Indian squaw! Me go. You follow! Is
that what we've come to, honey? Is that what you take for
granted?'

'But you could get a job up there.' Simon had thumped the
pillow. 'Manchester isn't exactly a turn-of-the-century village,
and with your languages and your secretarial experience. . . .'

'Stop patronizing me!' Chloe had been almost beside herself
with temper. 'Look. I am going to New York next month and
my boss *expects* me to go with him. I know the score, Simon –
I've already *written* the score! Haven't you heard of sex
equality? I an not some helpless female who has a day off a
month when her womb contracts. I'm not always trying to get
one over on my boss just because he's a man and I'm a woman.
It is *respect*, honey, and that is what you are not prepared to
show me. Mutual respect!'

The gown had slipped from a bare shoulder, revealing a
firm, rounded breast. Simon, reaching out a hand, had it
smartly slapped away.

'How like a man! Sex solves everything! Be nice to the little
woman. Do the things to her body you know she appreciates
and the problem will go away.' Chloe had faced him, two spots
of colour on her high cheekbones. 'And when it's over put your
head down on her breast and she will sigh and tangle her
fingers in your hair and give you anything. *Right*, honey?'

'And you love me?' Simon swirled the whisky round in his
glass as he recalled asking that, and remembered how Chloe
had thrown off the green silk robe and got into bed beside him.
He drained his glass as he remembered also his inadequacy
and the gurgle of her understanding laughter.

'I've pricked the bubble of your masculinity, and you don't
like it one bit do you, honey?'

He had smacked her behind hard and told her she grew
more like her momma every day.

'And have you ever seen a happier man than my daddy?'

Chloe's arms had held him tight, and he was sure they had fallen asleep smiling.

'The same again, sir?'

Patty's cleavage beckoned across the counter. 'Hear that lot over there? It's my brother again.' She fingered the mark on her arm reflectively. 'He's in fine form tonight.'

Simon turned and saw Emma Sparrow sitting a little way apart from the rest towards the end of the curved seat. At the moment he noticed her she tucked the strand of hair behind an ear, small, serious, looking about twelve years old, he thought, in her brown velvet jacket over tight cords.

Immediately he walked over, nodded at Ben, recognized one of the girls as a machinist, and smiled down at Emma.

'Hello there,' he said.

Emma blushed furiously whilst the rest of the group exchanged uneasy glances. Ben merely stared as he sat with shoulders bent and hands clasped between his knees in an attitude of insolent rejection.

'Would you mind if I joined you for a moment or two?' Simon sat down on the very edge of the red plastic seat next to Emma and spoke quietly to her.

'I've been away for a few days. Is there anything new about your father? I expect he'll have heard by now about the. . . .'

Ben said something out of the side of his mouth and the little group exploded into laughter, but Emma answered the question as if they were alone, speaking with a grave quiet courtesy.

'It was today. He got six months, sir. They said he must be made an example of, that what he was doing must be put a stop to.' She lowered her head. 'He took it badly. I think in his heart of hearts he believed they would never send him to prison for doing what he thought of as nothing to get steamed up about. Something trivial.'

'And do *you* think it was trivial, Emma?'

She bit her lip. 'Sins come in different colours, sir, in my book. It depends who's deciding which shade is the darkest. There was a woman who came up in court before my dad, and she only got a suspended sentence for battering her baby senseless. But there's no point in being bitter. What matters now is getting through the next few months till he comes home. Then I suppose he will need a lot of looking after.'

Simon had to remind himself of the age of this girl, talking to him with the wisdom of a middle-aged woman who had long ago accepted life for what it was. Not a shred of self-pity, just a determination to be getting on with things the way they were. And yet her face was the face of a lovely child untouched by worry.

'I am staying up here,' he told her, as the rest of the little group exploded into loud laughter again. 'So I will be looking round for a house or a flat.'

Emma nodded. 'And your wife, sir? She wants to come up here?'

'I'm not married,' he told her, mesmerized by the long dark eyelashes as they drooped against her pale cheeks. 'My girl-friend isn't keen on the idea, but she will come eventually.' He grinned. 'She's the type who has to make a token objection.'

'I see.'

'Time to go if you want a lift, Em.'

Rudely Ben jerked his head towards the door, swaying with ill-concealed arrogance, hands thrust deep in the pockets of his jacket, blue eyes steely cold.

For a moment Emma seemed to hesitate, then with an apologetic glance at Simon she got to her feet and nodded. 'Okay.'

Simon waited until she had disappeared through the swing doors then, with a brief goodnight to Patty behind the bar, walked swiftly out of the lounge, took the stairs two at a time to his room, swinging the key from his hand.

Outside in the car park Emma had no fancy words for what she had to say to Ben. She knew that his rudeness had stemmed from a deep-rooted inferiority complex; that like a child he had been showing off, broadening his accent and making it clear that he didn't think much of Mr Simon Martin trying to be friendly.

'If you're going to drive like you did the other night then I'm going to wait for a bus, no matter how long it takes.' A gust of wind caught her hair and lifted it away from her neck. 'Ben? Listen. Today has lasted long enough for me. I'd just like to go home in one piece and get to bed. Okay?'

So just to show her Ben drove at less than thirty miles an

hour, sitting bolt upright, arms stretched out before him, clutching the wheel like a man of eighty plus who knows his driving should rightly be behind him. Cars hooted as they tried to overtake, but Ben was enjoying himself and refused to drive any faster.

He was just like a child, Emma told herself, an overgrown schoolboy. And the thought softened her face, so that in that moment as they drove majestically down the wide arterial road she came close to loving him.

When Emma saw that the house was in darkness she knew that for once Sharon had been sensible and decided to have an early night. Still playing the fool, Ben handed her out of the car and drove away bolt upright in the driving seat, arms held straight before him on the wheel.

She opened the door, stepped into the tiny square of a hall and saw, in the glow from the electric fire, Sharon and the foxy-faced Ricky entwined on the hearthrug.

Even before she turned to run in acute embarrassment up the stairs Emma's mind had registered the face that her step-sister and her boyfriend were completely naked, their clothes strewn around them in careless abandon.

Five

At two o'clock Simon woke abruptly, switched on the light and saw with dismay that he had slept for only two hours. Wide awake, he lay with his arms behind his head and stared at the ceiling.

The barmaid, Patty Bamford, looked as if life had kicked her in the teeth once too often. Simon frowned. There was something. . . . He tried to bring her to mind as he had seen her that evening, strangely subdued in her mauve, woollen, short-sleeved dress. He had watched her as she turned to ring the change up on the till and thought. . . .

Suddenly he sat straight up in bed. Her belt! The narrow grey crocodile-skin belt round the waist of the mauve dress. A beautifully fashioned belt with a twist of gold chain forming a clasp.

'Never spoil good material and design with inferior buttons and belts.' He heard his father's voice as clearly as if he had been standing beside the bed. 'Here's what the smart women do. They buy cheap, mass-produced suits and dresses, then replace the buttons and belts with the real stuff.' He had thrown a grey skin belt down on his desk. 'Now, with Delta Dresses the quality's there right from the start. Take a look at this, son. Specially made for an export deal that went wrong for some poor chap. I've had a word with our designer and she agrees they'll work in fine with some of our spring models. Always one step ahead, that's your old man!'

Simon got out of bed and switched on the electric kettle, one of the hotel's amenities, then opened a sachet of instant coffee and poured the powder into a cup.

It was too much of a coincidence to suppose that Patty

Bamford had bought the belt separately. It had been a one-off job, and his father had taken the lot. Simon poured a stream of boiling water on to the coffee and pierced a hole in the triangular carton of milk.

And if Ben Bamford had taken the belt, then it followed he had taken the dress. . . . Simon took the cup of coffee back to bed. Those dresses retailed at eighty-five pounds with the quilted matching boleros. . . . He narrowed his eyes, trying to remember exactly the lines where items had gone mysteriously missing.

The file was in Harry Gordon's office. Simon restrained the impulse to get dressed and drive to the factory. The belt was merely one item. There had been blouses, the odd lined skirt, and then, as the thief gained confidence, the more expensive suits and dresses.

He lay down again and switched off the light, his mind clicking over with the competence of a programmed computer. Tomorrow . . . no, *today* he would do what he had to do. Ben Bamford would have to go.

The talk with Sharon had to come some time. Emma knew that. And yet, all during the day she asked herself if it was any concern of hers. Who had said she was to be responsible for her family? Who? Legally she wasn't responsible, not at twenty years old, surely? But *morally*? Emma tried to bring her stepmother's thin face to mind, and remembered how she would lash out quickly at the boys when they were cheeky. Just the once, with a resounding slap that silenced their bravado, even as it brought tears of humiliation to their eyes.

Mam had known how to deal with Sharon too.

'Take that muck off your face,' she'd say quietly. 'Go on! Upstairs. Right now. Going to school of a day, then dolling yourself up like a tart at night. An' if you land yourself in any trouble, lass, with them boys you're always hanging about on street corners with, then don't bring it back here! And take that look off your face! One of these days the wind will change in your direction and that sneer will set. And wipe that smile off too. You'll be laughing the other side of your gob before the day's over!'

Oh, yes, that had been Mam. Coming in from work, straight to the gas stove. Standing there sometimes forgetting she still had her outdoor coat on, flipping bacon over in the frying pan, seeing without turning round if the boys were putting their feet on the settee, holding out her hand for her husband's wages of a Friday, and once hiding his shoes when he wanted to go down to the pub and the gas bill hadn't been paid. Tempering the rough edge of her tongue with kindness, and treating her husband as if he had been one of her small boys, and Emma as if she were her own daughter. Making no difference, even to cooling the praise when Emma brought a good report home from school.

'There's more to life than being a good scholar. Some of them clever ones who go to university only smoke drugs and hang themselves sometimes when they don't pass their exams. You can think too much,' she was fond of saying. 'It sets the brain in a fever, thinking too much does.'

'Oh, Mam. . . .' Emma talked silently to herself as she hurried the boys out of the bathroom and into their beds. 'What would you have done if you'd found what I found last night? An' on the very day Dad went away to prison!'

Then she shook her head. Dad would never have gone to prison if his wife had been alive. For one thing, those boxes could never have been stacked on top of the wardrobe like that for weeks. Not with Mam cleaning the house from top to bottom at the weekends. And Sharon wouldn't have been allowed to stay out late every night, nor bring that boy into the house – just the two of them, with the boys asleep upstairs in their beds.

'Just a minute before you go out, Sharon.'

Emma caught her stepsister with one hand actually on the door catch, and knew she had crept down the stairs whilst the boys were playing up and refusing to get into bed. 'It won't take a minute. I know Ricky's waiting for you outside, an' I don't blame him. If he's embarrassed, then it makes two of us.'

'Yes?' Sharon stood by the door, wary and defiant, her eyes studying the toes of her boots.

Emma tried to think of the right thing to say. Oh, hell, she was *always* searching for the right thing to say.

'Sharon.' She held out a hand as if pleading for understanding. 'Look, love. I'm not going to interfere but, well, you are only sixteen an' if you get pregnant now you could ruin your whole life. And how old did you say Ricky was? Seventeen?'

'Nearly eighteen, and when he's had his birthday we're getting married. Remember?' Sharon stared at her defiantly, poised for flight, both hands busily tying a pink patterned headscarf into a bow beneath her chin. 'Flaminenry! Who said anything about getting pregnant? I'm not that daft, our Emma. Who do you think is on the throne? Queen Victoria?'

'What do you mean?' Emma kept her voice low. 'There's no need to shout. I wouldn't like the boys to hear this conversation. An' besides, what if they had come downstairs? Suppose Joe had walked in like he does sometimes? You know what a restless sleeper he is. Don't you think he's had as much as he can take just now without you adding to it?'

'Well, he didn't come down, did he?' Sharon's tone was flippant. 'An' to set your mind at rest you might as well know I've been on the pill for months. Got a prescription from the doctor when I told him nothing would stop me sleeping with my boyfriend, so you can stop worriting.' Her face softened for a moment. 'Flaminenry, our Emma! Haven't you got enough to bother about? I can take care of meself, and always have been able to. We're being responsible citizens, me and Ricky, and besides, his mam knows and she hasn't said nothing.'

'Ricky's mother knows?' Emma swallowed hard. 'How do you know she knows?'

Sharon answered with infinite patience, raising blue eyes ceilingwards as if seeking tolerance. 'She knows because she found out what we were doing – never mind how – and it was her what suggested I go to the doctor. So put that in your pipe and smoke it!'

'I'm trying to think what Mam would have said.' Emma raised her head as the sound of a motorbike shattered the silence outside in the avenue. 'But then, Mam wouldn't have said anything. She'd have merely knocked your block off, that's all. And as for that little lad wanting to marry you, well, she'd have knocked his block off too!'

'But Mam's dead, isn't she?' There were tears in the shouted defiance as Sharon's small face crumpled. 'She got killed when we all needed her, didn't she? An' I'll tell you something else, our Emma. Ricky isn't the first, not by a long chalk. I've been with other boys, lots of them, and sometimes without using anything, an' I got away with it.' She rubbed her eyes with a clenched fist. 'An' Ricky was the first boy to *care* whether I got pregnant. An' his mother cared too. She says she'll be glad to get me away from this house with what goes on. She's not the same as Mam, but she'll *be* my Mam, can't you see? An' when me and Ricky get married it will be like it used to be, with me coming home from work and smelling me tea cooking, and her doing me washing, and telling me what to do. Flaminenry! Can't you see?'

Oh, yes, Emma *could* see, and her heart ached with the seeing, but there was one remark she wasn't going to let pass.

'What do you mean: "what goes on in this house"? Tell me! What *does* go on that Ricky's mother finds so shocking?'

Sharon was crying openly now. 'Well, our dad of course. Mrs Rostron is the superintendent of the junior Sunday school at Marston Street Chapel, and Mr Rostron is a Mason. How do you think they feel about their son's girlfriend's father being in prison? They tried to stop him going out with me at first because it got back about Dad being up before the magistrates, an' him drinking an' everything. They never have a drop in the house, and Mrs Rostron works three afternoons in an Oxfam shop. They're *different* from us, Emma. An' when I am there *I'm* different too. They *talk* about things, and *do* things. Like Mr Rostron taking forms round to houses last week asking which people were interested in the . . . the reclamation of household rubbish. To do with the ratepayers, Emma.' She glanced round wildly. 'What do we ever talk about, Emma? What did our dad ever talk about apart from grumbling about the rubbish on the telly, and whether he had enough money for his whisky and his fags? He didn't care nothing as long as the boys were kept quiet an' his meals were there. And *you*! Some days you look about thirty, our Emma, an' I'm not going to be like you. I'm getting out, an' if sleeping with Ricky and marrying Ricky is the only way then I don't care! I don't care!'

The injustice of it made Emma feel sick, and when Sharon turned to go she put up a hand. 'Just two things, Sharon. Have you ever stopped to think what would have happened to this family if I had taken your attitude?' She sat down on the nearest chair, her legs suddenly weak. 'We both knew that Dad, for all his kindness – and he *is* kind, you know that – we both knew he hadn't got the guts to take over when Mam died. She *carried* him, Sharon. She thought for him and kept him decent, and without her he just gave up. So *somebody* had to do something. An' if doing it has made me look thirty years old, then it's too bad.' Her head lifted. 'An' I can't quite understand Ricky's parents' strict Chapel ways matching up with you being on the pill at sixteen. The two don't go together, not in my book they don't.'

Sharon blushed and edged a step backwards. 'You don't know Ricky. But they do. An' if what they did was the alternative to me getting pregnant, then they were prepared to turn a blind eye.' Her voice rose in defiance again. 'Is what he's doing any worse than getting mixed up with bad company? He was a right tearaway before he met me, Ricky was.'

Emma tried to imagine the slight, foxy-faced, spotty boy as a tearaway, and failed.

'All right, Sharon,' she said quietly. 'You seem to have it all worked out. But I hope you realize what you're missing.' She turned her head from side to side. 'You should be having *fun*, love. Going out with girlfriends, and saving up for holidays, not getting married at sixteen.'

Sharon opened the door and wiped the tears from her cheeks with the back of a gloved hand. 'You are you, and I am me,' she said, and just for a brief moment her face softened. 'Perhaps I have more of Dad in me than what you have, our Emma. Perhaps I just want the easy way out.' She glanced up the stairs. 'An' Alan's the same. He wants things on a plate, an' I don't just mean his dinner.'

The feeble attempt at a joke evoked a response in Emma's heart far more than all the shouting, the tears and the defiance had done. For once in this house two people had communicated, actually said what was in their hearts, and in a strange way it all made sense. She smiled and nodded as Sharon closed the door behind her.

'Have a good time, love,' she said softly, and they stared at each other, closer than if they had put their arms round each other.

And as Sharon climbed on to the pillion seat of the enormous motorbike and put her arms round Ricky's waist and smelt the familiar smell of his black leather fringed jacket, she failed to see the car drawn up at the kerb a few yards behind. Failed to see the fair boy sitting at the wheel smoking a cigarette, the stub of which he threw from the car window as the bike roared away up the avenue.

Emma stood quite still until the sound of the motorbike had died away. Inside her she was grieving, not for the Sharon who now seemed to have got her life sorted out all of a piece, but for the fourteen-year-old girl who had thought so little of herself that she had gone from one boy to another in an attempt to assuage the deep sense of loss after her mother had been killed. Somebody ought to have known, somebody ought to have seen. But who? Not her father, too wrapped up in his own self and his sorrowing to even guess at what was going on. That left herself. Emma Sparrow, eighteen, forced overnight into the role of mother to a bewildered five-year-old Joe and to Alan, two years older, whose mourning took the immediate form of aggression.

The loud knocking at the door tore at her ragged nerves so that the blood drained from her cheeks, and when she let Ben in she failed to notice that the violence in him was so ill-contained that it seemed to be·striking from his body like sparks.

'I can't come out tonight, Ben.' She went over and closed the door between the living-room and the foot of the stairs. 'I doubt if the boys are asleep yet. I can't leave them, and Sharon's gone out. You must have seen her go, she's only been gone a minute.'

'I've not come to ask you to go out with me. We're finished.' Ben spoke in a low, rough voice, and as Emma turned to him in surprise she saw that he was clenching and unclenching his hands in a rhythmic motion.

'What's the matter, Ben?' she asked quietly.

He laughed, a loud bark of a laugh. 'You have the nerve to ask me what's the matter? Good God, Emma Sparrow, you lose me my job without so much as a reference, and you have the bloody nerve to ask me that!' He kicked at the leg of the television table so that the set wobbled dangerously. 'I knew you were up to something last night when I saw you whispering to the gaffer's son, looking like butter wouldn't melt in your mouth, but I never thought you would pretend to know nothing.'

For the second time in ten minutes Emma sat down on the edge of a chair feeling her legs weak and her mouth dry.

'*Me* responsible for you losing your job? What are you talking about, Ben? I saw you go into the office this morning, but I thought it was just. . . .' She tilted her chin. 'I thought you'd been caught larking about downstairs like last time. Why did you get the sack? Why? Mr Martin wouldn't do that just for a bit of horseplay. He's not like that.'

'Hah!' Ben came a step closer, standing over her in a menacing attitude that made her shrink back in fear. 'An' you know exactly what he's like, don't you? He's been coming here, and you've been seeing him, and oh, yes, I can see it all. You *told* him about the dresses, all three of them, because I was daft enough to hint to you what I was doing. An' when he told me he wasn't going to bring the police into it, it was as though you yourself were doing the talking.' He gripped her shoulder hard. 'That would be just like you, Em, wouldn't it? I can just see you telling him you knew I was up to something, and persuading him to let me off with a warning. To save me from my bloody self, Em. That's the way you talk, isn't it? An' *why* did he agree not to send for the law? Not because he's that kind of man, but because you had made it worth his while, eh? Eh?' The fingers were vice-like in their hold, and Emma winced with pain.

'You are wrong!' She tried to speak firmly. 'I didn't know you were taking stuff from the factory! You hinted you were up to something, but I never thought. . . .' She forced herself to look into the blazing eyes. 'An' if I *had* known I would have talked to *you*, not to Mr Martin. What d'you think I am?'

'I don't know, Emma Sparrow.' Ben's tone was silky soft now. 'I've never really known, but I'll tell you something. That precious Mr Martin of yours isn't going to get away with it, I can promise you that. An' when I've finished with him you won't want to gaze in his eyes like you were doing last night.'

He let go of her and pushed her back so roughly that the chair almost fell over.

There was a pounding in his head, and now his hands were aching with the effort of keeping them off her; if she had been Patty he would have belted her till she cried for mercy. He stepped back.

But she wasn't Patty. This girl was like no other girl he had ever known. She was so beautiful that at times his guts felt like they were turning to water as he looked at her. She was full of spirit too; if he did lay about her she would try to fight back, he knew that. An' if he did touch her, then she would be lost to him for ever, an' he would regret it till the day he died.

If Mr bloody Martin hadn't spotted the belt, he would have denied everything, and brought him up at an industrial tribunal. Ben knew all about industrial tribunals. It wasn't as easy as all that to get rid of workers these days; the law was on their side, an' it was old Gordon's fault for being so slack an' not having every step of the manufacture signed for. The first time he got Patty on her own he'd show her what for, but it wouldn't be in front of the kid. Not that kid with her moon grin and devotion to her Uncle Ben.

'He had proof,' he said sulkily, 'but he wouldn't have noticed, the proof wouldn't have registered if you hadn't put him wise, hadn't hinted.' His mind continued its reasoning. 'Your dad got caught, and you tried to square it so that the same wouldn't happen to me. Why else would he let me go without reporting it to the law? Why else, Em, unless he was doing you a favour? He's a hard nut, your friend, like the rest of them. His sort don't do anybody no favours, not to my kind they don't.'

Then, before she could stop him, he pulled Emma up into his arms and, holding her pressed tightly against him, kissed her hard, forcing her lips apart, and grinding his tongue into her mouth.

'So now you know, Emma Sparrow!'

He let her go so abruptly that she had to grab the chair arms to steady herself, and before she recovered her balance he had gone, slamming the front door with such violence that it seemed the little house shook to its very foundations.

* * *

Three weeks later Simon Martin, bored with the loneliness of his hotel room, and seeing columns of figures dancing before his eyes, decided to take a midnight walk before going to bed.

The countryside stretching beyond the rear of the hotel was flat, bisected by wooded banks massed with wild flowers. And that night their scent hung in the air as if sprayed from an aerosol.

Simon was discovering to his delight, as many southerners had done before him, that Lancashire was more than a vista of mill chimneys; that there were green valleys, wide stretches of moorland and shimmering rivers. It was a night of stars, with hedges glowing greenly in the gentle darkness, and he knew, he *needed* to know, that when Chloe came up and saw the house now under negotiation, she would share his content.

He was turning to go back to the hotel when he heard the car pull up. When he was seized from behind the blow to the side of his head sent him sprawling. And when the kicks came fast and furious he held his arms over his head in an instinctive attempt to shield his face. There were no words, no grunts, no smothered oaths, just a deliberate series of well-aimed kicks, to his groin, his body, and when he tried to get to his feet he felt the blood spurt from his nose as a fist slammed relentlessly into his face.

Frantic now with pain, he gripped a trouser leg, his numbed senses telling him that there were three, or at least two attackers. His heart thumped against his ribs as with every ounce of strength in him he tried to twist the leg, to bring his assailant down to ground level, but a kick in the region of his stomach made him gasp and lose his grip, and as the car roared away he was kneeling down in the road being violently sick.

When he managed at last to stagger up the drive and into the foyer of the hotel, the night porter reached for the telephone even as Simon slid unconscious to the floor. By the time Simon opened his eyes to feel a wet cloth on his forehead, the ambulance was on its way.

Six

The news that Mr Simon had been mugged was all over the factory before the girls had taken the covers off their machines the next morning.

Mrs Arkwright was in the office discussing it with Mrs Kelly. The assembled pieces of material were neglected as rumours flew thick and wide, gathering strength as they were repeated.

'Left for dead,' the copper-haired machinist said in a hushed voice. 'In the infirmary with the sight of one eye nearly gone.' She paused. 'Mrs Kelly told me. An' Mr Gordon is by his bedside.' She sighed deeply. 'Strange Mr Simon coming up here from London where folks get mugged all the time, then having it happen to him here.'

'It's a terrible world and no mistake.' A middle-aged woman in a tweed skirt and a yellow tee-shirt stretched across massive breasts broke in. 'It was kids did it, I reckon. Just for laughs. I nearly said just for kicks,' she went on, then withdrew the smile from her face as no one saw the joke.

Emma stood quietly listening, her brown eyes wide in the sudden pallor of her face. Then without a word she left her machine and walked into the office, going straight in without knocking, leaving the girls exchanging meaning glances with each other.

'Is it true about Mr Simon?' Emma ignored Mrs Arkwright and spoke directly to Mrs Kelly, relying on the little Irishwoman's kindness to tell her the truth with no embellishments.

'Aye, love, it's true.' Mrs Kelly was ignoring Mrs Arkwright too. 'He went for a walk late on apparently, and got set on by a gang.'

'Is he badly hurt?' The question was no more than a whisper.

'Bad enough. They've kept him in the infirmary anyroad, and they don't do that unless it's serious, not these days they don't. Not with folks queueing up for beds and not getting one till they're at death's door.'

'Did they get who did it?'

Mrs Kelly shook her neat black head, with the hair so laquered into place that not a strand moved. 'No, they made off. But whoever did it wants locking up and flogging. Talk about short sharp sentences. It's short sharp leatherings what's needed in my opinion.'

'Thank you.' Emma walked, straight-backed, out of the office and back to her machine where she switched on, picked up a piece of grey satin-look material and slid the button trim underneath the foot.

Mrs Arkwright watched her with eyebrows raised. 'What was all that about, then? Something going on I ought to know about?'

'Nothing.' Mrs Kelly's tone of voice forbade any further discussion. 'You know our Emma. She won't tittle tattle. My guess, for what it's worth, is that little Miss Sparrow would walk straight into your job if you ever decided to go.'

'Would she indeed?' Mrs Arkwright flounced from the office to speak sharply to the girls, and Mrs Kelly nodded, satisfied.

At lunchtime Emma did not appear in the canteen. Instead she caught a bus outside the tall red-brick building and jumped off as it stopped for the lights outside Woolworth's. Sharon was weighing a quarter of peppermint chews for a stout woman who wore a headscarf with dogs' heads printed all over it. Sharon winked at Emma before passing the bag over and dropping the money into the till.

'I can't stop.' Emma leaned over the display of cellophane-wrapped sweets and spoke softly. 'But I had to make sure you would be going straight home after work.' She hesitated. 'I have to go somewhere, and I don't want the boys wondering what's happened.'

'Go where?' Sharon tucked a strand of fair hair underneath the wisp of blue chiffon wound round her head turban-wise. 'It must be important for you to come down here in your lunch break. Go where, our Emma?'

'I'll tell you when I get back.' Emma turned to go. 'Give the boys their tea, will you, love? There's a tin of baked beans in the cupboard.'

'*When* you've finished chatting to your friend. . . .' An elderly man in a cloth cap and a shabby raincoat edged close to the counter. 'A quarter of winter mixtures, if it's not too much trouble!'

Sharon gave him a radiant smile and scooped up a handful of the sweets, and when she turned round from weighing them Emma was gone.

'Now I wonder what all that was about?' she said aloud, and handed over the change with the practised smile dimmed a little round the edges.

Emma had tried to prepare herself for the worst before she went to visit Simon in the infirmary after work that evening, but what she saw was worse than anything she could have imagined. He was lying so still that at first he appeared to have stopped breathing. Grey of face, with a pad covering his left eye, a bandage holding it in place, and with the bedclothes held away from his legs by a cage the size of an upturned barrel, the sight of him numbed her senses for a moment. She could only stand by the side of the high narrow bed and gaze down at his still face in silent dismay.

A young Indian doctor beckoned to Emma and spoke softly.

'He is quite comfortable, really.' He smiled at Emma's stricken expression. 'He has not slept since being brought in at one o'clock this morning. He has insisted on talking on the telephone, and because he is badly shocked and will not realize, we have given him a sleeping draught an hour ago. You are his friend?'

Emma nodded.

'Then if you speak his name quietly he will perhaps hear and know you have been to see him, then when you come again he will be wide awake. It is best just to leave him. Really.' The dark liquid eyes were full of compassion. 'We will know tomorrow whether there is any danger to his eye. There is no internal bleeding, and no broken bones.' he smiled. 'Your friend is very strong and fit, it would take more than a beating to kill him.'

He walked away, the white coat flying, and Emma went to take her place by the bed again. There was such a shame in her that her whole body burned with it. The curious numbness had passed to her mind, and after five minutes had gone by without any movement from the still figure on the bed, she pulled up a little hard chair and sat down on it.

Ben had done this terrible thing, she was sure of it. Aided and abetted by his friends, who would follow him to the edge of a cliff and jump over if he led the way; he had taken his revenge. Emma slipped the strap of her shoulder-bag from her arm and held it on her knee, unclasping and clasping the catch in nervous agitation. The worry in her mind niggled away at the numbness so that she saw what had happened, understood what had happened as if she herself had been the instigator.

Ben had refused to believe her when she had told him she had had no part in his dismissal. He had often teased her and told her to stop acting God and interfering in other people's lives. Emma's brown eyes stared unblinking at the pale face on the white pillow. Was she like that? Sharon had hinted as much when she had lectured her about sleeping with Ricky. Her father had said she drove him mad with her nagging, and the boys often exchanged glances of disgust when she tried to make them behave. Was she . . . had circumstances made her into the kind of woman she never wanted to be?

Was that why Ben had been so sure she had hinted that the pilfering, no, the *stealing* from the factory was his doing?

Suddenly she remembered the way Ben had lost control at the disco and hammered the strange boy's head into the floor. Her chin came up. A sermonizer she might be, but someone else, something else in Ben's life had made him the way he was. Emma shifted slightly on the hard chair. She leaned forward as Simon's eyelids fluttered.

She held her breath as the dark eyes opened briefly, then as they closed again she spoke in a whisper.

'Sir? Mr Simon? It's me. Emma Sparrow.'

The long mouth curved into the semblance of a smile and

the hand lying on the turned-down sheet moved slightly before the sleeping draught took over again.

The colour suddenly flooding Emma's face made her beautiful. The pounding of her heart and the emotion tearing through her whole body took her by shattering surprise. Tears misted her eyes as she stared at the still face on the pillow. In that very moment, with a man coughing in the next bed and with the sound of a nurse's feet tapping along the polished floor, Emma stepped over the line marking what had been no more than a strange sensation of affinity, into the wider realms of unselfish love.

He did not know that she was there; on waking he would not remember she had been, but still she sat there. The visitors at the other beds in the small square ward said their goodbyes and went away. A junior nurse helped the coughing man into his dressing-gown and led him to the bathroom, but Emma heard and saw nothing.

Lost in her dreams, she failed to see the tall girl with dark shining hair come into the ward; failed to see the way she hesitated for a moment before coming swiftly over to Simon's bed.

When Emma looked up at last she saw this girl, with her cream suede jacket open over a green, silky polo-necked sweater, standing at the opposite side of the bed watching her. Not smiling, not frowning, just watching. There was a green silk scarf threaded through the leather strap of the girl's brown handbag, and large gold hoop ear-rings shone in her ears. She was dressed exactly as Emma would have liked to be dressed, given the money.

Chloe, in that same moment of assessment, saw a small girl clutching a black plastic bag, wearing a shortie raincoat over a dark-blue sweater. No jewellery of any kind, and hardly any make-up, but then who needed make-up with a skin like that? The eyelashes could have been false, but she thought not. Probably came with those enormous amber-flecked eyes, and what a face! This girl was a beauty, make no mistake about that.

All that in a swift exchange of glances, lasting no longer than three seconds, before Chloe nodded.

'Hi! I'm Chloe Day. I saw the doctor on the way in and she

90

told me he was sleeping.' She touched Simon's cheek gently. 'Looks pretty rough, doesn't he? Does anyone know yet what happened exactly?' She went on, not waiting for an answer from the girl sitting mute by the side of the bed. 'He actually rang me this morning before I left for work, just so I wouldn't worry if I rang the hotel this evening and got the news that way. He's going to get one big surprise when he wakes to find me here. I've told him before about going out running late at night, but you know Simon.' She looked up with disconcerting suddenness. '*Do* you know him at all well?'

And she wasn't being bitchy or snobbish, or patronizing, not even critical. Chloe was just being Chloe. Frank, friendly, mistress of her own emotions. Or at least she had thought so. On the long drive up from London she had imagined how Simon would look when he saw her, and how he would react when she told him she had given up a Paris trip and let her assistant go instead, just to be with him. Even as she imagined the scene she had heard her mother's voice:

'You're so like me, honey. Whatever the circumstances, somehow you will always cast yourself in the role of the heroine. When your daddy was so ill last fall I was picturing myself being the brave little woman if he died. You know, coping with everything so that people marvelled and said how brave I was. And let me tell you, honey, whatever happens to you there will always be a part of yourself out there in the wings, cheering you on.'

But here and now the reality was far different. In the scene she had envisaged, Simon had been sitting up in bed, holding out his arms and smiling at her, not lying drugged in a sleep that seemed almost deeper than death. She shuddered. And there had been no lovely elfin child staring at him with her soul shining clear for anyone to see.

'I work in the factory, at Delta Dresses.' The waif had a voice to match her fragile beauty, soft and husky, not loud like her own. Chloe held out a hand across the bed and found it held in a warm firm grasp.

'My name is Emma Sparrow,' the girl said. 'An' I'll be going now. It's been nice meeting you, Miss Day. Good-night.'

Chloe watched her go, a puzzled frown wrinkling her

smooth forehead. Emma Sparrow. The girl with the soul in torment. The girl Simon had mentioned more than once.

Moving round the bed she sat down in the chair Emma had pulled up to the bed and took Simon's listless hand in her own. Momma had been right. If there were to be any heroines competing for an Oscar the winner was going to be Chloe Day. Okay?

With dragging feet Emma walked down the long corridor, down one flight of steps, the length of another wide polished corridor and out through the swing doors into the warm spring evening. Emotions she hadn't known she possessed were rampaging round and round in her bloodstream, and the foremost of them all was telling her that she had to find Ben and confront him with her suspicions. No, more than her suspicions, her certainty.

She had seen the wild violence in his eyes the night he had come to the house, and he had hinted . . . but oh, dear God, never would she have believed that he could inflict such deliberate pain and suffering on another human being. Emma closed her eyes and behind the closed lids she saw Simon lying on the ground, and heard the dull thuds as the kicks found their target. She whimpered so that a passing cyclist turned his head to stare at her in curiosity.

Mr Simon's eyes, his steady dark eyes, cut and bruised. . . . She got on the bus, sat on the seat near to the platform, and got off before the terminus, deciding to walk the rest of the way.

Sharon would have to manage. For once she would have to see the boys to bed and stay in with them, with Ricky there or without Ricky there; it made no difference. Her thoughts were hard and clipped now, and her steps quickened as she turned into the long main road leading to the street where Ben lived with his sister.

She passed barren stretches of spare land where terraced houses had been demolished, land waiting for the money to be found for the builders to move in. She passed rows of shops, boarded up with crude graffiti chalked across the boards. She passed a public house, then another, with the tops of heads showing above half-glazed windows. And she saw nothing.

For the time being all her concentration was set on getting to Ben's house in the quickest possible time. The episode with Chloe at the hospital was obliterated from her mind as completely as if it had never happened.

When she lifted the knocker and let it fall against the door of the end house in a street not yet scheduled for demolition by the town planners, she was shivering. And when Patty Bamford stood before her, the blonde hair wisping from its tortured swirls, she was so breathless she could hardly speak.

'Is Ben in?' This was no time for niceties, no asking if it were convenient. 'I want to speak to him,' Emma said, holding her hand against the stitch in her side, the sharp pain only now making itself felt.

Patty's blue eyes widened. 'You'd best come in.' She stood back and waited for Emma to precede her down the narrow passage leading to the back room.

'I'm sorry things are in a bit of a mess, love.' She was apologizing, stacking plates together on the table by the window, stubbing a cigarette out in a saucer, waving a hand to Emma to sit down. 'That fella of mine insisted on going out, Ben's cleared off, and I should be at work but I can't leave her.' She jerked her head towards the child sitting strapped into a high-chair by the side of the wide, chipped tiled fireplace.

The child was way past the high-chair age, Emma saw that at a glance, but the little legs dangling down were spaghetti-thin, and the head seemed much too big for the frail body. The eyes were round and not set in hollows, and they shone, not with intelligence, but with a strange touching glow of happiness. Ben had said Patty's girl was a bit backward, but nothing had prepared Emma for the shock. She walked over to the chair and smiled, and the child immediately held up her arms.

'She wants you to lift her out.' Patty's voice was matter-of-fact. 'She loves people coming in. She'll go to anybody. It's a pity she can't run about, but she can shuffle about on her behind quicker than what some kids can walk. Go on, take her out.'

Carefully Emma lifted the child from the chair and sat down with her on the settee. And at once two thin arms crept round her neck and the grotesque head was snuggled into her shoulder as the child smiled a wide smile of pure affection.

Immediately Emma's pent-up anger evaporated as she rocked the small body to and fro. 'Is there . . . is there nothing . . .?' She faltered, stroking the fine soft hair away from the bulbous forehead.

'Nothing.' Patty shook her head from side to side. 'They told me she wouldn't live more than three years but she's four now, and she can feed herself and say a few words.' She raised her voice. 'Say hello to Emma, chuck. Come on. Don't let me down.'

The unblinking stare focused on Emma's face. 'Hello!' she said clearly, then again, 'Hello!'

'She's going to miss her Uncle Ben, that's for sure.' Patty sat down in the rocking chair pulled up to the flickering gas fire. 'But he'll be back. I know my brother. This isn't the first time he did a bunk when things got too hot for him, but he'll be back.' She blinked. 'An' before you say anything, I know what I know, and you know what you think you know, but least said soonest mended. Okay?'

When Emma made no reply to this, she went on. 'He cleared off this morning, but he's been working up to it ever since he got the sack. He had a bag already packed, and when he walked out of that door, *she* knew.' She pointed to the child. 'Cried for half an hour as if her heart would break, so she's got feelings same as you and me. She worshipped Ben, really loved him. Do you know something? She seemed to guess when it was time for him to come home from work, because she would crawl on her behind down the passage and wait behind the door, just like a faithful dog waiting for its master. So he can't be all bad. He's *not* all bad.' Her chin came up in a gesture of defiance. 'An' you must have seen the good in him or you wouldn't have been going out with him for so long. Why I've known him give his last penny if he thought one of his friends needed help; and yet the very same week he would leave me short and laugh in me face when I tried to tell him off.'

'I've just been to see Mr Simon – Mr Martin.' Emma looked at Patty over the head of the child sleeping now in her arms. 'He was mugged last night, but then I don't expect you know anything about that?'

Patty's face wore a stretched look as if she were about to weigh every word she said. 'No, I didn't know. Is he hurt bad?'

'Bad enough.' Emma reached out a hand for a shawl hanging over the back of the settee and draped it round the bare shrunken legs of the child. 'The doctor said he *could* have lost the sight of an eye, but there's nothing wrong that can't be put right, thank God.'

'Aye, thank God. He's a nice man. He comes down every night to the bar and always stops for a chat with me. Who would do such a dreadful thing?'

'Yes, *who*, Patty?' Emma tightened her hold on the warm soft little body nestling close. It put her at a disadvantage having the child on her knee. She was sorry for Patty. In a way she supposed she had always been sorry for her. From what Ben had told her the man Patty was living with wasn't up to much, and the man who had fathered this child had disappeared as soon as he had known Patty was pregnant. And this room. . . . Emma's quick glance, her way of observing detail, had showed her right away that Patty was no great shakes as a housewife. There was a shabby neglect about it that went further than mere dust on the furniture and stains on the carpet. There was a bareness, as though pieces of furniture had been sold, leaving only the essentials. The curtains were skimped of material, and the television table had a wad of newspaper jammed under one leg to keep it even.

'Who do *you* think would wait for Mr Simon outside the hotel and beat him up?' She kept her voice low. 'Because somebody *did* wait for him, Patty. There aren't many people round that area at that time of night, so I reckon it was somebody who was biding his time. Somebody who bore Mr Simon a grudge. Wouldn't you say?'

Emma was prepared for Patty to look dismayed, even prepared for her to come out with some sort of confession of what she knew, but what she wasn't prepared for was the way Patty jumped up from the chair, pushing it back so that it rocked violently.

'Don't ask me!' she shouted. 'Don't drag me into it! I've had enough. I've had it right up to here!' She slapped the underside of her chin with the flat of a hand. 'Ben's gone, and him I live with says he is going too, and what do you think's going to happen to me then?' Her hair was coming down, but she made no attempt to pin it back. 'Look at me, Emma

95

Sparrow! Just take a good look! Do you know how old I am? I'm twenty-four. Twenty-bloody-four, and I could be taken for ten years older any day. An' you know why? Because I always pick the wrong bloody man, that's why! I've lived with two wrong ones already, and I even picked the wrong brother. I nearly brought our Ben up on me own, did you know that? Mam picked the wrong man too. He knocked her about, just as I've been knocked about.' She rolled up the sleeve of her blouse. 'Look at this! An' if Tracy hadn't been downstairs this morning Ben would have given me a beating as a parting present.' Her blue eyes went blank for a moment, then she seemed to be making up her mind about something. 'It was partly my fault why Ben got the push, but there's no need to look at me like that because I'm not going to go into no detail.' She fastened the cuff of the shiny daisy-patterned yellow blouse. 'He's been hitting me on and off ever since it happened, an' in a way I can't blame him. But I'm telling you nothing! An' if the police come here then I won't be telling them nothing either.'

The front door opened and closed with a slam and immediately Patty snatched the sleeping child away from Emma, holding her roughly. Like a *shield*, Emma realized with horror.

'It's him,' she whispered fiercely. 'You'd best go. He's taking it out on me because I have to go out at night while he stops in with Tracy. She buried her face in the child's soft brown hair. 'A fella can only be noble for so long, I've discovered. They soon revert to type, the sods.'

And there hadn't really been anything she could do about it, Emma told herself as she made herself scarce. But, oh, dear God, that man! He looked what he was. Evil, loud-mouthed and furtively uncouth, and yet . . . even as Emma had mumbled something and turned to go, the child had raised its large head from Patty's shoulder and smiled at him, a touching and open welcome to the man who stood swaying in the doorway, his eyes burning with resentment.

For the first time Emma became conscious of the fact that she had eaten nothing all day. She had rushed here, there and everywhere, and for what? Nothing had been achieved, nothing proved.

'Leave it be, Emma Sparrow,' she muttered to herself. 'Stop

trying to act God, as Ben and your dad were always telling you. Get on with your own life, such as it is.'

She quickened her steps, making for Litchfield Avenue, forcing herself to dwell, not on Mr Simon's white face on the pillow, but on the domestic trivia she knew would be waiting for her the minute she opened the front door. Knowing that however troublesome that might be, nothing could equate with the squalor of the scene she had just left behind her.

How sad it was, and how true, that other folk's problems could sometimes make your own fade into insignificance, she told herself as she crossed the road, walking so quickly that her pony-tail danced and bobbed as if it were possessed of a life of its own.

When Chloe visited the infirmary the next day Simon was sitting up, propped into position with high-banked pillows, the bandage round his head replaced by a strip of plaster holding the eye pad in place.

'They've told you there's no permanent damage to the eye, honey?' She reached for his hand and he gripped it with a convulsiveness that only betrayed his weakness.

'Yes. I've been lucky.' His voice was so low that she had to lean forward to catch the words.

'Lucky? My God, Simon. That's hardly the word I would use. You could have been blinded.' She tweaked the corner of a pillow. 'Anyway, honey, I've been to see the house you wrote about and described, and I don't like it; so I've wheedled the agent into letting us have a rented flat till we find something better. The drapes and the furnishings aren't exactly David Hickey, but they'll do. Temporarily.' She smiled her wide smile. 'Okay, okay. I know I don't let no grass grow once I've made my mind up. I've been on to my boss and given him a month's notice, and though he did his nut there's nothing he can do. There's nobody indispensable. Not even me!'

Simon's answering smile was infinitely weary. 'Oh, Chloe . . . I thought you said . . . I thought you were determined. . . .'

'Sure I was determined. Just as I am now determined to come and keep an eye on you.' She wrinkled her nose. 'Anyway, my overlord was making objecting noises about me

97

wanting to take time off to go over to the States to see my folks, so the crunch would have had to come. He was getting a mite too big for those boots of his. He was treating me like a *wife*, for heaven's sake!'

Simon closed his good eye. It was good to see Chloe sitting there, and yet there was something he couldn't quite fathom. He could have sworn that last night – *was* it last night? – when he had opened his eyes it had been to see the girl Emma Sparrow sitting there with an expression of such caring on her face that immediately he had slipped back into a deeper sleep again.

'There was a girl here when I came last night,' Chloe was saying, as if reading his thoughts. 'Emma Sparrow, she said her name was. What is she? The works' shop steward or something?'

'She is the girlfriend of a man I sacked on the spot a few weeks ago.' Simon spoke without thinking, then bit his lip as the memory of the violence of the attack swept over him. He could still feel the heavy blows to his legs and the final terrifying kicks to his head as he lay helpless on the ground. Instinctively one hand went to his forehead. He had no proof. It had been too dark to see, and he had said that to the policeman who had come and stood by his bedside early that morning.

'Then *he* was the one who did it!' Chloe's mind had always worked like quicksilver; he should have remembered that. 'And she *knows* he did it. That is why she was here. To try and make you promise to say nothing.' Chloe's voice, never low at the best of times, rose so that the man in the next bed put down the paperback he was reading and stared at them with curiosity. 'Simon! You must tell the police so they can pick him up right away.' She glanced round the ward as if expecting to see a detective waiting in the corner. 'Good God, honey, you're not covering up for him, are you?'

'I don't know that it was Ben Bamford.' He paused, giving Chloe time to file the name away in her mind for future reference. 'I saw nothing. They came at me from behind.' He frowned. 'There was more than one, I am certain of that.' He flexed his fingers. 'One I could have managed, but I am certain that one held me down while the other put the boot in.' He smiled with a touch of his usual dry humour. 'That's a cliché that is really true, love. I would say they were hobnailed boots with studs in, at a rough guess.'

'And you told the police about sacking the man recently?'

Simon leaned his head back against the pillow and winced, though he really did feel much better. In fact he was going to get out of here as quick as he could, within the next few days at least. But Chloe was draining him. She was making him think before he was ready to think. It was a running battle for superiority between him and Chloe, and always had been, but she wasn't going to beat him. Not even this time when all he wanted to do was to shut his good eye and go back to sleep again.

'I am not going to tell the police about sacking the man,' he said slowly. 'It would lead to an assumption; an assumption that he tried to get his own back.' He shifted his position slightly. 'I was a stupid fool for going out walking at that time of night in a dark and deserted place. The police told me that there's been an increase in crimes of violence lately in the town. There's a lot of unemployment round here, and when men can't find a job they sometimes react unpredictably.'

'But there was no money taken!' Chloe was indignant. 'You told me that when you telephoned me in your half-conscious state. So how could the motive have been robbery?'

'There was nothing taken because I didn't have any money on me.' Beads of sweat were beginning to form on Simon's forehead. He was on the defensive without quite knowing why. 'I had slipped out for a walk, Chloe. A *walk*. Like I do at home.' He tried to smile, and at last she saw the strain he was under. 'I've missed my nightly runs since I came up here. If a bloke goes out for a walk here he's usually taking the shortest cut to the pub. Now, can we leave it?'

But Chloe never had been able to leave a question un-answered. 'Then what was the Sparrow girl doing here?'

Her tone was all sweet reasonableness, but Simon was too weak to shout, too weary to launch himself into one of their arguments. He opted out by closing his eyes and clamping his mouth tight shut.

Chloe stood up, gathering silk scarf and purse together. 'Okay, honey. I'll come back this evening, then tomorrow I just have to drive back. But I've left the keys of the flat in your

99

room. You can move in as soon as you feel well enough. I'll drive up in a couple of weeks at the weekend.' She leaned forward and kissed his unresponsive lips. 'I will be working like stink to sort things out at the office before I leave, and there's a trip to Copenhagen I must fit in somehow.' Simon heard her low chuckle. 'My replacement will wonder what's hit her, or him, when she or he takes over. That's for sure.'

He heard her quick footsteps go down the ward, then when he was sure she had gone he opened his eyes, pushed the cage over his legs to one side and painfully and slowly lowered his feet to the floor, wincing as his damaged right knee took his weight.

'Sister will murder you if she catches you doing that,' the man in the next bed warned, but sweating from every pore Simon pulled herself upright.

'Sod Sister,' the man thought he said; then he returned to his book, it being none of his business anyway.

When Simon appeared at the factory at the beginning of the next week, deathly pale and limping, with a strip of plaster over one eyebrow, the machinists followed his unsteady progress round the factory floor with eyes shining with admiration and awe. His courage brought out the mother instinct in them, and even the dour Mrs Arkwright fluttered round him, slipping down to the canteen for cups of tea laced with the sugar he did not take, and chocolate biscuits which melted in the saucer on the way up in the lift.

Simon waited for an opportunity to speak to Emma, and took his chance when he saw her sitting alone in the canteen.

'I would like to thank you for coming to see me in hospital,' he said, taking the chair opposite her and carefully stretching out his right leg to the side. 'I very much appreciate that.'

Emma blushed. She had taken the train to Manchester to visit her father in Strangeways gaol at the weekend, and was still bowed down with the memory of the small man in prison grey who had shuffled towards her. Weeks of prison life had aged John Sparrow so that the deep lines on his thin face seemed to have been scored with a chisel. He had grumbled in a low monotone about the food, the total lack of privacy, the habits of his cell mate, staring with red-rimmed eyes anywhere but at his daughter's face, so that when the time was up Emma had felt that she had been used merely as a sounding board.

'He is totally institutionalized,' she told Sharon back at Litchfield Avenue. 'He asked about you and the boys, oh, sure he did that, but he wasn't listening to what I told him. He is turned right in on himself.'

'He always was,' Sharon had said, her expression so much like her father's that Emma had been forced to smile. 'Me and Dad are selfish buggers, and the sooner you accept that the better.'

Simon glanced round the canteen, then back at the silent girl opposite to him.

'Have you seen Ben Bamford lately?' he asked straight out, throwing Emma into such confusion that she stopped playing with her spoon and let it drop with a clatter back into her saucer.

'No. No, I haven't seen him, sir.' Her voice was low and controlled, but Simon sensed her agitation.

'Gone away, has he?'

Emma nodded so that her hair fell forward almost concealing her face. 'I went to see his sister, where he lived, and she said he had gone. She didn't know where. Sir,' she added, as an afterthought.

It was the softly spoken 'Sir' that did it; that and the grinding pain of Simon's damaged knee-cap. He jerked his head up and stared angrily at the girl across the table. He would have sworn that this girl was different. He would have sworn that her natural intelligence overrode any hang-ups about management and staff, but now . . . well, he wasn't sure. His knee wasn't getting any better, and he hated the flat Chloe had picked out for him. It was too filled with the clutter of the unknown person who had chosen the décor. He hated every square inch of the patterned wallpaper, fighting for precedence over the patterned carpet. He should have stayed at the hotel for a while longer, hell, he should have stayed in hospital longer, but there was so much to do – two jobs to commute between now that the mail order firm was playing ball. It was going to be as his father had predicted it would be – hard work finding the time to eat and sleep.

'Do you think Ben Bamford did this?'

He had not meant to be so blunt, but as he saw Emma's expression change he knew he was right.

'That is why he has cleared off, isn't it?' he persisted.

Emma closed her eyes for a moment, seeing in her imagination Ben hammering the strange boy's head into the floorboards at the disco, and seeing too the squalor of his barren home, with Patty cowed and beaten, holding the mentally retarded child in front of her as the man she lived with swayed unshaven and threatening in the doorway.

'I don't know whether Ben did it or not, sir,' she said at last. 'He often disappears for months at a time, his sister told me. It may just have been a coincidence, but he would take it bad about getting the sack and not being given a reference.'

Simon moved his injured leg too quickly and smothered a groan. His face flushed with irritation and an impatience he was finding hard to control.

'Dammit, girl! I had no choice! He was taking stock, good stuff, and his sister was brazen enough to *wear* what he had taken. Did you know that?'

'Patty wouldn't know,' Emma said quickly. 'She's rough, but she's not dishonest. She has a little girl not quite right in the head, and a man who hits her.' She bit her lip. The canteen was filling up, and they were being stared at. Everybody knew that at Delta Dresses management and staff shared tables and acted democratic-like, but Mr Simon was angry. For no good reason he was angry with *her*, and it showed. His face was dark with anger, and she was trying to make him see, trying to make him understand.

'Ben never knew a proper father. He's never had a proper home. He has a black side to him, but most of the time he tries to be happy. He *is* happy, sir. In spite of everything he can still laugh. He needs help, sir. Badly he needs help, not punishment.'

'You missed your way, Emma Sparrow. You should have been a social worker, do you know that? Any minute now and you'll be telling me your own father is in prison because he's a victim of circumstances. Simon shook his head from side to side. 'It's women like you who make men like Ben Bamford and your father into what they are. Okay, I believe you when you say you don't know why Ben left town, but if you *knew* he was responsible for this. . . .', he pointed to his eye and slapped his leg, 'would you still say he was just working out his resentment against me?'

He stopped abruptly. What the hell was he doing? Arguing the toss with one of his girl machinists, with the rest of the workforce watching from the side lines. The anger drained from him, leaving him trembling and weak. Putting both hands on the table he levered himself up into a standing position.

'I'm sorry I misjudged you,' he said. 'I believe you when you say you know nothing about all this. But if Ben Bamford does come back, perhaps you would let me know? I haven't told the police my suspicions, but all the same I would like a word with him. Okay?'

He walked away, straight and tall, limping slightly, leaving Emma sitting still at the table, her coffee untouched and her packet of biscuits unwrapped.

There was a singing in her ears and a pounding in her chest. For a moment as he had placed both hands on the table she had been overwhelmed with an urge to stretch out her own hand and cover one of his hands with it. She had felt no anger at the things he had said; she realized that in his weakness he had been merely striking out at whoever was nearest. But this . . . this feeling of tenderness was spreading through her, causing her stomach to contract in a sharp grinding pain.

He was hurt, had been badly hurt, and she wanted to soothe, to comfort, to stroke his pain away. She was too soft. She would have made a bloody social worker, just as he had said. She understood when she should have condemned.

But oh, his hand with its long fingers and its clean oval nails. . . . For a wild moment she imagined lifting it and holding it against her cheek. She just knew the way his touch would be. . . .

And he *despised* her. He hated her for the company she kept, and he was as far above her as the bloody stars in the bloody sky.

'Emma! You *don't* swear! You never swear!' She remembered Sharon's young voice, shocked into insecurity, and saw again the bewilderment in her stepsister's blue eyes.

'But I do swear,' Emma told herself. 'There are times when all the swear-words in the world could not express the way I feel. Like now,' she went on, muttering to herself. 'Like bloody now!'

Seven

Before the month was out Chloe had tied up the loose ends of her job in London, hand-picked her successor and left the young man with his head in a whirl from her quick-fire instructions, intricately kept files and cross-indexed way of running the office.

'Now, honey,' she told Simon, 'you just get on with what you have to do and leave the house settling to me. I'm going to enjoy getting the place we picked fixed up, and I'm not even going to think about getting another job till it's all done and I've been back home. Till *we've* been back home.'

'I can't come with you, Chloe, and that is that.' Simon was sprawled in an orange vinyl armchair in the furnished flat, his grasshopper-like legs stretched out to the silver-gilt gas fire. 'No way can I leave the mail order set-up at the moment. Prices are fluctuating so much that the mock-up of the new catalogue is out of date almost before the ink has had time to dry. As it is, I am having to budget for an extra warehouse to consolidate what we have already bought. The way things are going we will be selling at a loss before the thing has even got off the ground.'

'Pooh!' Chloe wrestled with a mammoth-sized book of Sanderson prints, twisting it round and holding up a sample to the light for better effect. 'These are the drapes we're going to have in what that sweet little man at the agency called the "master bedroom". Green with a white carpet. Pretty, eh?'

Simon watched her as she pondered, selected, changed her mind and came back to her first choice. He had tried to explain that not until the contract was signed would she be allowed to do anything to the new house set well back from the main road, a modern open-plan house built into a hill, with the back sloping down to a little wood carpeted at the moment with vivid patches of bluebells. But Chloe had waved his warnings aside.

'But the old couple are *leaving*, honey. It's all arranged. They have given me a key and said I can go over any time. I am going to have the carpets laid long before we move in, and the drapes all up, and the kitchen fitted. It's your job, honey, that's making you ultra-cautious. It's making you middle-aged!'

That had hurt. No way could he have been called that even two years ago, but now, bearing the financial responsibility for two companies, there were days when he *felt* middle-aged. He had seen one or two silver hairs in the thick dark waves springing back from his forehead, and most nights he was even too tired to make love.

'But I am not taking time off to come with you to the States,' he said firmly. 'It would be impossible. Out of the question.'

Chloe threw down the book so that it landed with a thump on the highly patterned carpet.

'We might as well be married,' she said, curling her long legs up beneath her and reaching for a cassette in the file at her side. 'And does it ever stop raining up here?' She glanced towards the window. 'Grey skies, grey faces. I went into town today and it was hard to tell the difference between the Pakistani women shoppers and the locals. Every one of them dark and morose as if something unspeakable was about to happen round the next corner. Does no one ever smile, for heaven's sake?'

'Some of them have little to smile about.' Simon leaned back and closed his eyes as a Chopin waltz filled his mind with soothing sound. 'How would you like to work all day long crouched over a sewing machine, never even having the pleasure of holding the finished product in your hands? So many sleeves, so many collars, one after the other, then back to a house furnished as unjoyously as this, *worse* than this,' he amended, seeing in his mind's eye the front living-room at Emma Sparrow's house with its air of shabby neglect. 'My God, we don't know the half of it!'

'Don't call on God, He's on their side, honey.' Chloe,

inactive for too long, jumped up and walked over to the window to stare out at the rain. 'They don't even realize they are being deprived.' She pointed a finger at the green work-file on the small table by Simon's chair. '*They* don't take work home with them and worry about balance sheets when they should be relaxing. Off they clock, or whatever it is they do, then forget the factory the minute they step outside. A chip butty, then off they go to the pub or the club. Not a care in the world. Oh yes, honey, God is on their side all right.'

'Some of them have problems, love.' Simon reached for the file and opened it. 'Responsibilities don't always stop at the factory gates.'

'There are three silver hairs sprouting from the top of your head,' Chloe said, and went into the kitchen to lean against the old-fashioned drop-leaf dresser and wait for the coffee percolator to begin to bubble.

'One mug of instant coming up,' Sharon said, handing the steaming coffee to Emma. 'I wish you would stop waiting up for me. Why don't you go to bed early when you've been ironing? I thought for a minute you were going grey when I came in, but it was only the light from the lamp on the telly. I wouldn't be surprised, though. You look awful, our Emma, honest you do.'

'Thank you.' Emma took the mug and curved both hands round its warmth. 'Have you ever known a spring like this one? The smell of wet coats on the bus tonight was terrible. Like mouldy dishcloths.'

'We've fixed the date.' Sharon sat down on the settee, dangling both legs over the battle-scarred arm-rest.

'The date for what?'

'For the wedding, dope!' Sharon swung her legs till her sling-backed shoes fell off. 'It has to be October because that is the soonest Mrs Rostron could fix both the church and the reception. We're having it at the Pied Bull out the Preston side. A proper sit-down meal with steak and kidney, followed by trifle and everything. And I'm going to look in the July sales for a dress and veil. I want a tight waist and points coming down over my wrists, an' a high neck with a sort of mandarin

106

collar, an' a kind of short circular veil with the front part to come down over my face when I'm in church.' Her blue eyes glowed with excitement. 'Then when the service is over I'll turn to you, because you'll be my bridesmaid, of course, and you can lift my veil back. But I don't want it all sticking out like you see in some of the photographs in the paper. Some brides look like meringues, I always think.'

'Sharon!' Emma put her coffee mug down on the tiled hearth and held up her hand. 'Steady on a bit. Where's the money coming from for a do like that? For a dress like that? Have you any idea how much a reception at the Pied Bull would cost? You wouldn't get it for a penny less than eight pounds a head, not nowadays.'

Sharon swung her legs down and slid on to the rug in front of the electric fire. 'Ricky's parents are paying, dope. They said with me not having a mother or anything, and with my dad being . . . well, with him not being in regular work, it would be their pleasure to pay.' She drew her knees up to her chin and laid her head down. 'Ricky's an only one, don't forget, and Mrs Rostron said with not having a daughter she would have been done out of planning a proper wedding. She's right chuffed about it.'

'But I've never even met her!' Emma leaned forward. 'We can't let her do all that. I know Dad can't afford a posh affair, but he has his pride. I know what he'll say about it when you tell him.'

'He has nowt to do with it.' Sharon's face was flushed with the direct heat from the fire. 'He's got no say, not with what he's done. I would have asked for the wedding to be brought forward so that he would still be where he is, but Mr Rostron said it's only fair to have him give me away. They're ever so broad-minded considering they're such big Chapel workers. Mr Rostron lets Ricky's mother have all her own way, but he did put his foot down when she wanted the men to dress up in monkey suits and top hats, and Ricky and me agreed with him. Oh, our Emma, can you just imagine our dad in a grey top hat and striped coat and tails? I'd die laughing.'

Her light voice prattled on, and Emma half closed her eyes, only listening with a vague concentration. Little Sharon, already on the pill and planning every detail of a white wedding.

The virginal bride floating down the aisle on her father's arm with a veil covering her blushes. With that boy, that spotty boy waiting for her at the chancel steps – it would be funny if it weren't so . . . so sad.

'You are sure it's not just the thought of a big wedding that's making you want to get married?' Emma slid down to sit with her back against the chair. 'Remember you've a long time to live after all the fuss is over. It won't be the same living with a mother-in-law. If you are determined to get married, wouldn't it be better to ask the Rostrons to give you the money they would be spending on just the one day and use it to furnish a two-roomed flat somewhere? At least you would be on your own that way.'

Sharon's small mouth set hard. 'I have told you and told you, our Emma. I *know* what it would be like living there. Mrs Rostron doesn't go out to work, not even half-time. She sews and bakes, and when I go for my tea there I just sit straight down at the table and there's a plate put in front of me. She makes casseroles with chicken pieces, and hot-pots, and she takes her pinny off before she sits down. An' they don't just sit and watch telly all night. They *discuss* things. They play rummy sometimes, and every night at ten o'clock Mrs Rostron goes through and makes Horlicks. It's proper *living*, our Emma. You just don't know!' She gazed at the fire as if seeing pictures in the glowing electric bars. 'I did wonder if our Joe might be a page-boy? You know, in a proper suit with a white shirt and a little dark-red bow-tie. But then he's a bit big. No, I think I'll just have the one bridesmaid. I think you would look nice in pale-blue, Emma, although green's your colour, except that it might be unlucky.'

When Sharon had gone up to bed at last, with everything practically decided except for the hymns and the kind of flowers to carry, Emma sat on for a while, too tired to move and too exhausted to sleep.

She felt mean and small not being able to share Sharon's excitement. There was a dullness inside her as if she were incapable of feeling anything at all. Reaching up she switched off the lamp on top of the television set and went on sitting in the darkness trying to work out what she really thought about it all. Had the unknown Mrs Rostron with her fur stole and her slow-cooked casseroles really decided Sharon was the daughter she had never had, or was she merely making sure that her wandering boy stayed at home? Would it be as Sharon was sure it would be, or would Ricky's mother begin to feel resentment when she realized that Sharon was more than ready to be waited on hand and foot? What would happen when the babies came? Would Mrs Rostron take them over also?

And did any of it matter? Was she, Emma Sparrow, merely *envious*? Was she seeing, sitting here in the dark, the future, her own future stretching ahead with years of looking after the boys and her father? With no Sharon to take even the smallest share of the burden?

And worse than that, was she growing old long, long before her time, so that hearing of another's happiness twisted her guts with bitterness and precluded her from enjoying, even vicariously, their joy?

Was that the Emma Sparrow she had wanted to be?

Wearily Emma got to her feet, switched off the fire and went slowly up to bed. The slow drippy spring was ending. Soon it would be summer and the school holidays and the boys would be running the streets all day. She would have made thousands more buttonholes, cooked another legion of fish fingers, and thrown a dozen or so empty tomato sauce bottles away in the bin.

She undressed in the bathroom, washed her face, brushed her teeth and took a clean nightgown from the airing cupboard. She thought about her father in a morning suit with a top hat slipping down over his ears, and went to bed laughing . . . but not too much in case she woke Sharon, who was asleep with the light shining straight down on to her face.

'Absolutely not,' Simon was telling Chloe, almost to the day he drove her to the airport. 'No way can I come with you, love.' He ruffled her hair then bent his head and kissed her mouth, but there was no response.

'Two weeks, two lousy weeks, that's all. You could fly back and leave me there, for heaven's sake! Are you trying to tell me that Delta Dresses and the piffling mail order thing would disintegrate without you doing their sums for them for two lousy weeks?'

She was bored. Chloe would always be bored if she wasn't doing three things at once, and the new house wasn't progressing as fast as she had thought it would. Chloe was discovering that workmen turned up, then disappeared either on account of the rain or because the sun was shining and they wanted to get on with somebody else's outdoor painting. Kitchen units took weeks to arrive, and when they came they were sometimes the wrong size or even, heaven forbid, the wrong colour.

'This wouldn't be allowed to happen back home,' she said. 'I've known Momma go into a store, order something and find it waiting for her when she got back. Do you wonder this country is getting a third-rate reputation?' She put up a hand as if to stop a sudden surging stream of traffic. 'And don't look at me like that. I can see Union Jacks in your eyes. I was only joking, for heaven's sake!'

'Do you really believe I wouldn't like to come with you?' Simon picked up the gold-rimmed glasses he had taken to wearing and put them on. 'I don't count sheep when I am trying to go to sleep. I multiply the buggers then take their square bloody root. It's not Union Jacks you see in my eyes, it's figures. Columns of them, all screaming out to be balanced.'

Chloe stopped arguing. It was obviously useless. She would just have to go alone, and hope that by the time she came back they could think about moving in. Then she would find a job. She started to walk round the cluttered room, taking long strides that brought her up sharp against a piece of overstuffed furniture. It was okay for Simon. His adrenalin was pumping madly, in spite of his obvious weariness. His work stimulated him, gave each day fresh impetus. He was facing a challenge and glorying in it, whilst she, left at home, tidied the hideous flat and drove into town to match samples of material and try to co-ordinate scatter rugs with the colour she had picked out for the bathroom units.

She sat down and tried to collect her thoughts. Okay, so she understood that what Simon was doing he was doing for her and their future life together. She scowled. What kind of archaic reasoning was that? She didn't *want* a man who turned himself into a workoholic just so his wife could have a patio built or hire a cabin cruiser on the river. She wanted a man who enjoyed her company.

Even their sex life was inadequate now. It was quick, and although Simon always apologized he was asleep so fast she reckoned he couldn't have been all that sorry. In a while her insides would be all dried up like those of an eighty-year-old woman, and when he touched her it would be like touching an orange left to dry on a sunny window ledge.

And they weren't even married!

'There are times when I get to thinking about Ellen,' she said slowly. 'There are time when I can understand just why it was you broke up.'

Simon took off his spectacles and stared at her with dark eyes suddenly defenceless. 'Why bring Ellen up, for Pete's sake? I thought you were different. She wanted a nine-to-five bloke, and you knew from the beginning I wasn't that.'

'Were you doing sums when you screwed her?' Chloe heard herself say the crude word she never remembered saying before, but wanting to hurt she saw that she had succeeded.

'Don't talk like that!' Simon's face flushed red, and she knew she had hit him and made him angry, and the knowledge excited her so that she went on:

'What would you do if I decided not to come back from America? What have you decided to do if I do come back? Anything? What are you Simon? A typical Englishman? Because if you are, then give me a full-blooded son of Uncle Sam!'

'I am trying to balance these accounts,' Simon said calmly, then put up a hand as a tightly stuffed cushion edged with gold braid hit him square in the face.

After that they went to bed and made love, but although he tried to make it last it was over almost before it had begun, and he knew he was too tired to try a second time.

He drove her to the airport on the appointed day and watched her go through the gate, tall and loose-limbed, with her grey pleated skirt swinging against her long legs. He went outside into the May sunshine, and as he drove back to the flat he saw men without topcoats, and women in ice-cream coloured polyester suits pushing prams with babies sitting up, their heads bared to the warmth in the air. But the next day it

111

started to rain again, and the town settled back into its blanket of grey mist and overriding gloom.

A few days later, waiting to ease his car from the short road outside the flats into the main stream of morning traffic, Simon glanced sideways and saw a small group of people gathered on the pavement. The lights were taking an interminable time in changing, and as he stared he saw Emma Sparrow being helped to her feet by a woman in a yellow plastic raincoat. A push-bike lay on its side, wheels spinning, and a boy with tousled hair was obviously arguing, waving hands about as he demonstrated what had happened.

The lights changed to green and Simon was forced to drive on, but signalling left he pulled into the side of the road and parked the car.

'She walked straight out in front of me!' the boy was saying. 'Stepped off the pavement without looking. I didn't stand a chance, honest!' No one was taking the slightest notice of him, and as Simon approached he picked up the bike and stood helplessly, his young face white with shock.

And if he was pale, Simon thought, then Emma's skin tone was transparent. Her knee was gashed, and blood trickled down into her torn tights. It was raining, as usual, and her short jacket and skirt were splashed with mud. Simon could see that she was close to tears.

'It's all right.' He spoke in the tone of voice an officer might use dismissing his men. 'This young lady is a friend of mine. I'll see to her.'

'It weren't my fault,' the cyclist said again, and Emma raised her eyes to Simon's face.

'No. It wasn't his fault, sir. I was trying to run across the road to catch the bus when it stopped round the island. I had started to walk because I had already missed one, then this one came down the hill and I didn't think.' She put a hand to her forehead and swayed. 'I'm okay now, honest.' She touched her nose and winced. 'It's not broken, is it, sir?'

'A wonder she wasn't killed.' The stout woman in yellow plastic had disappointment etched on every line of her fat, flat face as she sensed that the little drama was almost over. 'He was belting down so fast he knocked her right out into the road, and if a car had been coming as she lay there in the

112

middle, well, I shudder to think. My sister was once knocked off her feet by a boy on a bike and she has walked with a stick from that day. Arthritis set in,' she told the dwindling audience.

'Thank you for your kindness.' Simon took Emma by the elbow and walked her over to the parked car.

'In you get.' He grinned. 'No, your nose isn't broken, just skinned. Now sit tight. Okay?'

He slid behind the wheel and drummed his fingers on the handbrake. 'Right! One thing's certain. You can't go into work like that.' He glanced briefly at Emma's white face, then down at her mud-splashed jacket and skirt. He was angry because this girl, this strange vulnerable girl, was upsetting the tight schedule of his planned morning. An early morning meeting with Harry Gordon, quarter of an hour with the mechanic to warn him that he would have to find another job if the machines he'd repaired kept breaking down, then off to the other side of Bolton to a management conference, where he was taking the chair, as finance was top priority on the agenda. He slapped the wheel with the flat of his hand.

'Look, Emma. I am in one hell of a hurry this morning. . . . Tell you what – my flat's just two minutes away. I'll take you there so you can clean up a bit, then I'll pick you up on the way back from Bolton and run you into work if you feel up to it. If not, I'll drive you home. Okay?' He started the car without waiting for her reply.

He was to ask himself afterwards why he hadn't taken, say, ten minutes, a quarter of an hour longer to run her home? But then his morning's schedule would have gone awry: that eventuality was unthinkable.

'I could drop dead on the floor, and if you were on your way to a meeting you would cover me with a sheet and still go,' Chloe had told him, more than once. 'Sometimes I think you are programmed, like a computer. Let the sky fall down but you'd still make for the meeting, wouldn't you, honey?'

And afterwards Emma was to ask herself why she hadn't insisted on either going back home or on to the factory? But there was something about this man that made her feel different, even sitting beside him in his car with her skirt all muddy and the skin off her nose.

So, like a lamb to the slaughter, she allowed herself to be led into the flat. Mrs Kelly had told her, with significant glances over in his direction one lunchtime down in the canteen, that Mr Simon's girlfriend was living with him now.

'American, I believe,' she had said, as if that put Chloe completely beyond Mrs Kelly's own particular pale. 'They're not married, not that that seems to matter nowadays.'

So Emma, expecting to see the tall elegant girl she had met at the infirmary, looked round the flat in surprise.

'The bathroom's through there,' Simon said, glancing at his watch. 'And there's the bedroom. My friend's away, but she won't mind you using her things. There's some antiseptic in the cabinet, and towels in that cupboard. Okay?' He backed towards the door. 'I'll be with you before lunch, but if you do want to go home just pull the door to. Right?' He opened the door. 'And now I must dash. Sure you'll be okay?'

'Oh, my God,' Emma said aloud as soon as the door had closed behind him. Not ten minutes before she had been on her way to work. Late as usual because Joe had told her at the last minute that his throat hurt and she had had to peer down his mouth and feel his forehead, then run upstairs to tell Sharon not to let him go to school if he didn't perk up a bit.

'He's shamming again,' Sharon had said, closeted in the bathroom washing her hair when she knew she would have to go to work with it wet. 'I'll sort him out. Not to worry.'

Worried and anxious, Emma had run from the house, missed the bus, started to walk, then half way there had seen another bus coming down the hill; stepped off the pavement, and wham! She sat down in the nearest chair and taking a tissue from her handbag dabbed at the blood congealing now on the grazed knee. There were bits of grit sticking to it, and the pain made her feel sick. And as she felt sick she remembered that she had had to leave her breakfast slice of toast on her plate when Joe refused to get out of bed.

For a minute she considered getting up and just walking out of the flat. She was sure she could manage, and she might be able to catch a bus – and if people stared, then they would just have to stare. She stood up and gave a small moan as the injured knee pricked with the pain of a thousand needles. Her tights would have to come off that was for sure, and the knee would have to be washed. Uncertain of herself, embarrassed even though she was quite alone, she sat down again and stared round the room.

There were books everywhere, and a record player, and rows of cassettes and records in an open cabinet. It wasn't the sort of room she would have expected the smart Chloe to have wanted to live in, but it was nice. Cosy and a bit crowded with furniture, but nice. . . . Emma glanced at the small table by her side piled with books. Not paperbacks, but real books. She twisted round to see the title of the book on top, and saw with surprise that it was one she had taken from the library only the week before. It gave her a small feeling of identification to think that Mr Simon had the same taste in reading.

Limping painfully, she went through the door he had pointed out and found herself in the bathroom. Still unsure of herself she sat down on the candlewick seat cover and took in her surroundings.

His razor was there, on the tiled surround of the bath, and he had showered because the wall was still wet with drops of water and his towel, cream with a brown border, was over the bath. There was a robe hanging behind the door, white and fluffy, and on a low painted cabinet were two flasks of talcum powder, a bottle of hand lotion and a box of tissues.

Slowly Emma peeled off the torn tights, took one of the tissues, dampened it and began to clean up the grazed knee. Feeling like an interloper, she opened the cabinet on the wall, then closed it quickly when she saw the shelves were filled with jars of cream, bottles of skin lotion and a packet of Tampax. She bit her lip. Okay, so she could get blood poisoning or worse, but not for anything was she going to open that cupboard again. For the first time she felt anger at the cool logic of the man who had brought her here, a virtual stranger, and told her to make free of his home.

He *demoralized* her. Yes, that was the right word. She should have insisted on going home. She wasn't badly hurt. Flaminenry, as Sharon would have said, she could have had her knee seen to from the first aid box at the factory, and by now she could have been sitting at her buttonhole machine as if nothing had happened.

Suddenly she looked up and saw her reflection in the

mirrored door of the high cabinet. And what she saw made her recoil.

If her knee looked a ghastly mess, that was nothing to her nose. Carefully she prodded the end, wiggled it about a bit, then winced as the grazed flesh burned in protest. Her face was green. Not white, just green, and the swelling on her nose seemed to have pushed her eyes up into slits. She was a *monster*, an ugly monster, and that was why he had brought her here. He had been sorry for her. He had wanted to spare her the stares of the girls at the factory, but being the sort of man he was he had not told her just how awful she looked.

Emma never cried. She couldn't remember the last time she had cried. Not even when they had taken her father away, or when Ben had threatened her. . . . Even when Mam died her tears had been more a moistening of her eyes and a choking in her throat because of the boys.

But now she was alone. For the first time she could remember she was alone in a house where there was no one to catch her giving way. It was all too much. Everything was too much. The coping, the anxiety, the wondering what could possibly happen next. Working, shopping, trying to keep the house clean and the boys decent for school. Wondering if Sharon was doing the right thing, asking herself if there was anything she could do about it. Scheming so that the money went round. Never asking for help. Not *having* anyone to ask for help.

And now, seeing herself in the mirror, looking on the outside as she felt inside – torn and bleeding, defeated, ugly, as if a great steam-roller had come and flattened all the spirit out of her.

Head bowed, she staggered from the bathroom through a door into a bedroom with a double bed with the covers hastily thrown over it. Sobbing, wailing, hearing herself wail and wanting, in a perverse way, to go on making that dreadful sound as if all the tears had been saving themselves up for just this moment.

She threw herself down on the bed and let the grief take over.

'First you tell me the mechanic isn't going to turn up, then I get a phone call to say the meeting at Bolton is postponed!' Simon faced an apologetic Harry Gordon in the small office. 'Okay, so

116

the bloke's got a throat bug. Okay, so two of the directors at Bolton are down with the same thing, but that's my day messed up properly.' He snapped his brief-case shut. 'And now I have to go home to collect the papers I thought I wouldn't be needing till tomorrow!'

Mrs Kelly lowered her head and watched from beneath black drawn-on eyebrows. So Mr Simon was like all the rest – nice as pie till somebody or something upset his precious schedule. She sniffed and rolled a piece of headed notepaper into her typewriter. Well, at least it showed he was human and not just an extension of the works like the sewing machines out there. And she for one wasn't going to feel sorry for Mr Gordon. Not her. He was just the same. Let something go wrong and he always took it out on someone. But then they were men. Puffed up, know-it-all men who went to pieces when they couldn't have their own way. She sighed. Well, she had got one at home like that, so she should know.

'I'll work at the flat this morning,' Mr Simon was saying as he walked from the office. 'You know where to find me if anything crops up.'

He was so angry he slammed the car door with a crash that reverberated all round the asphalt car park. What he did not realize was that the burning frustration at the collapse of his minute-by-minute planned day had triggered off an anger that had been simmering inside him since the night he had been beaten up. Five days, he told himself, five days after being kicked half way to death he had been back at work. And now he would have to cancel appointments and postpone meetings until the managing director at Bolton decided he was fit to toddle into the office. He signalled right. Delays cost money, and when money was in short supply, when finance was balanced on a tight string, leaving no surplus for mistakes or tardy decisions, he would be the scapegoat when the company foundered on a reef of its own making.

He was actually part way up the hill leading to the flat when he remembered Emma Sparrow.

The tears had done nothing to ease her desolation. Now she felt so lethargic that it was as if she moved under water, pushing with her legs against a heavy swell. Glancing down at them and seeing the blood and mud caked on her knees, she went into the bathroom and turned on the hot tap, letting the water run over her hands.

The feeling of being an interloper had gone. All she wanted to do was to lie back and let the soothing heat wrap her round. And if the scented bath oil she was trickling in belonged to another woman, so what? She was tired of always being the one to think before she acted, weary of being the conscientious one who tried to set an example to her family, who saw her as merely a provider and a substitute mother.

Life had kicked her in the teeth once too often, and this morning she felt she could take no more.

Emma lay back and closed her eyes.

Simon wrinkled his nose the minute he opened the door. It was a familiar scent, and for a startled, unthinking moment he thought that Chloe was back. He looked into the bathroom and saw Emma's clothes in a heap on the floor, walked into the bedroom and stopped abruptly.

This small girl, naked but for the cream and brown bath towel slipping from her shoulders, was not Chloe. This girl was so sweetly rounded, so exquisitely formed, with bare pink-tipped breasts above a waist as narrow as a hand's span. Her long brown hair, loosened from its binding ribbon, fell round her poor swollen face. . . . She had been crying, and as he went towards her she lifted a face so anguished that with an instinct as natural as breathing Simon held out his arms.

And the caring concern on his face was too much. It was so long since Emma could remember anyone looking at her like that. Not mother, father, not even Ben with his expressions of teasing affectionate laughter or frustrated passion, had ever looked at her like that.

Like a child she slid her arms round his neck. The towel slipped to the carpet. When she felt the touch of his hand on her hair she turned her face to his for his kiss.

There was so much to give. All of Emma's past was in that kiss. All the secret crying for love, for tender dominance from this man she knew now had filled her dreams since the first moment she saw him.

'I don't know you,' her mouth was saying as it opened beneath his. 'I don't know you, but I love you. How can that be?'

Her warm soft naked body was pressed against his. She was moving as if to get even closer, and when they moved over to the bed Simon had no recollection of how they had got there. Had he carried her, or had they moved together as if in a drifting dream?

All he knew was that she was lying beneath him, that he was tearing at his clothes, kissing her throat, her breasts, feeling the soft pink nipples harden as his mouth and tongue caressed them.

'Oh, God,' he moaned. 'Oh, my little sweet love.'

He was possessed; he had never dreamed he was capable of such intense rampaging emotion, and she was clinging to him, wrapping her legs round him, holding him, so that when he entered her the small cry she gave only added to his overwhelming excitement.

And yet, even though his sporadic love-making with Chloe had been unsatisfactory and swift, now it was as though he moved with such tenderness, such overpowering glory in his maleness, that he could not get enough of her.

This was what being a man meant. He thought he had known. Oh, God, he thought he had known. This girl, this beautiful lovely girl was so completely his that when it was over he still lay on top of her, whispering words formed not by his tongue but from some inner source of ecstasy.

Then, when he stroked her little swollen face he felt her tears on his fingers, and even then her tears did nothing to shake him back to reality.

It was only after he had driven her home and watched her let herself into the house, identical to the last grain of pebble-dash with its neighbours, that the truth struck him with more than remorse, more than shame. It was a blinding revelation of his own stupidity.

He went into the bedroom and stared down at the rumpled sheets. Never, never once, even in his wild teenage years had be behaved with such a total irresponsibility. And the girls he had loved had known what it was all about; that in itself had

119

been some sop to his conscience. But, oh, dear God, for Emma Sparrow it had been the first time. The very first time!

He picked up Emma's torn tights from the bathroom floor, took them through into the kitchen and dropped them inside the pedal bin. He stared at the pail for a long time, then he picked it up and took it down the stairs, crossed the courtyard at the back of the block of flats and emptied it into the communal dustbin.

Then he went back into the flat, spread his papers out on the coffee table and pulled it in front of the hideous orange vinyl armchair.

And asked himself, for what was to be the first time in at least a hundred how, for God's sake, *how* he could have been such a fool?

Eight

Chloe rang that evening.

'Hi, honey! Missing me?'

Simon ran a finger round his collar, just as if his tie were still in place. He had worked, or tried to work, in the flat all afternoon with the memory of Emma Sparrow's tormented face coming between him and the neatly penned rows of figures.

'How?' he asked himself a dozen times. And 'Why?' he had asked twelve times more.

Now with Chloe's clear voice in his ears, with the sense that she could have been there in the room with him, his normal self-assurance slipped, leaving him feeling ridiculously like a naughty schoolboy caught out in some misdemeanour.

'Work's piling up,' he said, in what he hoped was a matter-of-fact voice. 'The Bolton thing isn't going straight forward, but I am sure I can sort it out.'

'I'm sure you can, honey. But I am not ringing to ask about the factories, am I? I wanted you to tell me you can't exist without me, and to ask me to hurry back.' She paused. 'As a matter of fact, I am thinking of coming back next week. That's if you're not too busy to drive out to the airport to pick me up.'

Simon automatically reached for his work diary and flipped over the tightly packed entries. 'Just tell me when, and I'll be there.'

'Sure it won't interfere with your timetable?'

He couldn't tell whether she was being teasingly sarcastic, or just plain disagreeable. Without seeing her face he felt at a loss.

'Give me a day and I'll be there.' Simon found he was

gripping his ball-point pen between his fingers, willing her to co-operate just this once instead of turning even a trans-atlantic conversation into a form of mild bickering. A part of him was screaming at her to stay where she was for a while longer to give him time to come to terms with the extra-ordinary happenings of the day.

'What have you been doing with yourself?' Chloe asked after a day had been fixed. 'You sound harassed, honey. Is there any more news of the house?'

'Nothing.' Now they were on safer ground and he could stop acting like a law-breaker on the defensive. 'But all things being equal we should be able to move in about mid-June.'

'Momma says it's time we got married.'

Again he cursed the fact that he could not see her face. He gripped the receiver even tighter. For all he knew Mrs Day could be standing right behind her daughter, smiling and nodding her neatly coiffed hair, looking like an elder sister, and cheering Chloe on from the sidelines.

'We'll certainly discuss that.' It was meant to sound jokey, but now Chloe was having problems with only his voice to go by.

'Sure you can fit me on the agenda, honey?'

They said goodbye, with the thinly veiled animosity linger-ing like trailing ectoplasm between the north of England and New York. Simon went back to his papers and worked for a while, then dropped his face into his hands. He sat there without moving, whilst the silence of the room grew and lengthened.

Tomorrow he would have to go into the factory and face Emma. He knew that he was coward enough to dread it, and man enough to realize that what had happened could never be explained but had to be dealt with.

'Dealt with?' He said the words aloud. Oh, what in heaven's name had possessed him? And possessed was the right word. He dropped his hands and his eyes were bleak. They had come together like deprived children, seeking comfort. They had touched and rubbed flesh against flesh, and even to a man with an ex-wife and a mistress, not to mention roughly half a dozen other encounters, it had been a revelation. It had been as if they had been taken over by some primeval force stronger than he had known existed. She had *needed* that hour. Craved it. And so, God dammit, had he. Never, ever, had he experience anything remotely like that before. Not even when he was a young boy lusting after girls, wanting to explore their bodies and prove his masculinity.

Emma Sparrow. . . . Taking Emma and loving her was the sort of memory that would linger in his mind till the day he died. He was not promiscuous. He had been faithful to Chloe for a long time now, even without the binding legality of a marriage certificate, but that small defeated little girl had shattered his thought process. Through her he had lost his sense of legitimacy and for that, in a strange perhaps even cruel way, he could never forgive her.

He saw her the next morning, crouched on her stool over that infernal buttonhole machine, with her hair hanging loose and not pulled back into the childish pony-tail. To hide her nose, he thought, and was touched.

From his desk he could see her through the glass-fronted wall of the office, but she worked without looking up, steadily and methodically, reaching for one blouse after another, pressing the foot pedals, guiding the material into position as if all that mattered was achieving her quota for the day.

She knew he was there. After a long and almost sleepless night she had accepted that he would be there, and there was nothing she could do but wait, just wait to see what, if anything, he would do.

She was all emotion, but she was as still as a mouse inside her. He might never know it, but now her mind, her heart and all her being belonged to him. Now she knew how it could be, and the practical down-to-earth side of her was already accepting that it might never be that way again. She would never be a worry to him; not even the smallest anxiety. And if he apologized to her, she would want to die.

She looked up suddenly and in that unguarded moment their eyes met. As he looked hastily away she felt a coldness seep into her bones and was surprised to find that she was not shivering.

In the canteen at lunchtime she deliberately chose to sit at a table with three of the machinists and when, out of the corner of her eye, she saw him come in, she turned her head. She went back to her machine as soon as she could, and when Simon did not reappear she knew that he would not be coming back into the office that day.

She knew and felt as if she had been granted a reprieve, because there was nothing he could say.

Emma was alone in the living-room of the house in Litchfield Avenue that evening when the knock came at the door, and her hand crept to her throat as her eyes widened in dismay.

He had come to say he was sorry, to explain that he could not think what had come over him. He had come to beg her silence, to ensure that when his Chloe came back from America there would be no repercussions from what he would say had been a moment of unprepared folly. Emma felt the beginnings of hysteria rise thick as she told herself that never, ever, would Mr Simon say a sentence like that. She made herself take a step towards the door, then another.

It was . . . it had been, all her fault. Again and again she had gone over what she had done. She had gone straight to him and wound her arms round his neck, and she had let the towel drop, so that when he had put his own arms round her it had been her naked body pressing up against him.

Emma walked slowly into the square box of a hall and hesitated. He had come at a time when what defences she had were swept away by the wild force of her weeping, and any man would have responded in exactly the same way.

But if he apologized, if he tried to even *begin* to apologize, then she would die.

She opened the door and saw Ben Bamford standing there.

'Okay, okay. It's me, not me ghost. Come on then. Are you not going to ask me in?' He was grinning, jiggling his car keys up and down in the pockets of his brown leather jacket. His fair hair was shorter and more curly than she remembered it. His face seemed to be rounder, but his vivid blue eyes were the same laughing eyes, dancing with mischief as he stared at her.

'What's up, Em?' He stretched out a hand as she leaned against the door jamb, then drew it back as she flinched away from the supportive gesture. 'Eh? What's up?' he asked again. 'I've not got mange, chuck.'

'You'd best come in.' Her voice was low, and she glanced quickly up and down the avenue before stepping back. As he followed her into the living-room, she put up a hand to her face to hide the red of her nose.

'It's not as bad as it looks.' She sat down on the chair with its back to the window. 'I got in the way of a speed merchant on a bike on the way to work yesterday, that's all.' Then, for the first time, she smiled. 'Oh, Ben. It *is* good to see you. I never thought to see you again.' She pleated the folds of her skirt with nervous fingers. 'You're taking a chance coming back, aren't you?'

He threw her a look of disgust. 'You an' all, Em? You are as bad as our Patty. She whipped me into the house so quick you would have thought old Kojak was hot on me tail. I think she would have hid me under the settee given half a chance.'

Emma's chin, lifted. 'Are you trying to say you didn't do what I . . . what Patty and me suspected you did?' She shook her head slowly from side to side so that her hair fell forward. 'But then if you had done it, you wouldn't be here now. You couldn't just walk in as if nothing had happened. *Could* you, Ben?'

'*Could* you, Ben?' His tone mimicked her seriousness, but his eyes still twinkled. He pretended to tuck a strand of hair behind an ear, and spoke in a falsetto voice. 'Oh, Ben. How could you possibly come back after you had knocked old smarmy pants Simon Martin for a six? Left him senseless so that even his old dad down in London could not recognize him? Oh, Ben. I have a good mind to fetch the police and have you put away with my daddy for doing a wicked thing like that.'

'Stop it.' Emma gripped the wooden arms of the fireside chair. 'It's not funny. Mr Simon might have lost the sight of an eye. He might have been killed!' She dropped her voice to a whisper. '*Was* it you, Ben? Because if it was, I would rather you went. If it was, then I would advise you to leave the town again. The police will be asking you questions about where you were that night, and why you went away so suddenly. They found out that you had got the sack, and they're not daft.

125

It was good of Mr Simon not to report you, anyway.'

For a moment she saw the temper flare in his eyes, then with an unexpected movement Ben dropped to his knees by her chair, assuming an expression of mock pleading.

'Do *you* think I would do a wicked thing like that, Em?'

Again she shook her head. 'I don't know, Ben. If you didn't do it, then who did? You had a reason for wanting to get even. An' if you didn't do it, then why did you go away at exactly the same time?'

'I went away,' he said softly, 'because I bloody well wanted to go away. I'd had it up to here with having no job and with living in the same house as that drunken sod who was always yelling at Patty. I woke up one morning – the morning in question as it so happens – and heard them fighting. Aye, fighting in bed, if you must know, an' so I just got up, packed a shirt and skedaddled. Okay?'

'And you had no part in beating up Mr Simon?' Emma shrank back in the chair as if dreading the fact that he might try to touch her again, but Ben was enjoying himself too much to cloud the issue with any of that kind of larking about. It was as if, knowing that for once he was in the right, he was determined to make the most of the situation.

He put out a finger to touch the end of Emma's nose, only to see her jerk her head back. He grinned. 'For your benefit, I didn't even know the gaffer had stopped a pair of hobnailed boots till our Patty told me.' He put both hands together in an attitude of pious devotion, and raised blue eyes ceilingwards. 'But no way can I say as how I am sorry.' He rocked back on his heels. 'An' while I am in the confession box, dear Sister Sparrow, I have to admit that our Patty told me something else that made me say a rude word. She told me you had been to see her, straight after you had been to see *him* in the infirmary. Is that right? Now, why should you do a thing like that?'

'I went to see how he was, that was all.' Emma heard a car door slam outside in the avenue, and tension knotted tight low down in her stomach. If Mr Simon should knock at the door now when Ben was here. . . . If Ben thought . . . if *he* thought. . . . She closed her eyes briefly.

'Oh, please God, please, please God, don't let him take it

into his head that he ought to try to see me tonight . . . not with Ben here.' She opened her eyes to see Ben staring at her closely.

He nodded twice. 'Aye, that was it. You went to see him because you was sure I had bashed his head in. You was bloody sure. Without giving me a chance you was bloody sure. You went to ask him not to give me away, then you went round to our house and when Patty said I had gone away, you put two and two together and made bloody five. You were playing bloody Samaritans again, weren't you, Em?'

Her brown eyes were moist as she gazed at him, and because he had never seen her cry Ben reached for her, only to have her twist from his grasp as if his touch sickened her. Immediately he got up and went to sit on the settee opposite to her.

'Okay, okay.' His good humour remained unruffled. 'So you've gone off me?' He made a face of rueful resignation. 'Aye, well, it 'appens. But I will tell you something, Emma Sparrow. You are the only bird what has ever gone off me. Maybe that is why I keep on coming round when other fellas would have told you to get stuffed long ago.' Then, with a sudden mercurial change of mood, he was intense and serious. 'Our Patty is on her own again. That bruiser she was living with left her flat. Just buggered off, taking even the kid's money-box pennies with him.' His face darkened. 'An' you want to know what our Patty has been doing? Well, I will tell you for nothing. She's been going to work at the pub nights and leaving that poor little kiddo on her own. You saw her, didn't you?'

Emma nodded. 'She sat on my knee.'

'Aye, well, she would. She takes to everybody, that one does. She is a grand little kid, an' how our Patty could leave her like that I can't reckon. Just think if she had woke up to find she was on her own? It's not on, and I've told our Patty it's not on. So . . . so I'm stopping here, an' no, I didn't have nowt to do with what happened. I just picked the wrong day to go, that was all. So I've got me a job as a porter down at the station.' He stood up and saluted. 'Wait till you see me in me uniform! Robert Redford will be dead bothered if he sees me! An' I've fixed it up with the woman next door to pay her a bit of summat to have Tracy in her house at nights while Patty works.' He laughed. 'I'm not such a bloody hero as to promise to be the bloody baby-sitter as well as earning the bloody bread.' He lifted his head. 'What's that?'

'It's Joe.' Emma stood up. 'He's taken to coming downstairs about this time every night since our dad went away. He has nightmares. Listen to him. He must have had one now.'

When Joe came into the room, Emma went down on her knees gathering the small sobbing boy into her arms, trying to still the plaintive wailing that showed he was more asleep than awake.

'It's all right, love. It's all right. Emma's here. Hush now and we'll have a drink of cocoa, shall we? Just you and me, eh?'

Ben jiggled the coins in his pocket. 'I'll be off then, Em.' He patted the top of Joe's tousled head. 'Come on, now, lad. You're not frightened of no bogies, are you? Not a big lad like you. You just tell your Uncle Ben about where they hang out and he will have their guts for garters. Okay?' He walked to the door and turned. 'If you want me for owt, Emma Sparrow, you know where to find me. Right?' He twiddled his fingers in an airy goodbye. 'I'm not saying I'll be waiting, but you can give it a try.'

Then he closed the door behind him and walked with his jaunty step over to where his car was parked, whistling as if without a care in the world.

The car was there when Emma banged the front door behind her and ran down the avenue to catch the bus early the next morning. As usual she was on the last minute, yelling to Sharon to get up, retrieving a lost shoe from beneath Alan's bed, and checking the food cupboard to see what was needed from the supermarket on her way home.

'Get in, Emma.' Simon reached across and opened the car door. 'Come on. We can talk as I drive. Okay?'

He had cut himself shaving and his face was pale, but his hands on the wheel were steady and he drove the car expertly, almost as if it were an extension of himself. 'We have to talk,' he said, and Emma knew that the moment she had dreaded had come. He was going to apologize, to try to explain, perhaps even to ask her to keep what had happened a secret. Humiliation and shame made her sink down in her seat and turn her head so that she stared fixedly out of the window.

And all at once she knew she could not take it. In her agitation she knew that she would do something stupid and dramatic, like asking him to stop the car so that she could get out and run. In the middle of the night with Sharon sleeping soundly beside her she had considered giving up her job, then told herself that finding another would not be easy.

'Ben Bamford came to see me last night,' she said quickly, forestalling anything the grim-faced man beside her could say.

'He did what?' Simon turned and stared at her. 'He must be a cool operator.'

'He didn't do it, sir.' Emma's voice was low, and her heart ached as she noticed the nerve jumping in the cheek of the man who had loved her with such tenderness such a short time ago.

'Stop calling me sir.' Simon sighed. 'And you believed him when he said he didn't do it?'

'It was a coincidence him going away. He was fed up with what was going on at home, so one morning he just got up and went.' She twisted the strap of her shoulder-bag round and round in her fingers. 'And that was the morning after the night you got set on, so since you had sacked Ben a few weeks before, everybody jumped to the wrong conclusions.'

'Including you, Emma?'

'Including me.'

'So now you're back to square one?' Simon drove in silence for a few moments. 'You and Ben have made it up? Is that right?'

Was there a subtle pleading in his voice? Was it tinged with a kind of shamed relief? Emma thought so, and the knowing brought a twinge of physical pain low down in her stomach. Mr Simon was being let off the hook, he was taking Ben's reappearance as a sign from above, and what he said next proved this to be true.

'There is a lot of good in Ben Bamford. He was foolish, and I had no choice but to sack him, but I didn't take it any further, and I *could* have, Emma. You know that.'

The car pulled up at the traffic lights and Simon drummed with nervous fingers on the wheel as if willing them to change quickly so that he could get this embarrassing journey over. Emma lifted her chin and stared straight ahead. 'He has got a job as a porter at the station, and he's going to stay with Patty till things get sorted out a bit.'

'And you are pleased about that, Emma?'

The question was loaded, and as the car started forward, moving into the right-hand lane at speed, Emma said the words she was convinced he wanted to hear.

'I am very pleased. Ben is like his sister, always good for a laugh.'

'And there hasn't been much of that about for you lately, has there, Emma?'

Now they were on dangerous ground again, and Emma closed her eyes and willed the car to go even faster.

'You can forget about what happened,' she said clearly. 'We were both in a bit of a state, and it's best forgotten.' She waited for a moment. When he remained silent she said, 'Is Miss Day coming back from America soon?'

'Next week.'

'And you are pleased about that?'

Was she mocking him? Simon had no way of knowing, but risking a quick glance sideways he saw that her small face was set in determined lines of resolution. He took a deep breath.

'Yes, I am very pleased. We will be getting married soon. We are buying a house, you see.'

The car was turning into the long street with the tall red-brick Victorian buildings that housed Delta Dresses, and for once there was no stream of traffic delaying the right turn into the car park to the rear. As Simon swung the car into his own allotted space with his name painted in white on the far wall, Emma's hand was already on the door handle.

'That's that.' Simon switched off the engine, hearing himself say the two words without accepting their context, and surprised when Emma repeated them clearly as she closed the passenger door with a slam.

'That's that! Thanks for the lift then.'

'Take care of yourself. . . .' Simon got out of his side of the car, his face a mixture of ravaged emotion and relief. But she was running away from him so quickly that his words were lost as if they had never been spoken.

From force of habit he locked the car, although his hand was shaking so much he could hardly perform the simple task. And in that one revealing moment all the years of ingrained self-confidence, of professional know-how, of accepting his odd mistake and regretting nothing in retrospect – all Simon Martin's sureness of himself as a person deserted him totally. Leaving him diminished and more bleakly ashamed than he ever remembered being in the whole of his life.

Nine

When Chloe came back from the States her approach to Simon was entirely different from the dignified withdrawal that had been Emma Sparrow's way.

She was tanned, alive and brimming over with how it had been back home, the trips she had made, the visits. She was appalled to find that the contracts for the new house were still not exchanged, and she stormed at the passive acceptance by the English of delays she felt were inexcusable.

That first night, when Simon tried to make love to her and failed, she asked him straight out what was wrong.

'All the time I was away I was picturing the way it would be, and the way it is wrong,' she told him, switching on the light so that he cowered beneath the sheets, hiding his still painful eye with one hand. 'I love you,' she said clearly. 'Being away from you told me just how much I love you. It's the job, isn't it? You're worked half-way to death, and if you go on this way you'll have a coronary before you're forty. I have seen too much of it, honey.' She got up and went to the bathroom.

Chloe always took a bath or at least washed even after their unsuccessful love-making, and when she came back, cool and sweet-smelling, Simon drew her down into his arms again.

'Give me time, love,' he whispered, his face buried deep in the soft curve of her breasts. 'As soon as the Bolton thing gets off the ground we will go away. I promise.' He trailed a hand down the long warm length of her thigh. 'The Lake District is only an hour's drive away from here, and it is so beautiful. The lakes merge into the middle distance, and there are little stone-built pubs where you can eat the kind of food you only dream about.' He moved his hand only to find that she closed her legs like scissors.

'Is there . . . has there been anyone else?' Chloe had left the light switched on, so Simon kept his face hidden as he felt the rush of blood to his cheeks.

'Don't talk rot,' he mumbled.

'But it wouldn't be rot, honey.' Chloe spoke into the top of his head. 'We made no promises. We are intelligent adults, I hope, and I am not the sort to go screaming back to Momma. If I did she would only tell me it was sure to be partly my fault, anyway.' Chloe gripped Simon's hand hard. '*Did* you go to bed with someone else while I was away?'

He met her gaze without flinching. 'Yes, I did. But it was only once. Just once, and never to be repeated. And I'm sorry.'

'A one night stand?' There was no shifting of Chloe's gaze either.

'No!' Simon' voice came out louder than he had intended. 'It wasn't like that at all! It was circumstances, and it was unpremeditated, and I have said I was sorry, so can we leave it?'

'No, we certainly cannot leave it!' Her voice was even louder than his. 'What circumstances? Were you drunk or something? Did you go to a party and get sloshed so that you ended up in bed with somebody, because that is not – I never imagined that was your scene, Simon. C'mon, tell me! I have a right to know!'

'I wasn't drunk.' He spoke wearily. 'And now can we try to get some sleep? It is over. There was nothing between us to *be* over, and if you want to feel me squirm then I am squirming now.' Leaning over he switched off the light. 'I hate myself, if that makes you feel better. Okay?'

'A factory girl?'

There was no putting Chloe off; there never had been, and refusing to speak, even pretending to be asleep, were only delaying tactics and Simon knew it.

She was over-polite the next morning, very aloof and attractive in her green silk wrap, with her hair as smooth and glossy as if she had just come from the hairdresser's salon. But she was badly hurt, he could see that too, and after they had

133

washed up the supper dishes together that evening she told him the plans she had made.

'I went down to the real-estate office and they verified that there is nothing we can do about the house for at least another month.' She pulled at her fringe. 'I think he thought he had got some crazy American woman bawling him out in his tiny office. Then I called my boss, and when he said that the guy who took over from me walked out last week in the highest of dudgeons, I said I would go back. Temporarily.'

She reached for the coffee jar. 'I hesitated before about marriage and I am hesitating now. And with good cause,' she added, her back to him. 'It didn't take you long to satisfy your masculine instincts once I was out of the way, did it? And if, as you say, it wasn't like that, then what *was* it like, Simon?'

At the end of the next week Simon drove her to the station. They were standing on the wide platform, waiting for the train that was to take her to the connection at Preston. Simon had offered to drive her there, but even as he said it she had seen him glance inadvertently at his diary.

Chloe looked very attractive that late spring morning. She was wearing an almond green skirt with matching shirt blouse, with her cream suede jacket swinging from her shoulders. Businessmen turned interested eyes in her direction, and even a porter, lounging against a wall and smoking a cigarette, ambled slowly towards them.

'The first-class will stop up the other end of the platform,' he told them, and turning round Simon came face to face with Ben Bamford.

'This way, sir.' Ben picked up Chloe's case and walked ahead, every jaunty step indicating his childish pleasure in the unexpected encounter.

Simon put his hand in his pocket and closed his fingers over a fifty pence piece, only to feel a stab of humiliation at Ben's dignified refusal of the proffered coin.

'No, thank you, sir. It's my pleasure.' Ben's blue eyes twinkled at Chloe, who, to Simon's chagrin, was smiling brilliantly at the good-looking fair boy in the neat dark uniform. 'Have a pleasant journey, ma'am.' Ben touched his cap and grinned. 'Here she comes.'

'What a sweet boy,' Chloe said as Simon handed her into

the first-class compartment. 'The age of chivalry isn't dead, after all.'

As they kissed goodbye, Simon was conscious of Ben's eyes on them, and as he walked to the slope leading down to the forecourt of the station he could still feel Ben's audacious cheeky stare on his back. Now he accepted with certainty that Ben had been in no way responsible for what had happened on the night he left the hotel for a midnight walk, but what he could not and did not want to accept was Emma Sparrow's involvement with the strutting, cocksure, let-the-devil-go-hang attitude of the boy who stared at him as if finding him wanting.

And as he threw his brief-case into the back of his car, Simon told himself that what Emma did or whom she was involved with was none of his business. Of one thing he was certain. Emma had kept their secret. If Ben Bamford had known what had taken place in the flat that morning in May he would have pushed his ex-boss underneath the path of the incoming train.

When it did not come . . . when the cramping, dragging pain that always pulled at her insides every month did not materialize, Emma thought she would surely go clean out of her mind.

Every day, every hour almost of every day, she locked herself in the toilet, forcing herself to scrutinize the toilet paper for the slightest sign. It was degrading and terrible, but still she did it, telling herself that the shock of what had happened that day had sent her insides out of flutter. That her last visit to her father, where his slow deterioration had horrified her, could be responsible for nothing working as it should. She was anaemic. Just look at her white face and hollowed eyes. All she needed was a bottle of iron pills from the doctor to get her right.

'Why don't you go to the doctor, our Emma?' Sharon was coming into town with her one Saturday afternoon instead of going to work. 'I can put off getting me wedding dress for a bit. I wish you could sew, then you could make it for me.' She patted her jean-clad bottom in disgust. 'I used to take an eight, now what do you want to bet that I have to get a ten?'

'I'm all right, honest.' Emma walked to the bus stop with dragging footsteps. 'What time would I have for making your wedding dress, anyway? Even if I could sew.'

'Funny that.' Sharon pushed her way to the front of the crowded bus. 'You working in a dress factory and not being able to sew. It's a bit like that girl we used to know who got taken on at a sanitary towel factory when she had never seen her periods at eighteen. Or working in a chocolate factory when chocolate brings you out in spots.'

'I've told you before. Working on piece-work isn't like proper sewing. I don't even do the bound buttonholes. Mrs Arkwright has a girl specially trained for that. I don't think it's funny at all.'

'Okay, keep your shirt on.' Sharon studied her reflection in the glass section behind the driver's back. 'I told Ricky you were always ratty these days and he said you were probably a bit jealous because I was getting married before you.'

'Well, I'm not.' Emma felt a knot of tension low down in her stomach, and closed her eyes in a silent anguished prayer. 'Please God, let it be that. Let it come when I stand up, and I'll never snap at Sharon or the boys again. Let me be sickening for something, where one of the signs is not starting a period, but don't let it be that. *Please!*'

'We'll go to that new shop in the complex,' Sharon was saying. 'Or do you think we should have gone to that shop out Accrington way? It said in the paper that they had over two hundred and fifty dresses to choose from. We might have been able to get your bridesmaid's dress at the same time.'

'I haven't saved enough money up yet, have I?' Emma looked away from the surprise in Sharon's eyes. 'There's nobody given me twenty pounds like Ricky's mother's given you to go towards. *My* money goes to buy food and pay the bills, or have you forgotten?' She bit her lip and frowned. 'Anyway, I'm not in the mood for trying dresses on today.'

'There's summat wrong, isn't there?' Sharon put a hand on Emma's arm, only to have it shrugged away. 'You've been crabby for ages now.' She got up and started to walk towards the exit. 'But if you won't tell me, then there's nowt I can do about it.' She turned round. 'It's not our dad, is it? You're not keeping summat back from last time you saw him, are you? He'll be home in time for the wedding, won't he?'

'He'll be home,' Emma said in a dull voice as they walked towards the shopping complex.

And what will I be like then, she wondered, walking as the lonely do, staring at the ground and putting one foot in front of the other with automatic deliberance. She would be showing then, showing proper, with her front sticking out of her bridesmaid's dress and everyone staring and pointing. Exclaiming over Sharon in her virginal white, with her sister not married or even courting, and a baby on the way.

'Shall we leave it over?' Sharon's neatly-plucked eyebrows were drawn together in a puzzled frown. 'You've gone all green, our Emma. I'm worried about you. Honest, I am dead bothered.'

One glance at her sister's face was enough to show Emma that she was near to tears. It should have been Sharon's mother who was taking her to buy her wedding dress, and Sharon should have been bubbling over with excitement, clinging to her mother's arm and talking animatedly. It should have been one of those special occasions to treasure, almost as important as the day itself. She swallowed hard and forced her lips into a semblance of a smile.

'Right then. I'm okay now. I did feel a bit off on the bus, but then I always do when I'm crowded in like that. C'mon. Let's see if we can find exactly the dress you want, love, but we will walk straight out if they try to make us buy anything but the right one. Okay?'

She needn't have bothered telling Sharon that, Emma told herself an hour later when her sister had tried on four bridal gowns and declared each one impossible. And the prices were astronomical! Forgetting her worry for the moment, Emma examined the finishings, calculated roughly the amount of material and the workmanship that had gone into it, then made a guess at the retailer's profit.

'You will be paying through the nose, Sharon.' She said the words without thinking, then bit them back. This wasn't a day to quibble about prices and assess profits. This was the day when Sharon was seeing herself as a bride. A vision in white, floating up the aisle on the arm of her father, with the organ playing the wedding march and all her friends there to see her. What would it matter that the bride in white had been sleeping with her boyfriend for ages? What would it matter that the father of the bride had recently come out of prison after doing a stretch for repeated thieving? So the bridesmaid was pregnant and refusing to name the father? So what?

Sharon was trying on a veil now, holding it in place as an eager-eyed assistant lowered a wreath of mock orange blossom over it.

'You'll make a beautiful bride, love,' the assistant was saying, tweaking folds of the circular short veil into place. She turned to Emma. 'It's a funny thing, love, but I've been working in bridals for a long time now, and I still can't get used to that first sight of a young lass trying on her veil. Call me a soft 'aporth, or what you like, but there's summat gets right to me.'

And this, Emma knew, was going to be the dress and veil that Sharon chose. It was as if she had gone to a far-away place as she gazed enraptured at herself in the long mirror. She was like a child dressing up, seeing herself starry-eyed and beautiful, with the lacy tiered dress standing out from her tiny waist, and the tight bodice showing the curves of her young breasts. The assistant, with a movement that was all reverence, tried the effect of the veil down over Sharon's face, and immediately the too-bright blusher and the harsh eyeliner faded and merged, turning her into an ethereal creature, her features etched in soft misty watercolours.

'If I give you thirty pounds now, then will you keep it for me an' I will pay the rest off week by week?' Sharon's voice came dreamily. 'I only work a minute away, an' I can call in.'

The assistant hesitated as Emma opened her handbag and took out a well-worn purse.

'Here you are.' She spoke quickly. 'We'll take it now. The dress and the veil and head-dress. Okay?'

'Oh, our Emma.' Sharon turned to her the minute the dress was off and being packed away in a large oblong box filled with rustling tissue paper. 'That's the money we were going on the market with, isn't it? You shouldn't have done that.'

Emma smiled and wrinkled her nose. 'We can eat what bits I can find this weekend, then on Monday I will go to the post

138

office. I'm not without, you know.'

'But you'll be skint!' Sharon's eyes were round. 'That will leave you with nothing. I can't let you do that.'

'I have done it, love.' Emma sat down on a small gilt chair, her legs suddenly giving way beneath her. 'What does it matter, anyroad? Spend and God will send. That's my motto. Remember?'

And the worry was there, hard and tight as a knot inside her, but now Sharon was past noticing. Standing in a long queue waiting for the bus she held the awkwardly-shaped box in front of her, and when the bus came in already crowded with Saturday shoppers, she stood wedged in between Emma and the back of a seat, her expression rapt and her blue eyes dream-filled.

The boys were out and Sharon was upstairs putting the dress away when Emma, downstairs in the kitchen getting a makeshift meal together, felt the sour taste of bile in her throat. She had skipped breakfast, and now the thin smell of the tea she was pouring into two mugs proved too much. As Sharon came into the kitchen she was leaning over the sink, holding her stomach and retching; the cold sweat breaking out on her forehead.

'Oh, our Emma. You *are* ill!' Sharon was all contrition. 'I knew you were. You've got that sickness bug that's going round. The girl on the fruit and vegetable counter has got it. She got sent home only yesterday.' She passed Emma a towel. 'See, wipe your face with this, then come and sit down and drink this tea. Then you must go to bed and I'll make the meal.'

With infinite tenderness she led the whimpering Emma over to a kitchen chair and pushed the mug of hot strong tea into her hands. 'Drink this. You need something inside you when you're sick. Oh, you do look awful. You've gone all green round your mouth. An' I let you come into town with me and stand about in that stuffy shop and on the bus. You should have *said*, our Emma. Me dress could have waited.'

It was the kindness that did it. That and the nauseating smell rising from the steaming pot of tea. Suddenly Emma lowered her head and broke into a storm of weeping.

If her mother had been there, if even her stepmother had

been there, she would have been immediately enfolded in loving arms, she knew that, but there was only Sharon, kneeling down on the shabby linoleum flooring and pushing the hair back from her face.

'What's wrong, our Emma? There is something awful wrong, isn't there? I know there is something wrong, so *tell* me. You're sick to your stomach with worrying, aren't you?' She gazed into Emma's ashen face. 'It's Dad, isn't it? He's dying, an' you can't tell me. He's never going to come home any more, is he?'

'I think I might be going to have a baby,' Emma whispered. 'Oh, God, Sharon, what if I am? What will we do? What will any of us do?'

There was a moment of silence, a still moment when it seemed the whole world stopped turning. She saw the way Sharon's eyes dilated with shock, and the way the blood left her face, leaving the blusher standing out on her cheekbones.

'You what?' Sharon's voice was a whisper. 'You can't be!' She stood up and backed away as if to put as much distance as she could between herself and what Emma had just said. 'Is that why Ben came back? Is that why he went away? Oh, flaminenry . . . flippin' flaminenry!'

'It's not Ben.' Emma was addressing her muffled words to the floor now, her head lowered almost to her knees. 'He never touched me, not like that anyroad.' She lifted her head. 'It was someone else, and I can never say. It was just once but I can never say. Not ever!'

'But you'll have to say! You will have to do something!' Sharon's voice was high, almost bordering on hysteria. 'An' it doesn't happen the first time. You're all right the first time.' She was indignant. 'Anybody knows that!'

'Then anybody's wrong.' Emma got up stiffly and going over to the sink poured the tea away, as Sharon followed to stand right behind her.

'Listen! Listen to me!' Sharon sounded full of indignation. 'I don't think you know what you're saying, our Emma. You're sure that you – with whoever it was – you're sure that you went all the way?'

'Quite sure.'

'But if you've never. . . .' Sharon was like a mother forcing herself to ask her thirteen-year-old daughter questions she could hardly bring herself to put into words. 'Listen. Emma? What time of the month was it? Just after, just before, or in between? It could matter, honest.'

'About a week before.' It was Emma clutching at unlikely straws now, and they both knew it.

Sharon sighed. 'That's the dangerous time.' She twisted her stepsister round to face her. 'Did you . . . did *he* use anything?'

'No!' Emma was shouting now. 'It wasn't *like* that. I told you. If it had been planned then I wouldn't have done it, would I? I'm not that stupid!'

Then, as if realizing just how stupid she had been, Emma leaned over the sink so that her forehead was resting on the taps, and began to cry again.

'I'm making you some coffee.' Sharon lit the gas underneath the kettle again. 'You must get something warm inside you.' Emma heard the familiar sound as the lid of the coffee jar spun round. 'And come and sit down. You don't want to be like that if the boys come in. They'll be able to see you have been crying, but we can tell them it was because my dress cost so much and you don't know how you are going to manage. You can tell them you spent the food money and now your conscience is pricking you.'

Emma glanced at her quickly, but saw that Sharon was being totally serious. The four-year age gap between them had shifted so that now it seemed as if Sharon was the older sister and Emma the younger.

'You must wait till you've missed for the second time, then go and have one of them pregnancy tests. You can send a sample away, or get a kit from the chemist. A girl at work did one on herself not long ago and it was negative, but she was that dead bothered she had another go just to make sure.'

The kettle came to the boil and the water was sloshed over the coffee granules in the bottom of the mug, then milk added with the same abandon. Sharon's face was screwed into lines of determination, and her small nose pointed and peaky with worry. She passed the coffee to Emma and told her to get it down.

'Then if the test is positive you will have to go down the doctor's and tell him you will go off your chump if you have to go on with it. Tell him the boy who did it has gone off and you'll never see him again. . . .' Sharon interrupted her own narrative as what she had just said struck home. She gripped Emma's shoulder hard. 'Our Emma. You will *have* to say who it was. Doctor Entwistle *knows* us. He sees to Dad's cough and Joe's throats, and he gave me a diet sheet for me spots only a week ago. If he thinks you've been with someone married or something – oh, Emma, you have to say! People will say awful things if you don't say.'

She stared down at the top of Emma's head. 'An' you're not *like* that. I'm the worst one. I'm the one who should be sitting there, not you.' She started to cry, then dashed the tears away with the back of a hand. 'You'll have to make out to the doctor that if he doesn't send you for an abortion you will kill yourself. Remind him about Dad being in prison an' the boys running wild, and me being a big trouble with stopping out late and everything. Make him *see*.'

'Make who see what?' Alan burst into the kitchen with Joe only a step behind him. 'Where's the tea, our Emma? We're going out again right after. Somebody's let us ride his bicycle, an' Joe sits on the seat and I work the pedals. You should just see us go!' He glanced round the kitchen. 'Where's our tea, then? We have to go right back or he will change his mind, won't he Joe?'

Alan had noticed nothing but the fact that his meal wasn't either being fried or grilled, with Emma standing by the cooker as usual, pushing the wayward strand of hair back behind an ear. It was Joe who broke in with a tremor in his voice.

'Why has our Emma been crying? Is somebody dead or something?' His face was filthy, and his tee-shirt had parted company with his jeans, with their frayed bottoms hanging over the top of his grubby sneakers. 'Our Emma's been crying, 'asn't she?' he said again.

Sharon spoke quickly. 'She's been a bit upset because there's nothing tasty for the tea, because I went and spent the money on a dress to get married in. So now you know.'

After a moment of disbelieving silence, Joe hurled himself forward like a stone from a catapult. The years of insecurity since his mother died, and the abrupt withdrawal of his dad's presence from the house, plus Emma's strange unaccountable behaviour of the past weeks, had all taken their toll. Throwing himself at her, he butted her chest with his hard little head, then buried his face in her shoulder. His hoarse voice came muffled.

'I don't like it when you cry, our Emma. It doesn't matter about the tea. Me and Alan will have jam butties.' He lifted his head and searched her face. 'An' water to drink. We don't mind. Honest!'

'Speak for yourself, our Joe.' Alan hitched up his own slipping trousers with an expression of disgust. 'Why couldn't Sharon get married in the dress what she's got on? Who cares about a flippin' old wedding, anyroad? She'll look a right soft 'aporth dressed up fancy. I'm not getting married. Ever!'

Emma pushed Joe away from her and stood up, suddenly the Emma they could rely on once again. She managed a smile.

'There's no need for jam butties. Things aren't quite that bad. I've just had a smashing idea.' She winked at Joe, then reached for the frying pan and took a carton of eggs from the shelf. 'How about pancakes? It's not pancake Tuesday, but who cares? Pass me the flour and bottle of milk, then hang about a bit an' they'll be ready. No, not that milk, Sharon. That's today's. We will use the other first, okay?'

And as their eyes met, Sharon nodded to show that the unspoken message had been received and understood. For the time being at least she was to keep Emma's terrible secret. Comforted by her stepsister's apparent return to normality, she put the plates to warm and told the boys to wash their hands at the sink.

Who was to say that a miracle wouldn't happen? And who was to say that Emma wasn't imagining that what had happened was as bad as all that? She nodded to herself. Emma had always been a bit slow when it came to boys. She probably hadn't a clue what had really taken place. Just look how she'd got in a state about finding Ricky and her on the rug that time. No, everything would work out right. It had to. Flaminenry, it *had* to. For all their sakes.

Leaving Emma furiously beating the eggs, flour and milk into a frothy batter, Sharon ran upstairs. The big cardboard box from the bridal shop was lying on the bed, and somehow she didn't want to even look at it. She had been going to take the beautiful dress out to admire it and hang it in the wardrobe underneath a plastic wrapping from the cleaners. She had been going to try the veil on, and the little wreath of white roses intertwined with orange blossom. She had been going to try the effect with her hair done differently, all smoothed back behind her ears.

But now . . . everything was spoilt.

Emma, the one person in the whole wide world she had thought incapable of doing such a mad crazy thing, had got herself into the sort of trouble Mam used to be always going on about.

Emma, the sensible one. Serious, clever Emma, who could have gone to college if the money had been there. Emma, who always had her nose stuck in a book, going with someone nobody knew about. It was so unreal, it just couldn't be true. *Could* it?

'Shit!' The word exploded from Sharon's rosebud mouth as she lifted the box and pushed it underneath the bed, kicking it right under until it completely disappeared from sight.

'Flaminenry! Why couldn't it have been me? Nobody would have batted a flamin' eyelid if it had been me. Why not *me*?'

She asked the question aloud, totally unselfish for perhaps the first time in the whole of her young life.

'Bloody hell. Why not *me*?'

Ever conscious of Sharon's watchful eye on her at home, Emma dragged herself somehow through the days that followed; telling herself that tomorrow she would go to the doctor's, or the day after, or the day after that; dreading the confirmation of her fear, and hoping against dwindling hope that she could be mistaken.

She wasn't sick again, and though she examined her breasts carefully behind the locked bathroom door there were no signs that anything untoward might be happening.

She went to the library, and in the medical section surreptitiously read through the symptoms of pregnancy: blue veins on the breasts, twinging discomfort in them, an urge to pass water more frequently, morning sickness. No, no and no. Nothing but the cessation of her periods, and anyone could miss once. Anyone.

But when the second time came and went she sat at her machine like a small pale ghost, working mechanically. She walked the surrounding streets instead of going into the canteen, staring into shop windows and seeing nothing but her own anguished face.

She walked as if her feet hurt, as if she were four times her age, refusing to admit to herself that it was the feeling of love she felt for Simon Martin that was making her postpone what she knew to be the inevitable.

It was his baby inside her. This man whom she had loved from the moment she first saw him in the office at the factory, sitting there with his long legs stretched out and watching her with that amused twinkle in his dark eyes. If it had been what Sharon believed it to have been, a careless abandoned few minutes spent with someone she cared nothing for, then it might have been different. She was far from stupid, far from impractical. Life since Mam was killed had taught her just where her feet rested, and that wasn't just flat on the ground, it was two feet underneath!

She wasn't merely Emma Sparrow, a girl twenty years old who could decide to have her baby and bring it up with help from Social Security and visits from the Welfare ladies. She had no religious scruples about what she knew she had to do. There was just the hard fact that when her father came out of prison he would need care and cosseting. John Sparrow wasn't the type of man who, having learned his lesson, would move heaven and earth to find a job straight away. No, he would need a shoulder to lean on, heavily; always had done and with Mam gone, her own shoulder was the only one available.

And Simon Martin wasn't the insensitive kind of man circumstances seemed to have proved him to be. Their love-making hadn't been merely an indulgence in selfish passion. She knew that too. The tenderness had sprung from some deep well of need inside him, and without really *knowing* him, loving him but not knowing him, Emma was sure she was right.

Listlessly, she walked back to the tall red-brick building, scorned the lift and ran up the stairs, taking them two at a time, still willing a miracle. She locked herself into one of the toilets, then crept back to the buttonhole machine to try to lose herself in the monotonous automatic process of making endless buttonholes in endless button trims.

'Looking forward to Saturday, Emma?'

She jumped as if suddenly shot in the back, to see Mrs Kelly standing by her side clutching an in-tray filled with wage packets.

'If this weather keeps up we should have a right grand day out.' Mrs Kelly's eyes were friendly beneath the fiercely drawn-on eyebrows. 'You look as if you could just do with a spot of sea air. It might give you a bit of colour, love.'

'Saturday?' Emma blinked as if the word were unknown to her. 'Saturday?'

Eileen Kelly thumped the in-tray down on the work table, glanced quickly back at the office and, finding it deserted, hitched herself up on to a corner of the table. She tucked her chin into the pussycat bow at the neck of her blouse and spoke softly. 'What's up with you, Emma love? I've been watching you lately and my guess is there is something bothering you. It's not that cheeky Ben Bamford, is it? Mrs Arkwright tells me he's turned up like a bad penny again, just when I was hoping he'd gone for good. He's all teeth and charm, that one, with nowt to back it up. He wants seeing off, he does.'

'I never see Ben these days, Mrs Kelly.' Emma pulled a fresh piece of material towards her and slid it into position, but the older woman persisted.

'Have you really forgotten what Saturday is, love? The girls have been talking about nowt else these past few days. The shop down the bottom has run out of suntan lotion from what I've heard tell, though that lot from up the Khyber Pass won't be needing none, will they?' She took a list from the patch pocket on the front of her denim skirt. '*You* paid up weeks ago, but I'm surprised you're not bringing a boyfriend. There's quite a few husbands coming, including mine, and that's an achievement I might tell you, getting him off his backside of a Saturday.' She scanned the list, running a finger down the names.

'I must say it's decent of the high-ups weighing in with the cost of a fish-and-chip dinner, then a boiled ham and salad high-tea.' She glanced again at the glass-fronted office. 'Mr Simon was all for it. He says an outing like this is good for morale. It's an American idea apparently, letting the work-force do all the planning, then adding the management's contribution.' She picked up the tray and started to walk away. 'So shake the mothballs out of your bikini, love, and give the boys a treat, eh?'

'I'm not going,' Emma told Sharon. 'I *can't* go. I don't want to talk to anybody and the thought of traipsing round Blackpool and riding there and back in a coach makes me feel sick just thinking about it. They will think it's funny if I give backword now, so you'll have to send a message first thing Saturday morning. Alan is big enough to go with a note on the bus. I'll say I've gone down with 'flu or something, *anything,* but I'm not going, and that is definite!'

'Then I will take a day off from work and we'll go to the doctor's.' Sharon's small chin was set firm. 'He has a surgery Saturdays. An' we will practise what you are going to say, so that when we get home it will all be fixed. The abortion,' she added, raising her eyebrows at the stricken dazed expression on Emma's face. She sighed, a deep noisy sigh. 'Oh, flamin-enry, our Emma, you're not going to decide to have it, are you? You wouldn't be that daft, would you? It's nothing but a little tadpole at the moment, a *thing,* not a person! You're not going to spoil your whole life, not while I am here to stop you. Look, you can go in to wherever they go, have it done, and nobody will know. I'll ring the office and say you're off with a stomach upset, an' that will be true enough, then when you go back to work it will all be over. Okay?'

'Just like that?' Emma shook her head slowly from side to side. 'As easy as *that?*'

'Yes.' Sharon looked very wise. 'Doctors don't pass no judgement. They have to take an oath when they have passed their exams to say that they promise to get people well, not try to judge them for their morals. Ricky says so.'

'You haven't gone and told Ricky?' Emma's voice rose almost to a shriek. 'You promised on God's honour.'

'We was talking about something else,' Sharon said comfortably. 'Right then. Are we going to the doctor's on Saturday morning, or aren't we?'

Emma's brown eyes were the eyes of a small trapped animal. That was exactly how she felt. Trapped. Betrayed by her own body into a situation so unbelievable, so mind-bending, she was not ready to come to terms with it yet.

Soon, but not yet. Dear God in His heaven, not yet.

'I will go on the outing,' she said dully, 'then the week after I will go to the doctor's, but alone. Quite alone. What I have done I've done an' I will get out of it in my own way. Okay?'

Sharon bit her lip, then turned away so that Emma would not see the tears that had sprung unbidden to her eyes. When she spoke the familiar flippant tone was back in her voice again.

'Then sit on the seat over the wheel,' she advised. 'That way you'll get shook up, and who knows, it might just do the trick.'

And she ran upstairs before the tears could spill out and run down the blusher stroked in a triangular shape to hollow her cheeks like the fashion models in her weekly magazines.

Ten

The two coaches were there, parked in the street outside Delta
Dresses when Emma turned the corner. She had purposely left
it to the last minute, and was relieved to find that all the seats
were taken apart from one near the back. It was immediately
behind Mrs Kelly and her husband, a big man with grizzled
sideboards, the collar of his blue sports shirt turned down over
his jacket.

Emma sat by the window, laying her shoulder-bag across
the seat as if defying anyone to sit by her side. There was no
way she could make conversation, no way, and when Mrs
Kelly's black head appeared between the two tall headrests
Emma actually shrank back against the dark red upholstery.

'Did you see Mr Gordon sitting up front with his wife, love?
She looks a nice woman, but seventy if she's a day. I'm sure
that's an invisible net on her hair. It's the first time I've set
eyes on her as a matter of fact. He says she's not a mixer, and
never has been.'

The driver switched on the engine, and Mrs Kelly raised
her voice accordingly. 'Bet she's only come today because Mr
Simon's coming. Most likely old Harry convinced her it was
the done thing.'

With a sharp intake of breath Emma glanced involuntarily
at the empty seat beside her.

As if reading her thoughts Mrs Kelly went on. 'Of course
Mr Simon is following on in his car. He's meeting us at the
restaurant at dinner time.' She winked. 'I can't exactly see
him sitting on the back seat with the lasses and singing "I'll
take you home again, Kathleen", can you?'

'Nobody sings that nowadays anyroad,' came the disembodied voice of Mr Kelly from his seat. 'More like "I'll *sleep* with thee tonight, Kathleen". Oh, turn round, Eileen, do. Tha're as jumpy as a fart in a bottle this morning.'

Simon Martin drove down the M6 motorway at a steady seventy. To his own surprise he was almost looking forward to the outing. It should have been a duty chore, a mere showing of his face to illustrate the good feeling between management and staff, but as he drove along Simon felt his spirits rise.

True, his relationship with Chloe seemed to be at a watershed, despite the fact that when he telephoned her their conversation was punctuated with easy laughter. The clash of two strong personalities was, he told himself, smiling, obviously not so apparent when they were apart. It was clear that Chloe was revelling in her job, relieved to be back in London again.

Simon had visited Blackpool with his parents as a small boy and still remembered the Golden Mile along the promenade, with its shouting shabby fascination. The smell was the thing he recalled most vividly, a heady mixture of fish and chips, candy-floss and frying onions. He had made himself sick by stuffing himself with toffee apples and vinegar-soaked cockles, and had then listened entranced to the barkers in their set-back stalls selling pots at knock-down prices. Even now he could still remember staring up in amazement at a booth holder running a dozen dinner plates up his arm without dropping a single one.

After briefing Simon as to the exact location of the fish restaurant where they were to eat midday, Harry Gordon had lamented that all was changed.

'Bloody discos everywhere!' He had moved his head from side to side in disgust. 'Not to mention bingo round every corner. They've even mucked up the piers so they don't look the same at all. All the character's gone.'

But as Simon drove down the tree-lined avenues, with their gracious houses of Accrington brick mellowed by the morning sunshine, then on to the wide sweep of road flanking the promenade, he decided that as far as he was concerned the magic was still there.

The crowds on the front were still the same warm-hearted northerners out for a good time; the men in open-necked shirts and the women in their white cardigans with angry triangles of sunburn in the V-necks of their flowered summer frocks. And always the wind. Brash and breezy Blackpool, even on the hottest day, with sunbathers cowering behind striped windbreaks down on the golden pebbleless sands, and the Tower standing sentinel over all.

Simon remembered how his father had tried to turn a fortnight at the sea into a general knowledge exercise. 'Five million bricks, two thousand five hundred tons of steel, and ninety-three tons of cast-iron in that structure, laddy. And on a clear day it can be seen for fifty miles around. How about that, then?'

'How about that?' Simon asked himself as he drove past the enormous structure, smiling with quiet pleasure at the milling crowds with the youngsters in their stetson hats and tight jeans. As he passed a huge arcade an old Elvis Presley song wafted tinnily through the open window. Simon shook his head. Harry Gordon had been wrong. Blackpool was just the same. Different in some respects maybe, but fundamentally just the same.

He parked the car in a multi-storey car park, then walked for four or five hundred yards back to the fish restaurant, its presence heralded by the strong smell of potatoes frying in pans of boiling oil.

He joined Harry Gordon and his wife at a table by the window and, turning round, stared straight into the brown eyes of Emma Sparrow.

Emma had already planned what she was going to do. All morning she had walked along the promenade with Eileen Kelly and her ebullient husband, but as soon as the meal was over she was going to escape and wander off somewhere by herself, meeting up with the rest at five o'clock for the high-tea at a café pointed out to her on the morning stroll.

The wind had loosened her hair and brought a glow to her pale cheeks, and in spite of the terrible gnawing anxiety she was hungry. She watched as the girls at her table oozed tomato sauce over their fish and chips. She shared their uninhibited laughter, but when asked to join them down on the sands she said she had some shopping to do.

151

'Rock for my brothers,' she explained. 'They'll never forgive me if I don't go home laden with sticks of Blackpool rock.'

And because every girl on the long table had her boyfriend or husband in tow, they stopped asking her to stick with them and let her go, a lonely determined little figure in her white slacks and pale-pink overblouse, the inevitable bag swinging from her shoulder.

Simon saw her go, and refusing the cup of strong tea being poured from a thick white teapot by Harry Gordon's subdued wife, got up and followed her out on to the wide crowded pavement outside.

'I'm glad he's gone,' Madge Gordon told her husband. 'He's nice enough, I know, but I wouldn't have known what to say to him all afternoon. Londoners always affect me like that. They seem toffee-nosed when they are not being really, if you know what I mean.' She added hot water to the teapot for a second cup. 'I think it's the way they talk.'

'He means well,' her husband told her, draining his own cup and passing it over. 'I must admit I'm at a bit of a loss meself when we're not talking about the factory. These do's can be a bit tricky, I admit.'

'And we can have a nice look round the shops,' his wife said complacently, spooning sugar into the two cups of steaming tea.

'All alone, Emma?' Simon caught up with her flying figure and then stopped in embarrassment as Emma's face blushed a fiery red which faded quickly, leaving her as white as her trendy summer slacks.

For a moment they stood facing each other, jostled by holiday-makers walking three and four abreast, then Simon took her arm and, shortening his steps to match her own, walked her down the side street leading to the car park.

'It's time we had a talk, Emma.' He was in complete command of the situation, she could see that. And instead of telling him that she was in a tearing hurry, that she was on the last minute for a vital appointment, she could only stand there like a deaf mute, staring wide-eyed into his face.

His hand was firm on her arm as he smiled down at her. 'I

saw you walk out of the restaurant. Good meal, wasn't it? There's nobody makes fish and chips like northerners, and that's a compliment coming from someone like me who was born south of the Wash. You weren't on your way to meet someone? Ben on duty today?'

She turned her face away from his penetrating gaze. 'I don't know, sir. Sorry, Mr Simon. I don't know what Ben is doing today.' Emotion was in fast flow through her blood-stream. She wanted to back away, to run and put as much distance as she could between them, but the nearness of him, the feel of his fingers through the thin cotton blouse, the unexpectedness of it all had left her weak. So befuddled that she scarcely knew what she was saying or why.

'I don't see Ben these days,' she told him as he turned her round and guided her along the busy pavement thronged with children sucking ice-lollies, and harassed mothers carrying loaded plastic carrier-bags. 'We're still friends, but there's nothing between us. Not now.'

Simon shot her a quick glance, then talked about the weather and the bracing air, and how glad he was to have spotted her leaving the restaurant, until they reached the car park.

'Here we are,' he said as they took the lift to the top floor, just as if everything had been pre-arranged, and when they were in the car he raised a hand and wound back the sliding roof.

'We'll get away from the crowds, eh?' He turned the car away from the town's centre. 'Something tells me you're not a girl who minds her hair getting mussed.' He grinned. 'Do you know something? Every time I walk past your machine I have an urge to tweak that ribbon tying it back, but I have to be circumspect. You know that, don't you, Emma?'

She nodded, fighting to get a hold on herself.

'Ever been to Lytham St Annes, Emma?' he was driving with one hand on the wheel and the other resting lightly on his knee. 'We might find things a bit quieter there.'

She sensed the holiday mood he was in and suddenly, loving him so much, relaxing now a little, she wanted to identify.

Let tomorrow come with its return to anguish and terror. Let next weekend come with its visit to the doctor for the interview she was dreading with every fibre of her being. It was all right for Sharon to talk, but how was she going to sit facing that kindly man she had known all her life and tell him she wasn't prepared to say who was responsible? It was all right for Sharon to say that doctors didn't query morals, but they had *feelings,* didn't they?

No, she would put all that to the back of her mind if it killed her. She would take this moment and cherish every second – the sunshine, the glittering sea, the green and the gold, being with this man – and she would remember it for ever.

'We never had a proper week's holiday,' she said. 'But Mam, my stepmother, used to take us on the train sometimes on a day trip.'

Her hair blew in sweet disorder round her face and she put up a hand to keep it away from her eyes. 'We would go down on the sands and Mam would get a deckchair, then we would eat sandwiches, the potted meat in them gritty with sand, and drink strong tea from a flask. Then I would go for a paddle with my dress tucked in my knickers and scream as the ripples in the sand hurt the soles of my feet.'

'I used to be made to wear rubber shoes, and have cream rubbed on my shoulder blades. I remember feeling a right fairy,' Simon said, and Emma laughed.

'Oh, yes. Mam never seemed to think about sunburn till it happened. Then when we got home she would put camomile lotion on my back and arms, and when the skin peeled the next week Sharon would have a lovely time picking it off. But I never fancied doing the same for her, somehow.'

'Mean,' Simon said, and for a moment their eyes met and held.

'Yes, I do remember Lytham St Annes,' Emma said quickly. 'When I was about seventeen I went on a youth club picnic, and a boy took me snogging on a striped towel in the sand-dunes, out of the wind. But he was only fifteen and it was nothing really. He kissed me with his mouth clamped tight, like this.'

She tightened her mouth into a thin line and, delighted, Simon threw back his head and laughed out loud.

'My father loves this coastline; always has,' he said. 'He told me once that when he was very young, before the war, *his* parents used to bring him here for holidays. They stayed at a boarding house back Cleveleys way, and kept themselves. You know. Bought their own food. Tomatoes in the dining-room cupboard, he said, and the landlady charging a shilling a week for the cruet.'

'A what?'

'Cruet. A shilling a week for the use of, and if I know my grandma aright, she would be dousing everything with salt and vinegar, just to get her money's worth.'

'Mam said that people born Lancaster way used to put sugar on their tomatoes,' Emma told him, then she nodded. 'Oh, yes, I remember Mam said there used to be a pierrot troupe there with a man who used to come to the front of the stage at intervals and shout, 'Are you there, children?' An' the children would shout back, "Yes, Tommy'! We're here!" Mam said she once won a talent competition singing a song which went, "So you met someone who set you back on your heels? Goody-goody", with her hair in ringlets set with sugar melted in warm water and a bow on the top.'

'Lovely Mam.'

Emma nodded. 'She was that. She would give you a back-hander as soon as look at you, but you always knew where you stood with her, and if she was on your side then heaven help anyone who tried to hurt you.'

To her dismay, tears filled her eyes and she blinked them angrily away.

'No wicked stepmother syndrome, then?'

'Oh, no. I sometimes think she made more of me just because I *wasn't* her own daughter. An' yet, I never remember her hugging me, or praising me when I did well at school, but it was there all right, the solid affection.'

'And your own mother?'

They were back on the coast road again, driving past wide-fronted hotels, some of them set back behind green lawns and well-kept flower beds. Now the whole atmosphere was more leisurely, and Simon laughed again as Emma said, 'Posher this end, isn't it?'

They were so much in tune, so much at one with each other. He was, he told himself, so *enchanted* by this small girl sitting by his side that even though he knew he was treading dangerously, he found himself wishing the afternoon would last for ever.

She obviously did not want to talk about her own mother, and he was certainly not going to press her. Today was meant for joy. *She* was made for joy, and for a moment his heart ached as he thought about her life and the way it was.

'Here we are,' he said, and drove into the forecourt of a park with a pavilion flanked by green lawns, with putting greens and tennis courts and round flower beds abloom with bright vivid colour. 'Fancy a game of putting?'

The man handing out the clubs and the balls was as Lancashire as hot-pot and black puddings, with his creased kindly face and noble Jesus profile.

'Nay, that's a bit heavy for you, lass.' He took the club Emma was holding and handed her a smaller one. 'This isn't Gleneagles, tha' knows. Just keep your eye on the ball, love, and up with women's liberties.'

'He fancied you.' Simon walked by her side across the smooth lawn to where the putting green lay cool and smooth behind privet hedges and flower beds sloping up to a winding path. 'I could see him envying me.'

'I probably remind him of his niece who teaches in Sunday school,' Emma said with demure solemnity. 'It's Sharon who gets the wolf-whistles, not me.'

'I can't think why.' Simon stopped by the first putt, and as he handed Emma a ball, closed her fingers over it. 'You are very beautiful, and the nicest part is that you don't know it.'

In that instant she saw herself lying naked in his arms, and heard again the hoarse murmurings of his voice as he took her, gently at first, then with rising passion.

And in that moment she knew that he was remembering it too, and knew that in the park with the sound of children playing and the muted ping of tennis balls on rackets, with old couples strolling slowly along the winding paths, and the shimmer of the sea across the wide grass-fronted promenade – she knew that he wanted to kiss her so badly that his desire was there in his dark eyes, plain for her to see.

'Emma . . . .' his voice was low. 'Emma Sparrow.'

Like a slamming of a door in her face the happiness was gone. The worry and the fear were back, the humiliation and the despair. And she had been so wrong in thinking she could forget, even for the space of a sunlit afternoon.

'Where are you going? Stop!' His voice spiralled after her as she ran, stumbling over the grass, not knowing or caring where the path was leading, only wanting to get away from him and the longing on his face that she knew was mirrored on her own.

He caught up with her on the stony path with benches set back into high privet hedges, each one in a small secluded alcove of its own.

'Now,' he said, pulling her to sit beside him, 'now what's wrong? Come on now, love. You know me well enough to tell me, so let's have it.'

Then, when she drooped her head, but not before he had seen the tears glistening on her long eyelashes, he went on, 'Listen, Emma. I wouldn't hurt you either mentally or physically, you must know that?' He sighed. 'What we did was not a *sin*, Emma. You mustn't even think that.' He patted his pocket as if searching for cigarettes. 'It happens all the time.'

'But not to me! Not to me!' Emma jerked her head upwards, her brown eyes blazing in the sudden pallor of her face.

'Oh, I see.' Simon dropped the two clubs on to the path in front of the bench, and tried to take her hands, only to have them snatched away from his grasp. He sighed again. 'You must stop fretting and blaming yourself, Emma. It was my fault. I should have known better, but I am a man, and men . . . well. . . . They might regret but they don't *torture* themselves.' He pulled at his upper lip as if searching for the right words. 'What happened between us was beautiful and I will never forget it, and I am not asking *you* to forget it, just to keep it safe in your heart.'

For a moment the hate she felt for him brought the blood rushing to her face so that she wanted to hit out at him, to rake her nails down his face and shake him out of his complacency. Then the feeling went as quickly as it had arisen, and she clenched her hands together to stop their trembling and drooped her head again.

'I think we'd better go now,' she said in a flat, dull voice. 'You take the clubs back and I will wait by the car. I don't want to play now. I just want to go back.'

'But we haven't settled anything, Emma.' He was genuinely

concerned as he walked along by her side, genuinely caring. 'You haven't told me that you understand.' He shook his head from side to side. 'I don't want to imagine you fretting. I couldn't stand that. You make me feel like a . . . you make me feel terrible.'

Emma quickened her steps. 'What you mean is you want me to say it was nothing. What you mean is you think I am just a stupid girl, a *factory* girl who got what she asked for. Is that it?'

'Emma!' He pulled her round to face him, heedless of the stares from three women in crimplene dresses sunning their fat red arms on a bench by the tennis courts. 'I *care* for you. In my own way I care for you. I'm not a philanderer – oh, God, what an expression, but it fits. I was as overwhelmed as you by what happened. Can't you see?'

'Take the clubs back.' Her voice was weary and now, for her, the gay bright day was over. The sounds of summer faded, and as she retraced her steps to the car she walked like an old woman of the roads, trailing one foot after another.

She expected him to unlock the car when he came back, but instead he took her by the arm. 'We're not going back yet. We'll go over to the sea front and talk some more, and we are not going back until I see you smile again. And that's definite. Okay?'

She knew it was no use arguing. She was perceptive enough to realize it was his own conscience he was setting to rights in a way, and there she could not help him. It wasn't him having a baby, was it? It wasn't him lying awake at nights wondering what to do, knowing there was only one thing to do, and dreading the doing of it.

The tide was out, and they went down the stone steps to the beach where sunbathers lay spreadeagled, faces upturned to the sun in determined stillness; hot sun was a commodity too rare to waste, and getting brown was an important part of a holiday.

'How is Chloe?' Emma stopped and taking off a sandal shook the sand from it before putting it back on again. 'I thought she would have been with you today.'

'She is back in London. Her job came vacant again and she took it.' He stopped walking to watch a young man dangling his baby in the shallows, trailing the baby's feet in the water, then lifting him high as the child screamed with delight. The boy, for that was all he was, was totally engrossed in his task of introducing his little son to the sea for the first time, and without warning, the bitter taste of anger rose in Simon's throat. Suddenly, watching the young father, he was conscious of his own age, deeply aware of his failed marriage and the souring of his relationship with Chloe.

'I envy that man.' He was speaking half to himself. 'At this moment I envy him with all my heart.'

Emma was watching the baby too, perhaps for the first time realizing what she was going to do. Without thinking, she placed a hand on her stomach, and as the young mother ran past them holding out a towel and chiding her husband for keeping the baby in the sun too long, the dam of her emotions broke down.

'An' I envy them too, both of them. All three of them,' she shouted, and as Simon pulled her round to face him she told him about the baby.

'But it's all right. I'm going to see the doctor next week and have an abortion. I wasn't going to tell you. I don't know why I am telling you now.' She tried to break free from his grasp, but he held her tight.

His face had darkened. They might have been quite alone there at the edge of the sea, with the sun turning the dark-green rolling waves into a sparkling blue, with their feet sinking into the soft sand, and the wind lifting her hair.

His eyes were as dark as night, as the implication of what she had just said slowly dawned. He was seeing Chloe, lying on a bed in some nursing home, having his child dragged from between her legs, bloody and mangled. Not an embryo only one step from a sprouting bean, but a child, like that child being carried now wrapped in a towel in the loving arms of his father. He was seeing Emma, small and white, having her baby scraped from her body. *His* baby! His second son or daughter, discarded like bloody flotsam and dropped into some surgical pail.

'Not twice!' he shouted the two words as Emma drew back from him, bewildered by his unexpected reaction. 'No! You will *not* have an abortion, love. I won't allow it.' Pulling her into his arms he held her tight, rocking her backwards and forwards. 'I might have made a mess of my life up to now, but this time I do it right! I am going to do it right, I tell you!'

Emma wriggled free so that she could see into his face. Now she was the one to speak calmly, now that she had told him it was as though the way was clear. 'There is nothing for you to worry about.' She spoke softly. 'You know I have no choice. I am almost totally responsible for my family. For Alan and Joe, and my father when he comes out. There is no room for a baby in that set-up, and the doctor will know that. He will arrange it, and when it's over I can begin all over again.' She put up a hand and touched his ravaged face. 'I can go through with it, honest. There's no other way.'

He was holding on to her like a man drowning. 'You will *not*. I will not allow it. Never! Never!'

'But it's the only way.' Emma swayed in his arms, and when he spoke she would have fallen but for their fierce grasp.

'You can marry me,' he said clearly. 'I will marry you before I will let you do that. Understand? I will marry you, Emma Sparrow. Tomorrow or next week. I will marry you, and you will have my baby. Do you understand?'

Eleven

'It's like flamin' Cinderella! Cinderella coming home and telling her ugly sister that she's going to marry a prince! Flaminenry, but you're a dark horse, our Emma. Fancy it being your boss all the time! No wonder you were keeping your mouth tight shut!'

Sharon was tired, and Sharon tired kept little rein on her tongue, Emma knew that. Saturday was a long day standing behind the sweets counter and weighing out bags of mixed sweets chosen by jostling shoppers. She had had to miss her Saturday night disco dancing with Ricky – the boys had insisted on staying up late to watch television, and Ricky had gone home in one of his huffs – and now this.

'So you'll be getting married before me?' Her small, exhausted face seemed to have shrunk to the size of a teacup, and her blue eyeshadow accentuated the strain round her eyes. 'Well, one thing's certain, you won't be able to borrow my dress. Your bosoms are sprouting already. Did you know that?'

Even as Sharon spoke Emma felt the pricking twinge in her breasts. It was strange, but coming back on the coach she had felt the same sensation. It was as though for the first time she could accept the fact that there was a baby growing inside her. In some inexplicable way her body was at last responding to signs suppressed when it seemed there would never be a baby at all.

'It won't be that kind of wedding.' She drew her eyebrows together in a small anxious frown. 'We didn't get much of a chance to talk. Mr Simon . . . Simon wants it all to be a secret for a while. He has to go down to London on business next week, and when he comes back he says we'll start making plans.'

'Did he fetch you home tonight?' Sharon produced a plastic bag from behind a cushion and began to roll her hair up.

'No. The coach dropped me off at the bottom of the avenue. It would have looked strange if I'd travelled back with him. You know how people talk.'

Sharon speared a roller with a hairpin. 'Charming! An' I suppose they won't talk when they find out? Flaminenry, our Emma, they'll talk their bloody heads off!'

'I'll have left the factory before it gets out. Simon has his position to think about.' The frown between Emma's eyes deepened. 'I'm to stop at home till he can arrange a quiet register office wedding, then we'll move into a house he is buying.'

'Where?'

'Out on the old Preston Road side.'

'A posh house?'

'I don't know. I haven't seen it.'

Sharon's smile was sarcastic. 'An' who is to take over here then? Have you forgotten you have a family *already*, our Emma? What are me and Alan and Joe supposed to do when you're dusting the posh furniture in the posh house? Or don't you care?'

'Of course I care!' Emma twisted her hands in her lap, a sure sign of her agitation. 'Mr Simon . . . Simon says he will arrange for a woman to come in every day when the boys come in from school. To give them their tea and clean up a bit. He says when Dad comes out it will do him good to have to face up to his responsibilities anyway.'

'He what?' Sharon leaped to her feet, her face flushed beneath the crown of jumbo-sized rollers. 'The cheeky sod! So he knows what our dad is like, does he? Did you not tell him that our dad hasn't the strength even to blow the skin off his rice pudding? Does he think he's marrying into the aristocracy, or something?'

'No.' Emma's voice was so quiet it was almost a whisper. 'He knows exactly the kind of background I come from. He's been here, hasn't he? He's *seen*. But it makes no difference. He's not a snob.'

'He's so madly in love with you he can't see the wood for the trees. Is that it, then?'

Emma's face seemed to crumple. 'He just wants to do the right thing by me, Sharon. He wants the baby. He wants it bad. You should have seen his face when I told him I was going to have an abortion. I thought he was going to hit me.'

'An' you love *him*?' Sharon clenched her hands by her sides, rigid with indignation. 'First I knew of it if you do.'

Emma lifted her head. 'I think I love him so much that if I were to admit it, even to myself, I would be frightened to death. I think I loved him from the first moment I saw him. Just to be near him makes me so happy, even when I hate him I feel so happy inside. I didn't know. Nobody told me it could be like this. It's as though nobody but him exists. I can't stop looking at him, and when I am with him *I* am different. Words come into my mouth and he makes me feel lovely.' She held out a hand. 'You *know*, Sharon. You've got Ricky, so you must know.'

'I flamin' don't!' Sharon backed away. 'That's the soppiest thing I've ever heard. Me an' Ricky don't carry on like that.' She sat down again. 'You've got carried away, our Emma. You can't get married feeling like that. He's flattered, that's what he is. Older men get like that sometimes when a young girl fancies them, but it doesn't last. He's an old fella compared to Ben Bamford.' She leaned forward. 'Why don't you tell Ben about the baby? He would marry you if you still want to have it. He'd knock your block off first, but he would marry you; he's only biding his time, Ben is.'

'Let's go to bed.' Emma stood up and bent down to switch off the electric fire. 'It's all such a mix-up.' She turned impulsively and put a hand on Sharon's bare arm. 'We'll talk about it tomorrow, eh?'

'We flamin' won't.' Sharon shrugged the hand away. 'Strikes me you've met a right one. Fancy him going down to London just now. He should be here, sorting things out. Strikes me he's got his priorities all wrong, your Mr Simon. Best thing you can do would be to have that abortion before he comes back. Have it done private and charge it to him. I'll stop off work to look after you. Okay?'

'Would *you* have one, Sharon? An abortion?'

At the tone of Emma's voice Sharon whipped round. 'Like a flamin' shot if I was in your position. But then I'm not daft enough to get caught, am I?'

Seventeen next week, Emma thought as she followed the slight figure bristling with rollers and indignation upstairs. Oh, flaminenry! Only seventeen!

'You're doing this to pay me back, aren't you, Simon?'

Chloe's face was white with shock as she stood in front of the home-made brick fireplace in her friend's London flat. When he first told her she had thought she was going to faint. She had gone icy cold, especially her face, and the dark-brown carpet had seemed to come up as if it were going to hit her smack between the eyes. 'You tell me you are going to marry this girl because she is pregnant, because you got her pregnant quite sober one day when I was away. She means nothing to you, but you will marry her. Oh, God, Simon, don't play the knight on a white charger because it doesn't become you.' She put a foot up on the brick hearth and leaned her forehead against the mantelshelf with its hand-made pottery mugs and its bamboo-framed photographs of her friends' two children.

'You've been taken in by that heart-shaped face and those wistful brown eyes, haven't you?'

'But I never said. . . .' he looked bewildered.

'You didn't need to, honey. I always knew it was the girl called Emma Sparrow. I think I knew when I saw her sitting by your bed in the hospital. All smouldering passion behind that calm face and in that drooping sullen mouth. Her type have been leading men on since Eve passed Adam that rosy apple. She *wanted* you to make her pregnant, can't you see? And now, because integrity's your middle name, she's got you home and dry. Oh, Simon. . . .'

All at once she began to sob. Huge tearing sobs that made Simon glance round at the closed door.

'It's okay.' Chloe raised a ravaged face. 'They've gone to Hampstead to fly a kite on the Heath. And I don't know why I am crying like this. Heaven knows there hasn't been much going for us lately.' She fought for control. 'It's just the *surprise*, the *waste*. Jealousy, maybe, because she is going to share your life, and not me. Because *I* had an abortion and she had more sense. Because now I am sure I love you, when before I wasn't sure.'

'Chloe.' He took a step forward and she came into his arms. 'You're making this very hard for me, love.' He stroked her hair. 'I want us to go on being friends.' His voice deepened. 'You don't mean what you just said. You never wanted to live up there. You never wanted to marry me, not really. Before I told you, I was thinking how happy you looked. When you told me about your trip to Copenhagen next week I saw the pleasure in your eyes.' He shook her gently. 'Sometimes I think you will never marry.' He tried to make her smile. 'I don't think there's a man around who could tie you down to a home.'

'Tie me down to a home?' Chloe moved away, and covering her face with her hands began to laugh, gently at first, then with rising hysteria. 'Oh, God, Simon! I never looked on your feelings for me as a fortress I could creep into to shield me from the wicked world. We were *equals*! You were never the sort of man who would lose his cool because we ran out of your favourite cheese. I didn't have to hand you your vitamins at breakfast, and pick your socks up off the bedroom floor. Is that what you want? Is that what you have wanted all the time?'

When he left her she was calm again. He promised to keep in touch, and she promised to be his friend.

But when the door had closed behind him she ran into her room with its shower and the small portable television set at the foot of her bed. With pounding heart she lay down on the coverlet and drummed with her heels like a child in a tantrum.

'Blast you, Simon Martin!' she yelled. 'You stupid bastard! You stupid godamned bastard!'

She sobbed for ten minutes, then slowly calmed.

Telling his parents was easier than Simon had expected. He could have told them afterwards; after all, he had more or less gone his own way since he left school. But what struck him forcibly was the likeness between Emma and his mother. Mary Martin had the same soft quietness about her, the same brown stillness, the tilt of the head which showed she was not as passive as her gentle appearance might suggest.

'One of the factory girls?' Bernard Martin glanced across at his wife. 'History does repeat itself sometimes, then, lovey.' He leaned across and pressed her hand. 'First time I met your ma,' he told Simon, 'she was coming out of the biscuit factory gates with her head tied up in a turban thing. I was riding a bicycle and if I hadn't jammed my brakes on fast I would have knocked her for six. And instead of that she knocked me for six, didn't you love?'

'But there was the war coming, and you were only a glorified errand boy yourself,' his wife reminded him. 'Simon has his qualifications. We started off even-pegging, whereas Simon's already got on.' Her smooth forehead was furrowed with anxiety. 'And what about Chloe? Did it not work out, you living together?' She looked honestly bewildered. 'How do you know this will work out any better than your first marriage did? You can't keep chopping and changing, you're not exactly a young boy now.'

'Then it's high time he settled down.' Bernard winked at his son. 'When are you bringing her down to meet us, son? I don't blame you for wanting a quiet wedding, but we would like to see her some time. Your mother will be pestering the life out of me if you don't.'

Simon automatically reached for his diary. 'There's the annual general meeting of the shareholders in late August. I could take a week off then and kill two birds with one stone. Will that give you enough time to make new curtains for the guest-room and fill the freezer, Mum?'

Mary Martin relaxed with a smile. 'Oh, go on with you. We just want to make the girl feel at home. We want her to see you come from a nice home.' She was already making plans – Simon and his father could see the arrangements taking shape in her mind. 'She's only young, and I expect her parents are just as concerned.'

Ah, Emma's parents. . . . Simon's face was grave as he filled them in with the details of Emma's background, and when he had finished his mother nodded her head slowly.

'Well then, we'll just have to try to make up for what she has missed, won't we, Dad?'

'New curtains and fourteen quiches in the freezer definitely,' Bernard Martin said, and winked at his son once again.

Twelve

Emma had been at home for three weeks when Ben Bamford came to see her. She had left Delta Dresses without telling even Mrs Kelly the reason, and though Simon had assured her that this was the best way, the *only* way, she still felt strangely diminished.

Normally when any of the factory girls got married there were cream cakes all round, and crude slogans pinned on the wall behind her machine, as well as a ride round the factory floor in one of the big basket skips, with pound notes being pinned on to the bride-to-be's overall as she was dragged on her triumphal way.

Not that Emma had wanted that, she persuaded herself. Not that she didn't realize that in marrying the London boss's son she had stepped over the boundary of what was expected. Dignity was the thing, and Simon had said he would tell Mr Gordon in his own good time.

'Why the bloody secrecy?' Ben Bamford came straight to the point. 'And why the bloody hurry? I couldn't believe it when our Patty told me, and she only got to know because working behind a bar means she gets to know most things.' He reached out and gripped Emma's wrists hard. 'And it surely can't be a shotgun wedding because your old man couldn't point a bent banana at an Eccles cake.' He pushed her away roughly and looked her up and down deliberately, his vivid blue eyes blazing.

Then, as Emma's face gave the truth away, he stepped back a pace as his mouth dropped open in amazement. 'Well, bugger me! You *have* got one in the oven, haven't you? You could cold-fish me and then let the likes of him do what I've

167

been aching to do for ages? You dirty little whore!'

Emma bit her lips in a childish gesture of distress. 'It wasn't like that, Ben. You know me well enough to know it wasn't. I was half out of my mind when I found I was going to have a baby, and I was going to . . . to get rid of it, but he, Simon, he asked me to marry him.'

'Knowing you was *my* girl? Knowing that, he still did that?' The blue eyes raked her body in an insulting way. 'I wish it *had* been me that dark night kicking his teeth in. I'd have done for him proper if I'd known his game.'

Emma moved impatiently over to the settee, sitting down on the arm, her own eyes bright with indignation. '*Your* girl? Your girl, Ben Bamford? I hadn't set eyes on you for weeks, and you went away and never wrote once, and now you have the nerve to say. . . .'

'What did you want? Bloody bunches of flowers? Letters with SWALK on the back of the envelope? You *knew* you was my girl, Em. I can't say no fancy words like what he can but why did you think I kept on going out with you even though I was getting nothing?' Suddenly Ben slumped down in a chair and buried his face in his hands. 'You think I've got no feelings, don't you? I feel like I've just been punched in the guts right now. I *hit* our Patty when she told me, I was that mad. But even then I never thought you was up the spout.' He raised his head, and to Emma's surprise and distress she saw the sparkle of tears in his eyes. 'Why did you go and let him when you'd never let me, Em? Why?'

The milk cart stopped in the avenue outside and there was the clatter of bottles on the step. The small room was stifling hot, and Emma pulled at the neck of her thin blouse as if it choked her. 'I can't explain, Ben. It was only the once, and if I could explain it to myself I would try to explain it to you.' She twisted the duster she was holding into a thin rope. 'But it happened, and the baby happened, and when I marry him next week I will try to make him happy. He's not a happy man, Ben. You think he has so much more than you, but money isn't everything.'

'An' I suppose him having pots of it doesn't make no difference to you?' Ben's tone was sulky. 'What will you do when you meet his posh friends, Em? Will you go all lah-de-dah like them, or will he keep you hid like you are hiding now? Will you remember to take your pinny off when you sit down at the table? An' sit at the top table at the works do's, pretending to be friendly with the workers an' asking about their kids in a posh voice?' He turned the last screw. 'An' when the baby comes will you sit alone with it in a big house with fitted carpets while he stops down in London for what he says are meetings? Will you know for sure that he's not seeing that bird who looks like something out of a magazine?' He put up a hand. 'Oh, I saw her. I saw her and him down at the station, an' it wasn't all that long ago, either. I saw the way he was all over her when they said goodbye. What's he done with her, then? Paid her off like what he'll be paying you off one fine day?'

'Why are you trying to hurt me so much, Ben?' Emma stared sadly at him with all the brightness gone from her face. 'Why can't you wish me luck and go away? We never seem to meet without quarrelling. Every single time we've been together we've argued.'

'But can't you see? That's because we *belong*! If I wasn't on your side then I wouldn't be sitting here, would I? I would never have come round this morning, and if you was really certain then you would have told me to push off.'

Calmer now, he reached for a cigarette and lit it, throwing the spent match into the tiled hearth as if the electric fire were ablaze with coal. He inhaled deeply.

'Look, Em. You can't marry that bloke an' you know it.'

She gave up twisting the duster and threw it down behind her on the settee cushions. 'Then what would you have me do, Ben Bamford? Have the baby here, then have to take it out to be minded every morning on my way to work? Bring it up with Alan and Joe, and Dad sitting coughing in that chair? And you arguing with me when I couldn't come out with you every night? Is that what you wish for me?'

'I am asking you to marry me,' Ben said. 'I am asking you to marry me and come to live with me at Patty's home, and stop at home and bring up your kid along of Patty's poor little kid, with me working and Patty going out full-time.' He stared at the cigarette held loosely between fingers and thumb. 'Patty would like that. I know, because she likes you and even after I had laid into her she still told me off for letting you slip through me fingers. She said it was me own rotten fault.'

Choked with sudden emotion, Emma could only shake her head slowly from side to side.

'You mean you would marry me, knowing the baby belonged to another man?'

'It would be *yours,* wouldn't it?' Ben's tone was fierce. 'I like kids, an' it would be just another kid, wouldn't it?'

The sudden ringing of the door bell brought them both to their feet, the moment of closeness shattered and gone. Emma walked over to the window and lifted the curtain. 'It's the telephone engineer. Simon is having a telephone put in here so I can keep in touch with Sharon and the boys.' She stared down at the carpet. 'And the car just drawn up at the gate is the driving instructor to give me a lesson. I've had two already.'

Ben exploded into immediate and terrifying anger, his face flushing red and his blue eyes blazing. He dropped the cigarette on to the floor and ground it into the carpet with his shoe. 'Forget it, Em! Forget every bloody word I said. I wouldn't marry you, not if you crawled on your hands and knees to ask me! Forget the bloody lot!'

He wrenched the front door open and ran down the short path. The telephone engineer stepped hastily backwards to avoid being knocked over.

Sharon and Ricky went back to their respective jobs after Emma's wedding, and Simon drove his bride through the town, up the Preston Road and straight to the house set back from the main road.

'When we've changed we'll go out for a pub lunch,' he told her. 'I still think we should have taken your sister and her fiancé out for a meal. It's not much of a wedding day for you, is it, Emma?'

'It's the way I wanted it. The way we both wanted it.' Emma fingered the orchid pinned to the collar of her blue suit. 'All things being equal.'

She was very calm, very dignified, and there was nothing about her to suggest that inside she was a mess of teeming emotion. Here she was, she told herself, married to a man she loved but did not know. How could that be? And that awful short ceremony, with the registrar ticking Sharon off for giggling . . . and oh, God, when he reminded Sharon that what was happening was a serious matter, Emma had wanted to drop through the floor.

She stole a glance at the man sitting beside her, hands steady on the wheel, doing automatically all the things her driving instructor told her to do, doing them without thinking, his face serious, with only a pulse beating at the side of his neck giving his own feelings away.

Tomorrow he was going back to work, and at the beginning of the next week he was going down to London for two days, and she would be left alone in a house for the first time in her life.

There would be no Sharon sleeping in the bed beside her, head held rigidly on the pillow so as not to disturb the crown of soft rollers. No frenzied rush in the mornings to get the boys off to school. Instead of that Mrs Collins from over the road would be coming into the house in Litchfield Avenue for an hour, then letting herself in for another hour when Alan and Joe came home from school. All arranged by this man, and paid for by this man, with a simplicity that had left her breathless.

'Given the money, anybody can arrange anything,' Sharon had said. 'Besides, he is used to arranging things. He's a boss, isnt he? With a few pound notes in your pocket you can make anything work for you. I bet in a few months you won't want to know us, our Emma. He has taken you over, just like you was a firm he was merging with. You're like a flamin' zombie. Do you realize that? You've been going around in a dream like it was somebody else it was all happening to. Do you *want* to marry him? Do you want to be with a man like that for the rest of your life?'

Emma shivered, and immediately Simon's hand left the wheel and closed over her knee. 'I am sorry it had to be like this, love. I've done you out of being married in white with the bells ringing, and the choir singing "O perfect Love".' He squeezed her knee, then took the wheel again. 'But I am going to make it up to you. I am going to watch you grow rosy and fat as the weeks go by, and you're going to eat all the right things

171

so that when the baby comes it will be healthy and strong. And you are going to take care of yourself. For me, and for our son.'

'It could be a girl.'

Simon shook his head. 'The Martins always have boys. I *order* you to have a boy! Okay?'

He was obsessed about the baby. It was as though this coming child of his signified all his dreams, all his hopes, as though Emma herself was merely the necessary appendage to make it all possible. She knew that, and the knowledge scared her. It was as though once he had lost a child and was still mourning. He had told her about his first marriage, and she knew about Chloe; at least she *thought* she knew about Chloe, but sometimes she thought Simon Martin was like a chairman at a board meeting, keeping to the salient points and ruthlessly skimming over what he did not consider to be worth discussing.

She was standing in the bedroom in her bra and pants, wondering whether to wear her new jeans and a top, or whether a dress would be more in keeping for a wedding lunch, when he came upstairs.

Her normal instinct would have been to grab her blouse from the bed and hold it in front of her, but Emma knew no shyness with this tall dark-eyed man. From that first moment of total surrender she had given herself into his keeping for ever, and to be coy would have been hypocritical and embarrassing for both of them.

Coming swiftly over to her he pulled her to him and ran a hand down over her gently swelling stomach. 'It's beginning to show.' He was smiling, satisfied, proud, and when he unfastened her bra and cupped a rounded breast in his hand, Emma looked at his thick dark hair and felt her bones melt to jelly.

'I'll be careful, darling.' He was whispering now as he lifted her up in his arms and laid her down on the bed. 'I won't be rough.' He tore at his clothes, the way he had done that first time. Then, as he took her in his arms, he buried his face beneath her breasts and moaned softly. 'Oh, dear God, I *need* you, little Emma. You have no idea what you do to me with your soft skin and the quietness of you. I won't hurt you, or the baby. I promise.'

And he didn't.

Even at the moment of climax his movements were un-hurried, and the sweetness of his slow loving and the tender murmurings of his deep voice made the strangeness of the morning and the coldness of the brief ceremony recede and fade into nothing.

Later, when they showered together, they were like two children splashing each other, smiling and soaping each other as the warm water cascaded down over their bodies.

Then in the long lazy summer afternoon Emma unpacked her pitifully few belongings, storing her cheap underclothes away in the long drawers of the white fitted bedroom furniture. She put her blouses and dresses in the cupboard at her side of the double bed, hung her belts and chiffon scarves on the fitted rail, and placed her shoes, all three pairs, in a neat row at the bottom.

She opened the door of Simon's cupboard and gasped when she saw the line of shirts. Childishly she counted them, but when she got to fourteen she stopped and closed her eyes, remembering the days when her father had owned just three shirts. One on his back, one in the wash and one for emergency, as Mam had said.

It was perfectly true. There were those who had and those who had not, and now, as from today, she, Emma Martin, who used to be Emma Sparrow, was one of those who had.

Conditioned to long bouts of silent communication with herself, through the years of sitting at the buttonhole machine as her mind roved free, she tried honestly to assess her feelings.

It would be hypocrisy not to admit that the sudden transition from near poverty to comparative affluence was bound to affect her. She had never *seen* a bedroom like this, let alone slept in one.

She sat down on the edge of the bed and stared round the room, making herself see it as if she were an uninvolved stranger. At the long-haired white carpet, chosen by Chloe, at the turquoise heavy silk curtains with the matching duvet cover and pleated flounce round the bed. At the bedside lamps with their chiffon shades, and her dressing-table fitted into the corner by the window.

With the honesty that came as naturally to her as breathing, she asked herself a question: If Simon had been an out-of-work labourer, with nothing to offer her but a single room at the top of a condemned Victorian building, would she have married him?

Or would she have rehearsed her story for the doctor, told it with tears running down her cheeks, and be back at the factory now with nothing but a fading unpleasant memory to remind her of what had happened?

Would she? It was a straight question deserving a straight answer.

'That is what education gives you, Emma,' her head-mistress had said, despairing of her bright pupil's intention of leaving school instead of going on to A levels. 'Education gives a girl more than academic qualifications. It gives her the power, and it *is* power, my dear, to sit down and get things into perspective, to argue with herself and come up with the right answer. To evaluate and make a choice, not from blind un-thinking prejudice, but from her own logically drawn con-clusions.'

Emma had never forgotten the mini-lecture delivered in her headmistress's penetrating voice, so now deliberately she faced herself and spoke directly to her heart.

And she knew, in that moment, that education had no part to play in the way she was feeling now. If Simon Martin had wanted her, no matter what his status in life, she would have married him.

Love, she was discovering, was not the tender, dreamy emotion she had thought it would be. Love, her love for Simon, was a deep ache of longing, where family loyalties counted as nothing, where just the sight of his dark head filled her with a total contentment. And where cool, clear thinking had no part. No part at all. . . .

That first afternoon they took a car rug out into the back garden and lay on it, side by side, with the blue sky above and the distant hum of traffic muted in their ears. With their fingers entwined they slipped in and out of sleep together.

'I love you,' she whispered, and he smiled.

'You keep right on doing just that,' he said, and if it wasn't quite the reply she wanted, for today it was enough, more than enough.

174

When she made tea in the kitchen and took it outside Simon was sitting up with a folder open on his knees, checking the closely typed figures. He motioned to her to put the cup of tea down on the grass, adjusted his spectacles and went on with his calculations, leaving the tea to grow cold.

And it never occurred to Emma, not even fleetingly, that it was a strange thing for a man to be doing on his wedding day.

'You are sure you won't mind being alone?'

He held her close before he left to drive down to London the following Monday morning. 'You won't do anything silly like climbing ladders, or fainting in the bath?' He ran a hand in an already familiar gesture down the soft slight swell of her stomach. 'Take care of him for me. Okay?'

And when he had gone she stood in the doorway of the big room with its picture windows at either side, and silently gloried in its beauty.

The day before, whilst Simon prepared his notes for the trip down south and wrote the first draft of a memo to be xeroxed and sent out to every worker in the group of factories, she had rung Sharon and asked her to bring the boys over when she finished work.

'For supper,' she'd said innocently, and Sharon's loud explosive hoot of laughter had crackled in her ears.

'Last week it was *tea*! Oh, flaminenry, our Emma. Is it formal dress, then? 'Cos if it is I'd better be getting me tiara out of its box and giving it a polish. It hasn't taken you long to cotton on to posh ways, has it? Are we having "horses doovres" to start off with?'

Emma had leaped at once to the defensive. 'It *is* supper for me and Simon. He doesn't come home till seven at the very earliest. You've no idea how hard he works.'

But Sharon never had known when to let be.

'An' *tea* is cucumber butties cut so thin you can see the plate through them?' She giggled, and as she went on chattering Emma realized it was the first time they had spoken to each other on the telephone.

'The maid's having her day off. Hope you don't mind. You know what it's like with staff these days.'

175

Sharon answered through an invisible plum. 'Oh, my dear. I have the same problem. Only last week the parlour maid trumped as she was bringing in the fillet steaks, and of course I had to tell her to go. No refinement at all. So I *do* understand, my dear.'

'Come as soon as you can,' Emma said, and replaced the receiver carefully on its cradle.

At five o'clock there was a chicken casserole simmering in the new oven, four potatoes baking in their jackets underneath, and ice-cream in the small freezer. It was all a million light years away from standing at Mam's old cooker, often still wearing her coat as she grilled fish fingers or hamburgers straight from the packet.

And when Emma saw them coming up the road from the bus stop she ran to the door with arms outstretched in an excited welcome.

Because it was raining and the path was muddy, she made the boys remove their shoes, then smiled as they made a beeline for the velvet sofa facing the television – two inanimate objects, eyes fixed, transferred merely from one setting to another, oblivious of everything but the figures on the screen.

'Why is everybody so pale on your telly.' Alan wanted to know.

'Mrs Collins gave us cottage pie for tea,' Joe said.

'Shepherd's pie,' Alan contradicted.

'Cottage!'

'Shepherd's.'

'Cottage.'

'Oh, shurrup, both of you!' Sharon followed Emma through into the kitchen, arms folded, thin legs looking even thinner beneath the straight skirt she had shortened to meet the current fashion.

'You are all right, all of you? Aren't you?' Emma opened the oven door to peer anxiously inside and prod the potatoes with a fork.

Sharon stared down at her shoes, determined not to show rapture at anything in the house. 'A fat lot you care, anyroad.'

Emma whipped round. 'Of course I care!' Her face was flushed. 'I wouldn't have moved out if Mrs Collins hadn't stepped in and been glad of the money. And anyway, Dad will be home soon. It's only a matter of weeks now, then you'll be getting married and. . . !'

'An' Dad will take over?' Sharon's mouth dropped into a sulky curve. 'Oh, yes. I can just see Dad taking over. I can just see him in the kitchen wearing a pinny. He can burn a pot of tea an' you know it, our Emma.' She kicked out furiously at nothing. 'You never stopped to think, did you? Not when you did what you did, or about what's going to happen now.'

She lifted her head and stared straight at Emma. 'Anyroad, there were a knock at the door yesterday, and when I went it were a woman I'd never seen before.'

She hesitated as Emma took four plates from the oven rack and laid them out in a row on the breakfast bar. 'Well, go on.'

'It was your mother,' Sharon said.

Emma stood quite still, the meal forgotten.

'My mother? You mean my own mother came and just knocked at the door? Oh, my God, I don't believe it!'

'You'd best sit down for a minute.' Sharon pulled a tall stool forward. 'She said she had come on the train to see a friend she used to know years ago, and on her way back to the station she called on the spur. Her friend had told her about Mam dying, but not about Dad being in prison and you getting married. She was quite took aback.'

Emma could feel her heart thudding, even as she told herself not to be stupid. 'What was she like?' Her lips quivered. 'Was she like me? I mean, am I like *her*? Was she nice? What did she say?'

'You've gone ever so white.' Sharon's voice was concerned. 'She wasn't . . . you're not a bit like her. She was little and fat with her hair done in a reddish colour. She said she was a widow now, and when I told her you was married she couldn't believe it. She lives somewhere outside Birmingham, and I've got her address if you want it.' Sharon looked round for her shoulder bag. 'But I didn't give her *your* address. I was going to, then I thought better of it.'

'Did she ask for it?'

'No, she didn't. She was only in a minute with having to catch her train and everything.' Sharon put a hand on one of the plates. 'I'm starving hungry, our Emma. Mrs Collins gave the boys jam on toast, but I've had nothing.' She gave Emma's arm a little shake. 'Look. You can't be *that* upset about it. You're just being dramatic. *Mam* was your mother, an' you know it. Not that woman with dyed red hair. She went off and left you and never even wrote nor nothing. You want to forget she ever came.'

Emma nodded, and getting down from the stool began to dish up the meal. They were carrying it through into the far end of the big room used as a dining-room, when she suddenly stopped and said, 'What colour were her eyes, Sharon? Was she a *kind* sort of person? Did you like her? Would I like her?'

'She was just a woman,' Sharon said impatiently. 'Oh, flaminenry, our Emma, forget her. I wish I hadn't told you now.'

They were half-way through the meal when Sharon asked where Simon had gone.

'London. He has four interviews and three meetings to get through in two days,' Emma told her.

'Stopping in a hotel, I suppose?' By the tone of her voice Sharon managed to make it sound as if what she really meant was a brothel. 'Why couldn't you have gone with him? You could have gone round the shops in Oxford Street. Catch me missing a chance like that.'

She passed her plate for a second helping. 'Won't you be scared sleeping alone in this house with no neighbours to knock on the wall to? I've had Joe in bed with me since you went, an' even though he kicks me to death it's better than being on me own.'

'I'm not in the least worried.' Emma went through for the ice-cream, and wondered if her mother had really been as fat and red of hair as Sharon had tried to make out. It was no good, she just couldn't put it out of her mind.

In the middle of the night, with the house dark and silent, she sat up in the middle of the big bed and tried to work things out in her head.

It was true that Mam had brought her up, and with as much loving care as if she had been her own daughter. And it was also true that if her real mother had been dead she would never even have thought about her.

Emma hugged her knees and switched on the beside lamp. She couldn't *love* a woman who was a complete stranger, even if that person had given birth to her. *Could* she? She could be curious about her, and even terrified at the thought of meeting her. She could wonder what deep unhappiness had caused a mother to walk away from her husband and child; and knowing her father, in spite of loving him, she could ask herself had all the faults been on one side?

Sitting there in the darkness, she could remember the anguish of the weeks after she discovered she was pregnant and how, half-ashamed, she had cried for her mother. Wanting and needing her with such intensity that once, in despair, she had even stretched out her arms to her. And if it was ridiculous, even if it was disloyal to those who had cared for her, the feeling was still there. A strong, deep love that wouldn't go away.

'I bet her hair wasn't all that red, either,' Emma told herself, as switching off the light she lay down again and tried to will a sleep that would not come.

Thirteen

It was after nine o'clock in the evening when Simon arrived back looking, in Emma's private opinion, tired and ill.

Quick at sensing his mood, she made the mistake of offering him something to eat straight away, remembering how Mam had always pushed a plate of food under John Sparrow's nose as soon as he came in. 'Feed a man the minute he comes in before you tell him owt,' she always said, so Emma kissed her husband and smiled.

'There's a nice pork chop in the oven. It won't take me a second to dish it up.' Then she stepped back as if he had raised a hand to hit her as he hurled his brief-case into the far corner of the velvet sofa and slumped down in a chair.

'Just give me a whisky and soda, there's a good girl. I couldn't eat a thing.' He patted his flat stomach. 'I am all blown up with eating business lunches for the past couple of days, and talking to illiterate morons who won't even try to realize how desperate things are and what we're up against.'

He drained the glass and passed it over to her. 'Get me another one, love, and go easy on the soda this time. It's been hell down there. We've had to lay off seventy workers at the Acton factory. Seventy! And with the excuse that it was all due to production problems.' He ran a hand through his thick hair. 'What a fiasco! It's a vicious circle with the mills up here laying off *their* workers in turn.' Glancing at his watch he started to get up. 'I must ring Harry Gordon up to ask him to arrange a management and supervisors' meeting first thing tomorrow morning. He won't like it, but there's no choice. Somebody has to get the message across somehow.'

His dark eyes were like chiselled holes in his face, and there were two spots of high colour on his cheekbones. He took the glass of whisky through with him into the hall, sipping from it as he went. 'I should have rung him from down there, but I wanted to get back.' He looked up briefly from dialling. 'You've been all right on your own?'

Emma nodded, opened her mouth to say something, thought better of it, then went through into the kitchen to switch off the oven and take out the casserole. There had never been any left-overs in Litchfield Avenue, and she stared at it, wondering if it would heat through the next day, reminding herself that Mam had always said that pork was tricky, when she heard Simon's raised voice as he talked to Harry Gordon.

'So, okay, it's bloody short notice!' His words were ragged with exhaustion, and sharp with irritation. 'Well, you will just have to put him off. I know . . . I know.'

Emma stood listening. So this was one of the boss men her father and Ben Bamford had complained about!

'Sitting about on their fat arses,' John Sparrow had said, 'watching the men do all the work.'

'Treating us like we was down the bloody salt mines,' Ben had grumbled. 'Taking three hours for their so-called business lunches then knocking off again at five.'

Emma reached for a piece of foil and wrapped up some white crumbly Lancashire cheese, put it back in the fridge, then replaced some biscuits in a tin.

It just went to show, she decided as Simon's tone rose in frustration. She bit her lips. An' the best thing she could do was to keep out of his way till he had got it off his chest. For the time being, anyway.

So silently, like a small quiet mouse, she went about her task of tidying away the uneaten meal, knowing and accepting the fact that until Simon had relaxed, her very presence was superfluous. She wasn't being subservient. Nothing like that. She was merely using her loaf, that was all.

When she went back into the living-room at last he was asleep in his chair, the glass empty by his side, papers slipping from his knees. He looked grey, far older than his years, and touchingly vulnerable.

When the telephone rang she went quickly into the hall to answer it, whispering a hello, and praying it wasn't Harry

Gordon ringing back.

'Hi! Is that Emma?' The voice at the other end was as loud and clear as if its owner were standing there right beside her. Emma saw her eyes grow wide in the reflection in the mirror over the small table.

'This is Chloe. Chloe Day. Is Simon there? Would you mind if I had a word with him? I've a few things I would like him to send on. You don't mind, honey?'

Taken completely by surprise, Emma stammered something. By Simon's chair she hesitated for a moment as she realized the sleep was a necessary shutting down of his over-taxed strength. She touched him gently on his arm, and immediately he opened his eyes and stared at her face as if wondering who she could be.

'The telephone. For you.' She tried not to sound apologetic. 'It's Chloe . . . Chloe,' she repeated, then stood back as he almost knocked her away in his rush past her into the hall.

'Chloe! How *are* you?' His voice was quite different now. It sounded young again, filled with pleasure, eager and almost excited.

Determined not to eavesdrop, Emma ran quickly upstairs and closed the bedroom door.

And she wasn't jealous. To show jealousy would be childish and make Simon angry and disappointed in her. He had explained that there was no animosity between him and Chloe; that he hoped that some day they would meet and be friends. Emma tucked a strand of hair behind an ear and went to examine her body profile in the long mirror. She was the one Simon had married, and this was his baby just beginning to show. Besides, men brought up like Simon Martin did not write off their mistresses, or even their ex-wives when they married someone else. They behaved in a civilized way.

Just as she, Emma Martin, who used to be Emma Sparrow, must behave in a civilized way. Not carry on like Ben Bamford, rushing down the path in a frenzy of rage, or like her father refusing to talk about his first wife.

Emma glanced at the drawer in her dressing-table where she had hidden the slip of paper with her mother's address scribbled on it. She nodded her head up and down twice. Her decision not to mention it to Simon, now that was being civilized. It was bad enough him being lumbered with a father-in-law who would soon be coming out of prison to drink and cough what was left of his life away, *and* sponge on Simon if he got the chance. Emma was ready and prepared for that. But for Simon suddenly to find he had also acquired a fat mother-in-law with bright red hair, well, that would have been *too* much. Emma trailed through into the bathroom and turned on the taps to drown the sound of the animated conversation going on in the hall below.

Simon's homecoming hadn't been in the least like the rapturous, idyllic meeting she had planned. The honeymoon was over, as Mam would have said. Slowly she began to undress.

But then, did *anything* turn out according to plan? Flaminenry, as Sharon would undoubtedly say, that was life. Wasn't it?

Simon got into bed just after eleven o'clock. Too tired to make love, too sleepy and whisky-sodden to do more than lay his hand on her stomach with a proprietary gesture. 'Don't let me miss the alarm in the morning, love. I want to be away before eight. I've got to chase some supplies up after the meeting with Harry Gordon. It's a good job I'm not a union man. Being the boss's son has its disadvantages at a time like this. There's too much at stake, and I don't mean just personally either. . . . God, but I'm tired.'

Whenever Emma had thought about marriage to Simon, if she had really thought past the wedding and the relief from the anguished anxiety and indecision about what to do about the baby, it had been in terms of him going off to work, then coming home to a cooked meal.

She would be a credit to him. That she was determined to be. She would meet his friends, and they would spend long weekends in the large neglected garden with Simon pushing the lawn mower whilst she weeded gently and went indoors for drinks and trays of snacks. She would learn to cut bread thin and spread it with butter, not grab thick slices from a cut loaf and smear it with margarine, and she would think in terms of chops instead of fish fingers and the interminable hamburgers.

She wasn't blaming Simon for the humdrum reality of her existence. He had rescued her from far worse, hadn't he? And the fact that their being together had coincided with the partial closing-down of the London end of his father's business meant that he had to work even longer hours to consolidate the northern side. This much she understood.

What she had not prepared herself for was the loneliness. Long, long days in the house when there was nothing left to polish, when the evening meal so lovingly prepared dried and frizzled in the oven, and a telephone call told her he would be delayed once again and not to keep anything for him as he would be having a beer and a sandwich with a client before going back to the office to work on yet another return.

She still, to her surprise, had failed to come to terms with her pregnancy; she told herself that maybe it was because it had been wished on her and not entered into voluntarily. The books she read one after the other made pregnancy out to be a joyful thing, where eyes and hair shone and the mother-to-be went around in a state of bovine contentment.

Emma waited for this to happen, and when none of it did she sat down and quietly assessed the situation with the same matter-of-factness that was so much a part of her character.

Nothing in this life was handed to you on a plate. This much she knew and accepted. If she was lonely then it was up to her to do something about it, and when she saw the girl next door getting out of her car and carrying a carton of groceries inside, she called out to her:

'Like to come in for a coffee? It seems silly us not knowing each other. Bring the baby in. We've already made friends over the wall; he's a real smiler, isn't he?'

And as soon as Ginny Boland came through the kitchen door, balancing her round fat son on her hip, Emma knew that the courage it had taken to speak first would be rewarded.

'I feel awful.' Ginny said this with a broad smile. 'I know I should have come round to see if there was anything I could do, but, well. . . .' She spread her hands wide. 'I know I'm probably dropping a brick, but I did talk to . . . oh, God, I hope I'm not speaking out of turn . . . I did get to know the other girl I thought was coming to live here. Then when she stopped coming and you turned up, oh, God, what have I said?'

'That was Chloe.' Emma busied herself with the kettle. 'My husband had a long-standing relationship with her, then it was off, then he married me. Because I was pregnant,' she added wickedly.

Ginny plonked the fat baby down on the floor. 'Fair do's. And now you're dying with boredom? I know because I was the same, but I taught geography and maths till I resembled one of my own contour maps. Couldn't you have carried on for a few months yet? Or were you modelling swimwear or something? You've got the *face* for it, anyway.'

Emma bent down and tickled the round cheek of the placid baby who was making no attempt to crawl or even move from his fascinated scrutiny of his own podgy feet. 'I worked in a clothing factory making buttonholes on a machine, and it wasn't on the cards for me to carry on because my husband was my boss.'

'You mean punching holes in stuff? All day long?' Ginny's face was a study. 'What were you doing? Turning your back on the system and finding yourself? How fascinating!'

Emma poured a stream of water into two earthenware mugs. 'I did it because we needed the money fast and I wasn't trained for anything. My father was always out of work, then my stepmother died and he went a bit off the rails. He's in prison now, as a matter of fact.'

Ginny stirred her coffee thoughtfully. She was a big, carefree, pleasant girl with devoted parents, a mild-mannered husband and a baby who only cried when he was hungry. Even the children she had taught at the private school in Preston were from the same kind of background, taking extra music lessons, horse riding, and ballet as if it were their right. She put the spoon down and stared straight at Emma.

'You're testing me out, aren't you? You're making your life sound like a soap opera just to see if I drink my coffee politely then go, making it clear that I never wish to darken your door again. Right?'

'Something like that.' Emma nodded, biting her lip. 'I know it's a kind of snobbery in reverse, but I thought. . . .' Her voice tailed away.

'Tell me something.' Ginny leaned forward, her rather protruding blue eyes alight with genuine interest. 'How many could you do a day?'

'How many what?'

'Buttonholes. And what is your father in for? Trying to rape you?' She curled both hands round the coffee mug. 'It's like having a bit of that *Dallas* thing on television right next door, except that you're a lot prettier than Sue Ellen. I think she's a drag.'

'What I would really like to do,' Emma said when the second mug of coffee had been drunk and the baby had fallen asleep on the velvet sofa with a towel underneath his head, 'is to take some sort of a course.' She waved a hand at the books piled on the low table. 'I am floundering and I know it. No, what I would really like to do would be to work for O levels and then As, and maybe to go on to read for a degree. Work I can do at home till the baby is old enough go be left for part of the time.' Her brown eyes glowed with enthusiasm. 'I used to dream of doing something like this when I was at work, but after Mam died there was always too much to do at home.'

'Because you have seventeen stepbrothers and stepsisters, and nine of them are mentally retarded,' Ginny suggested sadly, and as their laughter joined, the baby woke up and, waving his dimpled hands in the air, grew cross-eyed as he absorbed their fascination.

'Roger will know. He lectures in engineering at the technical college, and he's all for educating the masses. Says it's our only salvation. I'll get him to give you all the information you need, and then perhaps when your baby is here we can do swaps two or more days a week, and you can study and I can maybe take a part-time job. Swap the babies, I mean, well, not swap but, oh, you know what I mean!' Ginny ruffled her short curly hair till it stood out round her head. 'We are terribly poor, you see. Even with my parents giving us a whacking down-payment on the house the mortgage repayments are crippling.'

Emma smiled. 'Would you really like to know just what being poor means, Ginny?'

Her new friend laughed out loud, reminding Emma for a moment of Ben Bamford. 'Oh, God, there we go again! Okay, tell me about being really poor then. But nowadays it's all relevant, truly. You'll soon find out, or is your husband a bloated capitalist?'

'So much so I'll be voting Conservative at the next election,' Emma said straight-faced, then joined in Ginny's uninhibited laughter.

Filled with optimism, Emma caught the bus into town then another out to Litchfield Avenue the next day. Simon had told her it would be nine at the earliest before he came home, so she planned to be there when the boys came in from school, and to take over from Mrs Collins for just the one day.

But when she let herself in with her key it was to find Nellie Collins sitting in a chair reading one of Sharon's magazines, as much at home as if she were growing there.

'No need for you to do nothing, love.' She patted her hair which had been so tightly permed that it clung to her scalp like small dry curly worms. 'I've a potato pie on the go, and I've taken to eating with them since it saves me running up two gas bills. I'm stopping on tonight anyroad to let Sharon go out with her boyfriend. There's nothing coming to any harm over the road; that's what living alone means, you can go back to find that nowt's changed from when you left it. Would you like a cup of tea?' The small brown eyes were sly. 'You're looking a bit peaky, but then that's only to be expected, isn't it?'

'That would be nice. Thank you very much.'

Emma sat down on the lumpy settee and listened to Mrs Collins making housewifely noises from the kitchen. For all the world like a visitor, she thought, and reminded herself to tell Simon about it. If he had time to listen.

And in the kitchen Nellie Collins clattered cups on saucers, saying to herself that 'that was telling that young madam what was what'. Thinking she could just turn up bold as brass and take over. Putting on airs and walking in looking like Lady Muck in her white dress and pale-green cardigan that hadn't come off no stall down the market if she was any judge. Her stepma would be revolving in her grave if she knew the way things had worked out, with Sharon getting married and not before time, Alan running wild with a bunch of skinheads, and only Joe amounting to anything as far as she could see.

Nellie Collins's granite features softened as she thought

about Joe and his puppy-like devotion to her. Childless through no fault of her own, she felt her insides melt when the little bullet head butted her with a shamed show of affection. She had known Ma Sparrow for a long time, and had often envied her the brood of children, even whilst telling herself that she could have made something from John Sparrow, given the chance. Her barren widowed existence had been depressing her lately, and even her twice-weekly bingo sessions had begun to be more of a chore than a pleasure. What mattered was to be *needed*, and here, in this house over the road, she *was* needed, and that young upstart waiting for a cup of tea needn't think she could just walk in and take over as if nothing had happened. Nellie Collins was at the helm now, and Emma could either like it or lump it. An' if she thought she was still in charge, then she had another flamin' think coming, because she would sort her out right, and give her a piece of her mind if needs be.

'I'm going with Sharon to fetch your father out when he's finished his stretch in three weeks,' she told Emma, when she had handed over the tea and settled herself down with a cup. 'Then I'll still come over of a morning to see to things to help him to settle in. Being in prison knocks the stuffing out of a man. He won't know which way to turn, left to himself. An' I've got the time. Even without the money I've still got the time.' She half drained the cup of hot tea at one gulp. 'Time is a terrible thing when there's too much of it.'

If Emma had not been preoccupied with her own feelings she could have felt pity for the large sloppy woman sitting opposite her. Mrs Collins had the strong features of a panto-mime dame. Her enormous bust gave a top-heavy appearance to her slim legs and surprisingly small feet, and over the years Emma had known her the spade-calling remarks had ceased to be insults.

'My husband and I were going to drive over and pick my father up.' She stopped suddenly, trying to remember whether she had asked Simon to leave the date free. Knowing that if any entry wasn't written down weeks ahead in his diary, the odds were that he would be 'tied up' as he called it. She jumped as the telephone, on the sideboard for want of a better place, shrilled out.

'Now who can that be?' Mrs Collins stared at it as if mesmerized, and when Emma picked up the receiver she felt the small eyes boring into her back.

'Emma? It's Simon. I'm speaking from home. Listen, love. I've just thrown a couple of shirts into a bag and I am off to drive down to London. Dad has had a heart attack. He's in intensive care and they *think* he'll be okay, but I have to go. My mother sounded almost out of her mind when she 'phoned.'

'Then I'm coming with you.' Emma forgot all about Mrs Collins sitting behind her listening to every word. 'I'll get a taxi and come right now. It won't take me a minute to get some things together.'

'No!' Simon's voice was firm. 'For one thing I can't wait, and for another it isn't necessary. Things will be chaotic at the office and I will have to take over at once. They're right in the middle of this proposed closedown, and as dad could never delegate there's only me to step in.'

'But it's my *place* to be with you!' Emma felt her heartbeats quicken. 'Simon! I can maybe help your mother. I *want* to be there.'

'There isn't time for me to wait.'

Emma could almost see him glancing at his watch, the overnight case on the floor in the hall by his side.

'If there had been time to catch a plane I would have done that. No, you be a good girl and stay put, then maybe as soon as we know he's out of danger I'll send for you.'

'Simon! Don't shut me out! Please.' Emma heard her own voice rise on a note of hysteria. 'Don't go without me. I know you're upset, but this is something I have to share with you. I can be with you in twenty minutes if I get a taxi straight away. The whole thing will only delay you for less than an hour. Please wait for me . . . please.'

But it was no good. The impatience with which Simon refused to tolerate even the slightest delay when his mind was made up had spilled into his voice, sharpening it with barely controlled anger. When Emma replaced the receiver and sat down again she was trembling with frustrated disappointment.

'You can understand him wanting to rush to his dad's sickbed. Heart attack, is it? It was a heart attack took my husband off. One minute there and the next minute gone. Just a little cough, then nothing.' Mrs Collins leaned forward and patted Emma's knee. 'An' getting upset in your condition won't help matters. Driving all that way could easily bring on a miss, especially at three months.'

Emma could see her doing little sums in her mind. If she had been Sharon she could have told Mrs Collins to mind her own flamin' business and stop treating number twelve as if it were her own home. But she wasn't Sharon. She was herself, and the self she was could only sit there shelled in her own self-made solitude, listening to someone else telling her what to do while making up her own mind. Quietly.

'I will go now.' She picked up the soft green jacket from the back of the settee and put it round her shoulders. 'I don't feel like waiting now.' She tried not to see the gleam of satisfaction in Mrs Collins's eyes. 'Tell Sharon what happened, and . . . and thank you for looking after them.'

'We only pass this way but once.' Mrs Collins followed her to the door, showing her out like a visitor, and Emma walked down the long winding avenue to return to an empty house, and the knowledge that even in a moment of acute distress her husband had not felt the need for her.

Fourteen

Bernard Martin had no intention of dying, not this time, and when, propped up against his pillows, he was declared fit for visitors he told his wife he had decided to take an early retirement.

'What left-over life we have we are going to enjoy,' he said, holding her hand and smiling into her anxious eyes. 'I've talked it over with Simon and he's going to leave things as they are down here, mebbe till Christmas. That will give him time to put a man in charge at the northern end, then he will take over here as chairman. So I won't be hanging on, even part-time like some silly blighters do. It will be a clean break, with somebody else doing the worrying for a change.'

'You mean Simon has agreed to give up his home and move back down here?' Mary Martin patted his hand gently. 'I thought he was settled in Lancashire?'

'So he was. So he was. But me flaking out has thrown a spanner in the works, hasn't it?'

Emma was upset when Simon told her of his intention of moving south. He had returned haggard and pale, to plunge immediately into the business of the northern factories – dates fixed, appointments made a month in advance – and when she reminded him of Sharon's wedding he flipped over the pages of his long leather-bound diary and shook his head.

'Can't be done, love. That's the day of the shareholders' meeting in London, and as their new chairman I have to be there. You'll just have to make my apologies, that's all.'

Emma felt herself grow pink. She wasn't being unreason-able. She could see that Simon's father's sudden retirement meant that his son would be over-burdened with responsibilities for a long time to come. And as dull day followed dull day, she played the part he seemed to be expecting her to play. She waited with meals, kept warm now on a hotplate she and bought with the money she had saved from her first month's housekeeping money. She drank coffee with Ginny from next door; she took her vitamins and swallowed her fruit juice; and only at minutes like this did she admit that the very protectiveness she had craved had become oppressive.

Like Mrs Collins, now almost permanently ensconced in number twelve Litchfield Avenue, she needed to be needed, and so far as she could make out this self-sufficient man she loved with all her being needed nobody.

Almost without realizing it she found herself plunged into their first real quarrel.

'If you won't go to Sharon's wedding with me, then I won't go either!'

'I didn't say I *won't* go. I said I *can't*. You don't expect me to send a circular letter round cancelling the meeting because my wife's stepsister is getting married, do you?'

'You never wanted to go. You are glad of the excuse. Admit it!' Emma could hear herself being childish, but it was too late.

And Simon, because he was tired, and because whenever he closed his eyes figures danced in macabre fashion behind his eyelids, turned to sarcasm as a weapon of defence. 'Well of course I wanted to go! That is my idea of a good time, going to a wedding that is all for show, when the happy couple haven't even the price of a table and chairs to set up home together! Then eating a four-course meal at half-past three in the afternoon . . . oh, yes, I was indeed counting every minute to the day!'

Mam had once said that on the few occasions when Emma lost her temper it was enough to make a cat laugh. But Emma was losing it now with a vengeance. She had never asked again to be taken down to London on one of Simon's now weekly visits, telling herself that she had her pride. And yet pride, she was discovering fast, was a very expendable commodity.

Speaking with a slight tremor in her voice, she said, 'I am really sorry that things haven't gone straight forward for you since we got married. Since that afternoon in the flat,' she amended, wanting to hurt and wound with an intensity that was quite alien to her equable nature. 'An' I am truly sorry about your father giving up so readily when it was on the cards that he could have carried on for a while.' She walked over to a chair and held on to the back to try to stop the trembling of her hands. 'Maybe it would have been easier for me if I had been brought up to accept that a husband's job of work takes precedence over everything. Even his marriage. But I am sick of being treated like a housekeeper whose job it is to keep you fuelled so that you can scoot from one factory to another.' She brushed angry tears from her eyes. 'An' while we are on about it, I've never mentioned it before, but that day when your father was rushed into hospital – that day you couldn't wait half an hour for me to come back from Litchfield Avenue – you weren't in too much of a hurry to collect Chloe's things together to take down with you, were you?' Her voice broke on a sob. 'Did you meet her to hand them over, or am I so much a nothing that I am not supposed to want to be told that either?'

Emma was glad when he refused to look at her, because that proved she had pricked the bubble of his irritating superiority. And now she could hate him and love him at the same time with a clear conscience.

Simon spoke directly to his shoes. 'I took the things round to her, as a matter of fact, because it happened to be no more than ten minutes out of my way on my drive back from the hospital at Highgate.' He got up to pour himself a drink and Emma did not realize that his studied calm was his own way of latching on to his slipping control.

'Why did you marry me and not Chloe?' she whispered, her heart pounding.

'You know bloody well why I married you.'

Still with his back to her, Simon poured his drink, the bottle jittering against the heavy whisky glass, so that the small sound like the whimper of an animal in pain escaped him. When he turned round Emma had gone, running upstairs and slamming the bathroom door with a crash that resounded all through the house.

Wearily he took the drink back to his chair and sat down. Wearily he justified his own behaviour. What had started it all off, anyway? He drank deeply, shuddered, then drank again.

Oh, the wedding. That stupid extravagant wedding of two

kids who hadn't begun to know what it was all about. Sharon treated him with a cheeky disdain, and that boy . . . oh, God, that pimply boy with a face like an anaemic weasel beneath that atrocious crash helmet. Money squandered on a lavish ceremony that nobody could afford. Utter stupidity. Crass ignorance. Working class ignorance. . . .

He drained his glass and got up to pour another. As if it mattered whether he went or not. Emma had decided not to be a bridesmaid, and he hadn't been asked to be an usher or anything, so why the fuss? Simon drank the whisky as if it were water, then shook his head as a mist formed before his eyes.

He wasn't going to admit it, not even to himself, but the way things were going redundancies would be rife during the coming months. Women just weren't buying clothes nowadays. Not the quality stuff his father had insisted on, anyway. Jeans and bright tops, that was all the kids wanted; and the elegant women of forty plus who had once been their best customers, well, they were into jeans and tops too. Or too weighted down by inflation and trying to keep up standards to pay the rising, astronomical prices for their clothes.

Simon got up and poured yet another drink, only half aware of what he was doing.

Yes, he had to face the fact that his father's ideas on modern management techniques were completely out of date. He had been appalled to discover the wastage, and irritated at the sentimentality displayed in the retention of workers who should have been, in Simon's opinion, pensioned off long ago.

He sipped the drink, his eyes bleak above the rim of the glass, and the whisky flowed like fire through his veins.

Take old Cummings . . . sixty-four if he was a day. He was one of Bernard's old wartime buddies, wounded at Alamein, and therefore, by his employer's code, immune from the chop. Simon had seen a tremor in the hand wielding the cutter, slicing through material, the cost of which had caused his own hand to tremble as he put it through the costing system. One of these fine days old Cummings would spoil the lot. Probably had done just that many, many times. And yet, because sentimentality was all, had been kept on.

'Sentimentality!' Simon's voice slurred the word as he spoke it out loud. 'Sentimentality is a dirty word, Dad. Hadn't you even learned that much?'

The truth was he was scared. Really scared. Bernard Martin had dealt his son a dirty trick in giving up the reins without letting them fall loose for a while. He had merely dropped them and walked away. Simon drained the glass, then closed his eyes in an attempt to stop the room from revolving round him.

If Bernard Martin could bring himself to listen he would have to be told that only an enormous cutback in personnel could keep the firm solvent. And that would hit hard at a time when the old man was in no fit state to be hit hard. Not for the first time Simon asked himself if maybe, just maybe, his father's heart attack had been a subconscious way of getting out of his seemingly unsolvable problems?

Pushing himself up out of the low chair with difficulty, Simon began to weave his unsteady way upstairs.

Whatever happened, whichever way things went, he would have to keep the aggro away from his father. That much he had promised his mother.

He would cope. He had to. With so much at stake, he had no choice.

The bed looked so soft and welcoming, it was as though it was holding out arms to him. Simon pulled his shirt over his head, rolled it up into a ball and hurled it away from him. He had drunk too much and too quickly. He wrenched his mouth out of shape as he tasted again the quarter chicken done in a wine sauce, with mushrooms scattered lavishly like brown pieces of rubber. He saw the florid-faced man he had entertained that evening gloating over the loaded sweets trolley and digging his fork into a chocolate cream gateau. He could even see the splodge of cream lodging at the corner of his slack mouth. The wine, mixed with the whisky, was sour tasting, and suddenly Simon knew he was going to be sick.

And the bloody bathroom door was locked!

By the time Emma crept into bed beside him she felt as ill as Simon looked. She had mopped up, heard him groaning as he splashed cold water over his head; she had sponged the worst away and left Simon's trousers to be taken to the cleaners, and she had held her own nausea tight inside her as, white-faced, she had ministered to the man so sick and sorry for himself that all he wanted to do was to lie curled up before sinking into a sleep that was more of a stupor.

This was no time to talk things through. No time to relive the way she had sat there on the bathroom stool, cold and shivering with the knowledge that after what he had said nothing could ever be the same between them again.

The dream she had of them living together happily ever after had fallen apart. He had married her because of the baby and there, sitting in a chair downstairs, he had admitted it. She had opened the door of the bathroom cabinet and seen Chloe's bottle of sleeping tablets, and God forgive her, but for a moment her hand had stretched out towards them.

Emma lay on her back with her legs closed, as far away from Simon as she could get without falling out of bed. He was snoring now, and the stench of vomit lingered in the room. He was as unlovely as John Sparrow used to be when he had drunk a drop too much, and yet now it was worse. It was worse because she, Emma, was responsible for his deep unhappiness. She had trapped him, and she had been foolish enough to think that by reading textbooks and taking exams she could somehow turn herself into the kind of woman he wanted. She had imagined herself discussing the business with him, listening and understanding, as she was sure Chloe had listened and understood.

Emma felt a slight tremor inside her, no more than the brushing of a butterfly's wing. Yet even as she laid her hand over her stomach, it had gone.

There was nothing she could do about the baby now except go on and have it. So she would have to grow fatter and walk about splay-footed till the time came.

Then? Then what?

Simon stirred and threw an arm across her, and it lay like a weight, uncomfortable and heavy. Emma lifted it from her and turned on her side.

And went to sleep as lonely as if the man by her side did not exist; as bereft as if already he had gone far from her, never to return.

*

She went to see her father the day after he came home from prison, and seeing him crouched over the electric fire, in spite of the warmth of the day, it was as if he had never been away.

Mrs Collins was there, bustling about, full of importance, making tea, telling him to stop where he was, that she would see to things, pandering to the ineffectual man as if she realized that this was exactly what he wanted.

'How are you feeling, Dad?' Emma wanted to put her arms round him, to have him tell her in detail just how he was, and how it had been. But with Mrs Collins there it was impossible.

'What he needs is some good food down him.' Nellie Collins, with her hair like a steel-wool nimbus round her head, now that the perm was mercifully growing out, sat down heavily on the settee, and folded her arms. 'He's not fit for nothing, and won't be for a while yet.'

'Did the prison welfare people talk to you, Dad?' Emma leaned forward, trying to ignore the squat watching figure in the bulging nylon blouse and crimplene skirt.

'They don't bother overmuch with short-term inmates.' John Sparrow lit a cigarette from the stub of the last. 'I'm not rushing into anything.' He coughed and beat his chest with a clenched fist. 'Anyroad, I'll never be able to do long-distance trucking no more. These last months have taken years off me life. You could be dying on your feet for all them bastards care.'

'But the money?' Emma tried to persist, conscious all the time of the sharp dark eyes watching her. 'Will you be able to sign on straight away? How will you manage?'

When her father exchanged a glance with Mrs Collins, Emma knew they had been discussing her. He sniffed and flicked the ash into the tiled hearth.

'Well, it won't be the same with you and our Sharon gone, will it?' he coughed feebly. 'I never thought when I went away it would be to come back to both my daughters gone off on their own bats. But we'll just have to manage somehow.'

'But how?' Emma heard her voice rise. 'Look, Dad, when I was at home I managed the bills and the food shopping, and I knew just how much there was left over. An' that was when you were working. Dad! It's not just an idle question. I want to help, and how can I help if you won't talk to me? Are you going to apply for Social Security, or what?'

Mrs Collins did not move an inch. She just sat there with her knees slightly apart showing pink Directoire knickers, but it was as if she had shot out an elbow and nudged John Sparrow into saying what she had primed him to say.

He took a deep drag of the dwindling cigarette. 'Well, I won't be asking you for nothing, that's for sure. Nor our Sharon.' His glance flickered sideways. 'Mrs Collins has been a good friend to me while I've been away. Like a mother to Alan and Joe, an' we had a long talk last night, me an' her.'

He glared at the telephone on the sideboard.

'She was here when you rang up as a matter of fact, so I wasn't on me own.'

'I couldn't come last night,' Emma said gently. 'Simon was bringing two men in for a meal, and I couldn't let him down, not when it was the first time he'd done that.'

'No, but you could let *me* down,' her father said clearly as Mrs Collins nodded. 'An' our Sharon just *had* to go out, so between you I knew where I stood.'

'Aye, he did that.' Mrs Collins's short neck almost disappeared into the collar of her shirt blouse.

'So we've come to an arrangement.' John Sparrow coughed again, but not too forcibly. 'Mrs Collins will give her house up and move over here. That way she will save the rent and all the lighting and heating.'

'And the overheads,' said Mrs Collins with authority.

'As my housekeeper.' Emma's father dared her to say another word. 'She'll stop where she is till our Sharon gets married, then she can have her room.'

'An' bring me bits and pieces over, so some of this stuff can go to the sales room.'

Emma felt the cobweb-fine thread of hope that somehow, sometime, after the baby came and her part in the fiasco of her marriage had been played, she would go back to Litchfield Avenue, snap. If Simon did not need her, then for as long as he lived her father would be her responsibility. And the boys. She could never go back to work at Delta Dresses; that would be out of the question, but there would be a job for her somewhere. She tilted her chin to stop its trembling, and stared out of the window.

You had to laugh, the way things turned out. For all those years, when a hand with the shopping or an eye on the boys would have meant so much, Mrs Collins had been merely a flounced nylon net curtain twitching in the window opposite; a grumbling voice when Ricky's motorbike revved up outside, and a long nose quivering with distaste whenever the police called.

And now she was going to sleep in Emma's bed. Or was she? Emma looked at the unlikely pair sitting there. Her father, small and shriven, with his prison pallor accentuating the deep lines from nose to mouth, and Mrs Collins, chins, breasts and stomach hanging in pendulous folds.

Surely? Surely not?

'I'd best be getting back,' she said as she had said before, and stood up. 'If there is anything you want me to do about the wedding, let me know.' She nodded towards the telephone. 'You know where I am.'

'Oh, aye, we know where you are.' John Sparrow nodded, and in that moment Emma glimpsed the hurt bewilderment in his eyes. And if Mrs Collins had not been there she would have gone and knelt on the rug and laid her head on her father's knees. Like when she was a child and he had towelled her hair dry for her in front of the fire.

'Dad,' she whispered. 'Dad. I'm sorry.'

But the words were in her head, and even as she turned to go he was lighting yet another cigarette, and Mrs Collins was patting his knee and telling him she was going through to put the kettle on.

'She's like a huge overfed rabbit,' Emma told Simon that evening. 'All twitching possessiveness, and my dad is loving every minute of it.' She put her library book down and rubbed her eyes. 'He could never have coped on his own, that much is certain, and in a strange way she is so much like Mam. Aggressive when there is no need to be aggressive. You know?'

'Let's drink to Mrs Collins then.' Simon pushed the papers he was working on aside, and went over to the sideboard. 'I'm forgiven about the wedding, am I, love?'

He was so dear to her, so vulnerable in his white shirt now

that the striped tie had been wrenched off, that Emma felt her eyes fill with the moist sparkle of tears as she watched him. His dark hair was badly in need of a trim and was growing down the nape of his neck into an endearing straggly point. If he would have let her she would have taken his worry to herself, absolved him of all anxiety, and rocked him in her arms like a child.

'I wish there was something I could do to help.' She spoke softly, but he heard her and turned round with the glass in his hand.

'Perhaps you can.' He came to sit beside her on the sofa. 'In the next few weeks I have to send a quarter of the workforce packing, and I can't. This town is sick, Emma, and further unemployment only adds to the downward spiral. Life wasn't meant to be drab, Emma. We are having to scrap all plans for the Christmas dinner and dance because we just can't afford it. And I am the chap who is continually having to say no. No, no and no!' He reached for her hand. 'What is happening to us, love?'

Emma shook her head. 'You don't know Lancashire folks, Simon. It's always been like this. In a different way, of course. My grandma used to tell me that her mother ran to the mill at five to six as the hooter blew, then the gates were closed, and as they began their work the trams stopped running and for one hour the streets were as still and deserted as if it were midnight. If they went too often to what was called the "necessary" they were fined threepence, and if they hung anything on the gas pendants it was another twopence. They were *slaves*, Simon. And during the Depression they were *hungry*, not like now when the state takes over to keep them fed. An' in the twenties the weavers used to come out of the factory gates, arm in arm, and singing at the tops of their voices.'

'Like an old Gracie Fields film?'

'Just like that.' Emma snuggled closer and laid her head down on his shoulder. 'They'll bounce back. It's something inside them that makes them survive. Mam used to say there are bystanders and standbyers, and Lancashire folks are the latter. If one member of a family is without a job, then the rest rally round. You are dealing with tough nuts, Simon, not wets.'

They were silent for a moment, then he said, 'And I am going to take you away from all that. Your heart and your roots are here.' He tweaked the ribbon holding her hair back and pulled it free. 'You are as Lancashire as a red rose, little Emma, and I am taking you away. You must hate me, and yet you've never said a word.'

She jerked up and laughed into his eyes. 'Come on, now. What about the last war, and the Londoners? This part of the country isn't the only part with guts. I thought your father started on a stall on Petticoat Lane? He didn't get to where he did by talking posh and sitting on his backside.'

She bit her lip. 'But none of that helps, does it? Nothing I can say is going to make these next few months easy for you.'

Taking her by surprise, he pulled her close, holding her to him as if he could never let her go. 'But you have helped, love. You have said exactly what I wanted to hear. And now I must finish this report. Redundancy might pay its own way in the long run, but it digs deep into the revenue. And you must go up to bed. You've been looking pale lately, and you are carrying a precious cargo. Never forget that.'

The strength of his arms and the almost desperate way he had strained her to him had filled Emma with the longing ache of desire. Wanting him so much that she felt the heat rise in her body, she began to kiss his face, to nibble at his ears and to kiss the corners of his mouth with teasing slowness.

'I love you,' she whispered. 'I love you so very much.'

'You keep on doing just that.' He reached across her for his spectacles and a large manilla envelope on the side table.

Once again he had shut her out as completely as if he had slammed a door in her face, and although Emma knew she was being irrational, his rejection shocked her.

'I'll go upstairs.' She picked up her book and walked towards the door. And when she turned round, he was reading a closely-typed sheet, as oblivious of her as if she had never existed.

Fifteen

Sharon was ten minutes late for the wedding. The guests fidgeted in their seats, and in the front pew Ricky's neck turned a bright pink.

Emma, with Alan on one side and Joe on the other, tried to imagine what was going on in Litchfield Avenue, and closed her eyes in silent prayer.

If Sharon took over an hour to get ready to go disco dancing, what would getting ready for her own wedding involve? Emma glanced to the right and saw Ricky's parents staring straight ahead, Mr Rostron fingering the flower in his buttonhole and Mrs Rostron pulling at the brim of her hat as if she wasn't quite sure whether it was at the right angle.

Ricky turned round to shoot a brief worried glance towards the church door, and Emma though how unfamiliar he looked without his crash helmet. He caught her eye and winked.

Mrs Collins was riding to church with the bride and her father and the two bridesmaids from Woolworth's, and when at last her top-heavy figure, resplendent in apricot tweed, pushed its way into the pew to sit beside Joe, Emma relaxed.

'The young bugger! She's had that head-dress on and off at least fifty times, and even now she's not satisfied.' Mrs Collins bent her head to hiss the words as if in reverent silent prayer. 'An' it doesn't look no different now from the first time!' She raised her head. 'An' your father wanted to wear his brown knitted waistcoat underneath his jacket! An' if that's chewing gum in your mouth, young Joe, take it out an' no sticking it on the pew neither!'

Immediately Joe took the wodge of gum from his mouth and disposed of it Emma knew not where, for the organist went into a spirited version of 'Here Comes the Bride', and the congregation rose in relief to its feet.

Emma's mouth turned upwards into a smile. It was Mam all over again. Brash and domineering. For the very first time she felt a warmth of affection for Mrs Collins. They would be okay. Alan might go his own way, but Joe and her father had got Mam back, and from now on their lives would run in grumbling acceptance of guidance from a stronger personality. It was true. God *did* move in a mysterious way. She turned and saw Sharon walking slowly up the aisle on her father's arm and, ashamed of her lack of control, felt the warm tears flood her eyes.

It was all over. The ceremony, the endless photographs outside the church, the cars wending their way to the Roundhouse out on the Preston side, and the seating of the guests at the long tables set out in the big room that would be used for dancing later on.

Emma sat at the end of a table nearest to the top table, where she had a clear view of Sharon, radiant and smiling, her perfectly made-up little face aglow with happiness beneath the white veil. The virginal bride, ethereal and lovely, glorying in every moment of what was, for her, a day she would remember for the rest of her life.

Simon had been wrong. It *was* worth it; worth every penny lavished on the expensive meal and the constantly flowing wine. And tomorrow the happy couple would be flying off to Majorca for ten days, where Sharon would spend her time determinedly getting brown to show off her tan when she went back to work in her blue and white overall.

Emma heard the table behind explode into sudden laughter and, turning, saw Ben Bamford, with his head thrown back and the light catching the thick fair hair as his blue eyes crinkled with merriment. She turned back quickly and picked up her glass, surprised to find that her hand was not quite steady.

'Did you not know I was coming?' He came to her as the meal finished, before the cake was cut and the short awkward speeches made. 'I couldn't get off to go to the church, but

Ricky's a mate of a mate of mine, didn't you know?' He grinned. 'What are you doing on your own then? Is this not quite big boss man's scene or something?'

'Simon is in London.' Emma felt her cheeks grow pink. 'He had a meeting he couldn't put off. It had to be Saturday so the shareholders could be there. He *wanted* to come,' she lied.

'Oh, aye?' Ben scuttled back to his place as John Sparrow got nervously to his feet amid loud bangings on the top table for silence. Emma's stomach muscles tightened with worry for him as he started to read his speech from a slip of paper. Then, nudged fiercely by Mrs Collins, he removed the cigarette from the corner of his mouth, coughed and began again.

Then the best man read the telegrams, three in all and two of them extremely rude. Sharon, with Ricky's hand over her own, cut the bottom tier of the cake, and the rest was whisked away to be cut into slices by the kitchen staff. And later, much later, after the long tables had been split up and placed round the walls to leave a floor-space free for dancing, a tall boy with a thatch of bright red hair moved in with his equipment, setting up the lights and testing the microphones for sound.

More guests arrived, among them a crowd of Sharon's friends from Woolworth's, like vividly coloured birds in their tight trousers and overshirts. They carried their drinks over to a corner table and sat giggling and twittering, waiting for the fun to begin.

'I thought you might have gone home to get changed. Somebody would have run you.' Sharon's eyes flicked up and down Emma's jacket and skirt. 'Ricky's mum and dad have gone back for a breather.' She was ablaze with excitement. 'I'm stopping as I am. I might as well get my money's worth out of this dress, I can't see me wearing it again.' She put up a hand to her veil and head-dress. 'I hope me hair isn't flattened when I take this off. It was murder getting it fixed on right.'

'So Mrs Collins told me.' Emma wrinkled her nose. 'I bet you didn't get much change out of her.'

'She's a shit,' said Sharon from within the clouds of white tulle, then she turned to smile radiantly and sweetly at one of Ricky's relations. 'Are you having a good time, Auntie?' She shouted the words, then in her normal voice told Emma that the elderly woman was as deaf as a post. 'She's come all the way from Bradford,' she explained, before rushing away to greet more incoming guests. 'Talk to her for a bit, our Emma.'

Emma could see Ben at the bar. He had a small crowd gathered round him and from the shouts of joy she concluded that he was half-way drunk already. She left the deaf auntie and moved to sit alone at one of the tables, pretending to watch the children sliding up and down on the polished floor, small girls in party dresses, and boys in unaccustomed suits. When the music blared out Emma shrank back in her chair as if she had been dealt a blow right between her eyes.

She was a newly-married woman, and yet she had come alone. She was pregnant, she had eaten too much, her head was aching, her skirt was too tight and she wanted to go home.

She was twenty years old, she reminded herself, and because Simon wasn't there she wanted to go home. She was as old in her thinking as the older relatives gathered together in the far corner of the room. Yet she felt as she had the night Ben had taken her disco dancing. As if she wanted to move out there into the middle of the floor and shake her hair and forget herself in the pounding rhythm of the music.

But that was long ago. She started as Mrs Collins's harsh voice broke into her thoughts.

'Come and sit with us, love. There's no cause for you to be sitting here on your own. Your dad sent me. Just look at him, three sheets in the wind already and the night hardly begun.' She lowered her voice from a shout to a bellow. 'He's a bit disorientated. What with spending all that time shut away then coming to this.'

Four bitter lemons and four hours later Emma wondered if she could slip away and 'phone for a taxi. The loud music was spreading in a pain up the back of her neck, and when a plate of fancy cakes and a pot of tea were put on the table she closed her eyes in horror.

'You okay, kid?'

Ben was there, bending over her, blue eyes concerned in his flushed face. 'You look like you're ready to go over.' He leaned forward to stub out his cigarette on the ashtray. 'Would you like me to take you home?'

'Oh, Ben, would you?' Emma nodded. 'But it doesn't seem

fair. They'll be here till long past midnight. I can't let you do that.'

'I can come back.' He laughed. 'There's a nice little bird over there I'm doing all right with. Just let me go and explain and we'll go. Okay?'

He was still the same Ben. Kind and generous in spite of everything. Emma thanked him, said her goodbyes to Ricky's parents and kissed her father on his cheek.

'Tell Sharon I've gone,' she whispered, and the last thing she saw as she walked from the room was the flash of her stepsister's white dress as she gyrated opposite her new husband in the middle of the floor with a spotlight picking out the corn-gold of her shining hair.

'Sure you are fit to drive?' She felt just a momentary anxiety as Ben slid behind the wheel.

'You have to be joking, Em.' Ben threw his cigarette away through the open window before winding it up. 'I've only had a couple of lemonades.'

'Ben Bamford!' Emma joined in his laughter, and it was like the old times, with Ben stepping on the accelerator and the shabby car eating up the road as if they were on the last lap of the Monte Carlo rally.

'How is Patty?' Emma closed her eyes as they swept round a corner. 'And little Tracy? Is she okay?'

'Patty's all right, but Tracy's got a chesty cold. Her sort do get them a lot, I believe.' Ben, to the sound of a blaring horn, overtook a huge container lorry. 'And up yours!' he shouted as the car gathered even more speed.

They were over a bridge and at the lights when it happened. Without waiting for the green, Ben shot forward just as a car coming towards them swung right, going too fast, smashing into them with a grinding metallic sound that Emma was to remember for ever.

Alone in his parents' big house Simon put the telephone down and glanced at his watch. Almost half-past eleven. He pushed the pile of papers to one side and rubbed his eyes.

It would have been good to talk to Emma, to hear her light voice telling him about the wedding. She had the gift of being able to be funny without being vindictive. And he needed to laugh. God knew how much he needed to laugh after that meeting. At one point he had thought they were going to turn on him like a pack of wolves, and the unspoken implication that if his father had been in the chair things might have been different was as plain as the noses on their respective faces.

And now his father was on a cruise ship, probably half-way round the world, leaving his son to redress the wrongs, to reorganize, prune and try to steer the firm into calmer waters.

He dialled again. He remembered Emma telling him that the disco would go on maybe until the early hours of Sunday morning, but surely no one could stretch a wedding out to last *that* long? The very idea was mind-boggling; it was almost like a Roman orgy where guests feasted and drank for three days at a time. He drummed with his fingers on the table as he heard the ringing tone going on and on.

Well, at least she must be enjoying herself, whatever she was doing. . . . Simon walked over to Bernard Martin's drinks cupboard and poured himself a drink. He was restless without knowing why. He should have been exhausted, but he was too tired for sleep, too high from the aftermath of the long drawn-out meeting to relax. His parents' taste in music was not his. Simon lifted out one or two LPs and smiled to himself. Vera Lynn, Songs from the Shows, Jim Reeves, Mantovani. Putting them back he glanced at the telephone. His friends were Chloe's friends, married couples in the main, and anyway it was much too late to ring them. More likely than not it would be a baby-sitter who answered the phone, or an au pair.

Restless beyond comprehension he dialled Emma's number again, then slammed the receiver down with a gesture of frustration. What was she doing out at this time? He hoped she'd have the sense to call a taxi because from what he'd been told, a northern wedding reception did not stint itself as far as the booze went.

A cold shiver ran down his back. What the hell was the matter with him?

Suddenly, almost without volition, he rang Chloe's number, and was both surprised and pleased when she answered.

'Simon! Where are you? Lordy, you were the last person on earth I expected to hear.'

'I'm a bit surprised too. What are you doing, may I ask?'

'Baby-sitting. I'd nothing on this evening and they've gone out to dinner to some friends Stanmore way. Where are you? Is anything wrong?'

'Has something to *be* wrong before I call you?'

Chloe chuckled. 'Well, no, honey, but you sounded mightily relieved to hear my voice. Emma left you already?'

'She's gone to her stepsister's wedding, and I'm down here. My parents have gone on a cruise, and I had to come down for a meeting today. A tricky one. I thought they were going to lynch me at one point.'

'Poor Simon.' He could see her, long legs curled up beneath her, cradling the receiver and making faces at him. 'Why haven't you driven back then?'

'Because there's another meeting first thing Monday, to report on today's. I would hardly have got back before it was time to come down again.'

There was a small silence. 'But you could have gotten back this evening.'

He frowned. 'I suppose so. What is this? An inquisition?'

'So Emma has gone to the wedding alone, and you are sitting there alone? You haven't changed, honey. Have you?'

'You think I should have gone straight back? Is that what you're trying to tell me?'

It had been a bad day for Chloe. First the flat she had thought was all lined up had been taken off the market, then the trouser suit she had bought had looked an entirely different colour away from the shaded lights in the big Regent Street store. Plus the fact that the man she had been seeing for the past three weeks had said he must spend the entire weekend with his family. And now the sound of Simon's voice was making her heart do strange things, just when she had thought she was getting over him.

'I can't tell you anything, honey. But it's still Simon Martin first, second and last, isn't it? Why have you rung me, then? To ask me round for a bit of extra-marital hoo-hah? Because there's nothing doing. Okay?'

Simon gripped the receiver hard. 'I rang you because I wanted to talk to you, that's all. Because Emma isn't back yet, if you must know, and because I am a bit anxious about her.

It's not like her to be out this late.'

Chloe had only seen Emma once. Just that one time in the hospital, but she had never forgotten her. She could see her now: small and vulnerable, where as Chloe knew herself to be big and totally self-sufficient; holding Simon, as she had failed to do; having his baby when she, Chloe, had got rid of hers. She couldn't help feeling that somehow the deck had been stacked unfairly against her. Guilt about what she had done did not help either, because guilt could be comforting and wipe out its own source if dwelled on for long enough. And now she realized that Simon, even in his own selfish way, had shown her what love could be.

'You are a traditionalist, did you know that?' She had only one weapon left now, and that was to hurt, to hit hard and punish him for what he had done. 'All you want really is a house filled with kids, and a nine-to-five job, and when your job or whatever goes the wrong way you sulk.' Chloe felt the tears spring to her eyes. 'That's what you're doing now, isn't it? Sulking because you've had a bad day, and because your little wife isn't there, waiting by the telephone to hear all about it. You needed a sounding-board, so you rang me.'

'It seems I made a mistake,' Simon said quietly, his voice etched with hurt.

'You'll get over it,' Chloe said, equally quietly, then later, when she had replaced the receiver, she buried her face in her hands.

'Slut. Cow. Whore. Stupid, sloppy, silly dried-up spinster!' She mouthed the words, but when she opened her mouth to yell, no sound came. Then, staring straight ahead at the peg-board on the wall, with her friend's children's drawings pinned in rows, she forced herself to accept the fact that she would never see or hear from Simon again.

'But there's no man going to spoil my rotten life!' She got up and walked slowly upstairs, the tears now streaming down her face.

Simon had dialled Emma's number again before Chloe had snatched her nightgown from beneath her pillow and gone into the bathroom. When there was still no answer, he rubbed the back of his neck and came to a swift decision.

Okay, okay, he wasn't going because of anything Chloe had

said. He was going to drive back north and creep into bed beside Emma. Then tomorrow night – no, tonight – he would drive down again. It could be done. With a fast car and the motorway straight before him, it was nothing. And when her arms wound themselves round his neck and he felt her soft body pressed up against him, this restless feeling would be gone. She was peace. Emma Sparrow was peace. She was his wife, soon to be the mother of his child, and what else was there? What else in this rushing, crazy world was there?

He was backing the car out of the drive as the telephone rang in the quiet, darkened house, and with no one to answer it, it went on ringing. Then all was silent.

Sixteen

There was pain and soothing voices, more pain, a prick in her arm and sleep. But Emma did not want to sleep. She fought it with all her strength, and when the pain increased and she felt the warm wetness between her legs she screamed. At least she thought she screamed, but what came was a whisper, a pleading wail as her head turned from side to side on the pillow.

'My baby! Oh, please, please, save my baby!'

The young doctor turned to the waiting nurse by the side of the high hospital bed. 'Try to get it through to her that she is lucky to be alive. And call me if you need to.' He walked away, white coat flying, bleeped away to yet another Saturday night accident case. And before he had gone through the door Emma opened her eyes wide.

Immediately the nurse moved to take her hand. 'It's all right, love. You had a bit of a smash-up in a car, but there's nothing broken.' She patted Emma's hand. 'You're going to be okay. Right?'

'My baby?' Emma tried to sit up, pushed herself up so that the hospital gown slipped from her shoulder. 'What is happening to my baby?'

Nurse Briggs sighed. She was very young. She had enough experience not to be too dismayed, but there was something about this patient that reached through the armour of her ingrained discipline. So drained of colour, so still for such a long time, the long brown hair and the huge brown eyes, the frantic need for reassurance, even before she was fully conscious.

'I am losing my baby.' The eyes closed and filled with tears that ran down the pale cheeks and sideways into the pillow

Nurse Briggs reached for a small hand towel. 'You are aborting your baby, love. There is no way we can stop it. You were thrown from the car. Not through the windscreen because it wasn't a head-on crash, but the door gave and you ended up in the road.' Gently she wiped Emma's face. 'There will be other babies, love. Just try to keep calm. The doctor is coming back soon and he will help you. I promise it won't be too bad.'

'But you *have* to save it.' Emma struggled again to sit up. 'You don't understand. My husband. . . .' She lay down again as the foot of the bed seemed to rise up as if to hit her smack between her aching eyes.

'You are in shock, love.' Nurse Briggs smoothed the hair back from Emma's forehead. 'You had a nasty accident. Now, please try and relax.'

'Ben!' The sound was torn from Emma's throat. 'What happened to Ben?' Once again she saw the car coming straight for them. Coming unbelievably at them. On Ben's side. With a sickening thud of crashing metal on metal. Almost at right angles. On Ben's side.

The years of training stayed Nurse Briggs's voice to a soothing murmur. 'The young man driving the car is down in theatre now. He is . . .', she turned her head away from the anguished pleading on the white face, '. . . as well as expected. Now you *must* be still.'

'Ben is dead.'

Nurse Briggs felt for her patient's pulse as Emma drifted into merciful oblivion. She stood there, vigilant, caring, staying on duty when she should have gone off more than two hours before.

'Where is Emma?'

The man standing on the doorstep of number twelve Litchfield Avenue had dark eyes sunk back into hollows in the grey pallor of his face. He had driven hard, taking less than four hours to complete the long mileage from London, and his dismay at finding the house empty and the bed as neat as when Emma had made it that morning had left him in no mood for explanations.

'Why is the telephone off the hook?' He pushed past Mrs

Collins, an unlovely sight in her thick brown woollen dressing-gown, and without a by-your-leave, replaced the receiver. 'No wonder I couldn't get through.' He towered over her, causing her to step back a pace. 'What's going on, for Pete's sake?'

Mrs Collins did not hold with Simon Martin. Because of who he was and what he was, she had written him off irrevocably. He talked posh for one thing, and he had got Emma into trouble for another, and here he was marching in as if he owned the place.

'I took it off because I wanted Mr Sparrow to get his rest.' She folded her arms over her massive bosom, and sat down. 'There's been that much going on with folks ringing up, and Sharon saying she wasn't going to Majorca, though she's seen sense now, thank goodness.' She folded the skirt of the dressing-gown over her knees in case her nightdress was showing. 'What a thing to happen on a wedding day. I thought you was in London. They telephoned from the infirmary but you wasn't there.' She glared at Simon from beneath straggly eyebrows, and nodded as if satisfied.

Simon clenched his hands. In another minute he was sure he would lift the old bag bodily out of the chair and shake her till her teeth rattled.

'Emma! Where is Emma?' He fought hard to hold his slipping control. 'Is she ill?'

'She was in an accident.' Mrs Collins was coming to the good part now, as her small eyes never left Simon's face. 'She was being run home with Ben Bamford, and they had a crash. But she's not hurt bad.' She shrank back in the chair as the tall man took a step towards her. 'Thought he was going to clock me one,' she was to tell John Sparrow later. Then her mouth dropped open in a wide gasp of surprise as Simon turned abruptly and ran from the house, slamming the car door fit to wake the dead and roaring away up the avenue.

'That's teached him,' Mrs Collins told herself, not quite sure what she meant, but meaning it just the same.

It was almost noon before he was allowed to sit by Emma's bed. They had tidied her up, they told him, down in theatre

213

and now she needed to sleep, so he must be very quiet and not upset her.

'Your wife has taken it hard about losing the baby,' they said, and Simon nodded. It was all mixed up in his mind. The angry voices at the meeting that morning. No, yesterday morning. The strange, almost hysterical reaction from Chloe when he telephoned her. The long drive when at times he had been terrified he was going to fall asleep. And now this. . . .

There was a peculiar numbness all through his body. It had spread to his mind, and for once his clear thinking had deserted him. He wanted to stretch out a hand and touch Emma, but she was lying there so drained of colour, so small, he could hardly bear to look at her.

She opened her eyes, saw him, recognized him, Simon thought. Then wearily she closed her eyes again so that there was nothing to do but to wait and try to shake off the overwhelming urge to let his head droop forward in sleep.

The baby was no more. It had been scraped away, or flowed away, the baby that in his muddled, exhausted frame of mind was to have replaced the one that Chloe had refused to have.

Simon shook his head as if to shake away the blurred edges of his reasoning. One thing he knew: it was all his fault. If he had taken Emma to the wedding she would never have got into a car with an irresponsible man the worse for drink, to drive through the darkness along winding lanes.

As Chloe had said, he had a one-track mind. Simon buried his face in his hands. He had always known that Bamford would get even with him some day. Some time, somehow. It had been written on his face, that grinning handsome face with the clear blue eyes that mocked and twinkled with a secret amusement all their own.

A nurse brought a cup of tea, and Simon nodded his thanks. Oh, God, but Chloe in her wisdom had been right. He, Simon Martin, was selfish to the core; thinking, no, taking it for granted that Emma would in her own quiet way just get on with what nature had intended her to do. And now, she had destroyed his child. *Their* child.

Like Chloe before her. In a different way, but with the same end result.

The minutes ticked away. Now he felt drugged, but before

he could sleep there were things to be done. Simon put a hand over his eyes and tried to think, to plan. There were things to be done. If only his father was there instead of thousands of miles away sunning himself on the deck of a ship sailing through blue waters. If only, and if only. . . .

Emma opened her eyes and saw the darkness of his emotions flitting across his face like a shadow. It was all there, the ache of despair, the disappointment. Directed at herself. She knew that.

'I am sorry, so sorry,' she whispered, and turned her face away so that he would not see the tears slipping down her face.

Simon reached for her hand. 'It doesn't matter. All that matters is that you are safe.' He held her hand and ran his finger round the blue veins at her wrist. 'It doesn't *matter*, love.'

But she had seen his face, and she knew that it did.

When he went away she slept the rest of the afternoon, and when she awoke she opened her eyes to see Patty Bamford sitting by the bed, eyes swollen with recent tears, the bright blonde hair skewered untidily on to the top of her small head.

Instantly both Emma's hands went out to her as she raised herself up dizzily from her pillow.

'I am sorry. Oh, Patty, I can't tell you how sorry I am.'

Patty's head drooped. 'I know. But it was better. Some day I will be able to tell meself it was better.'

'I can't remember what happened.' Emma closed her eyes and heard again the dreadful crashing iron sound of the car tearing into the side where Ben wrenched at the wheel in a futile attempt to evade the smash. 'I hope he didn't suffer much. Oh, Ben. Poor Ben.'

'Ben?' She heard Patty's gasp. 'Ben's going to be okay. Didn't they tell you? Oh, God, love. Fancy letting you think. . . .' She put out a hand and gripped Emma's arm. 'Ben has a smashed leg and a few cracked ribs, that's all, and knowing him he'll be up and about afore long.' Her bright gash of a mouth with the lipstick chewed off at the edges wrenched itself out of shape. 'It is Tracy who's gone. She had one of her chests, and it turned to pneumonia, an' there was nothing they could do. They had warned me they sometimes go that way, her sort, but I can't get over me leaving her with a neighbour so I could go to work, an' it happened when I wasn't there. I should have been holding her, you see.'

All her own distress forgotten for the moment, Emma sat up and pulled the weeping girl into her arms.

'You weren't to know. You mustn't think that. Please . . . oh, please, Patty. Don't cry like that.'

'It were telling Ben.' Patty's voice came muffled. 'He worshipped that kid. Even though she didn't walk right or talk proper, she would do anything for Ben. An' smile! Did you ever know a kid what smiled all the time like what she did?' Patty groped for a tissue and pushed herself away from the bed. 'An' now I've upset you when what I came for was to see how *you* were.' She dabbed yer eyes. 'You've had a miss, haven't you, love?'

Emma nodded, biting her lips. 'But that's nothing compared. I had never really begun to think that what was there was a baby.' She smiled a rueful smile. 'Not till I knew I was losing it, then it mattered.'

Patty scrubbed her eyes, still ringed with the previous day's mascara. 'I've had two, love. Two misses, and the last one I didn't tell nobody about. I just kept on going and thanked God.' She leaned forward, whispering. 'It was that bloke you saw that day you came, an' I wasn't going to have his baby, not if I had to winkle it out of me meself.' She looked round the ward then lowered her voice even more. 'I drank gin from a pint pot and sat in a bath till I pickled meself, an' that got shut of it all right.'

'Oh, Patty.' Emma knew she was going to sleep again, and tried hard not to, but it was no good. And although the last thing she should have remembered was Patty's pinched face with the blue eyes sunk deep into red slits, the face she saw was a man's face, dark with disappointment and a terrible anger.

'Oh, Simon. It's all up with us now.' Her mind said that quite clearly before she slipped into unconsciousness once again.

* * *

She was back home two days afterwards to find that Simon had cancelled his return visit to London and taken the whole week off to look after her.

Emma was touched to find that he had removed the baby things from what was to have been the nursery. Nothing much. She had been too superstitious to buy anything big, remembering how the neighbours would not give a pram or a cot house-room until the last possible moment for fear of what they called tempting fate. Just a couple of matinée coats, and a pile of patterns and a bag of knitting wool she had promised herself to make a start on one day.

And now that day would never come.

Simon was caring and tender, but although he had told her he was used to fending for himself, his undomesticated floundering in the kitchen and the meals he produced - whole soups from tins, and thick wedges of cheese grilled on blackened pieces of toast - were more indicative of a man used to being ministered to.

'I am not ill,' she told him, but her mirror showed a white face with hollowed dark eyes, and when she tried to sleep it was only to wake from a screaming nightmare in which she dreamed her baby was being torn from her, to the background sound of metal crashing into metal.

Once she came down from an enforced afternoon rest to find him seated at the dining-table with papers spread all around him - papers which he pushed guiltily away.

'Simon,' she said softly, 'why don't you go back to work?'

He stared at her in open dismay. 'And leave you all alone?' He shuffled the papers together. 'I thought you were asleep, love. Did the telephone disturb you? It was Harry Gordon asking for some figures. It seems they can't manage without me after all.'

'Then go back.' Emma pulled at the ribbon ties of her pale-cream housecoat. 'I'm not an invalid. The doctor didn't say I had to rest all day.' She smiled, a faint smile that was a mere shadow passing over her features. 'If I were still living in Litchfield Avenue I would be thinking about going back to work myself by now. I'm tough, Simon. Honestly. I'm much tougher than you think.'

'You don't look tough.' He came to her then and pulled her

gently into his arms, but even the way he held her was different. There was no straining her to him, no hardness of his body pressed against hers. He held her as if she were a delicate child, all womanliness vanished, with the passion that had once bound them vanished.

The only reason he still slept with her, Emma had decided, was for the simple reason that in the whole of the house there was still only the one bed. He seemed afraid to come too close, and when she whimpered in the night he got up to make her a cup of tea instead of drawing her close and allowing her to sob her anguish away in the comfort of his arms.

'Go back tomorrow,' she said, and walked slowly upstairs to get dressed, and wonder at the skirt that hung round her waist in loose folds, and the zip that stayed sadly zipped into place.

She wandered round the house like a small pale ghost when he went shamefacedly back to the factory, throwing his briefcase and his document folder into the back of the car.

'If you are sure you will be all right?' He had asked the question so many times, and she had tried to laugh as she almost pushed him through the door.

'Ginny will be coming in,' was the last thing he told her, and when true to his word Ginny appeared, Emma had to start all over again with the assurances of her well-being.

'I am not an invalid. Truly.' She reached up to the dresser shelf for the inevitable coffee mugs. 'Where's the baby?'

'Mother's got him.' Ginny took over and motioned Emma to a chair. 'I thought that maybe. . . .' She looked embarrassed, and busied herself with the electric kettle.

'Now let's get this straight.' Emma pushed her hair back behind her ears. 'I lost my baby, but I hadn't really had time to get used to the idea of it being a baby. I was lucky that I wasn't injured badly, or even killed, so don't *you* start pandering to emotions I haven't got. I am fine, absolutely fine.'

'Then why do you look so bloody awful?' Ginny walked to the fridge and took out a bottle of milk. 'You can have postnatal depression without having had a baby, you know. And if you are going to shout at me and say you're not depressed, then stop wasting your time. If I say you are depressed, then that is what you are. Depressed.'

The kettle came to the boil and she poured the water into

the two waiting mugs. 'They haven't told you that you can't have any more babies, have they?'

Emma was not sure whether the tears in her eyes were from weakness or laughter. She had never known anyone quite like Ginny Boland. Miscarriages and abortions were usually spoken about in hushed tones, with shakes of the head, and meaningful expressions. 'Three children and never a miss,' Mam had said, as if by losing her baby a woman betrayed her own body.

'They said I would be all right,' was all Emma could bring herself to reply. 'It was more the shock than an actual injury.'

'Then the sooner you start another one the better.' Ginny put a steaming mug of coffee in front of Emma and sat down. 'You shouldn't have much difficulty in getting Simon to co-operate.' She took a sip and grimaced. 'I'll never be able to get used to doing without sugar, but I must try. I'll be heavier than Roger soon and can you think of anything less romantic?'

'That girl you first saw coming here.' Emma spoke suddenly, quickly, before she could change her mind, the urge to talk swamping her with a kind of shamed relief. 'She went to a clinic and had an abortion, and although Simon didn't actually say, I know he never forgave her. I asked him last night why he didn't marry her, and though he didn't say, I know it was that.'

'Oh, my God!' Ginny thumped the thick mug down on the breakfast bar. 'Men are such shits, aren't they? Now why did he have to tell you a thing like that? Now, of all times.'

'So when I got pregnant and threatened to do the same, he offered to marry me.' Emma's tone was quite factual, utterly devoid of emotion. She scooped a hair or something from the remains of her coffee. Ginny opened both eyes wide.

'So now you think he doesn't want you? That he feels he married you for nothing?

'Yes.'

'Oh God! Have you asked him?'

'No.'

'Why not?'

Emma clasped both hands together underneath her chin. 'Because I am frightened of the truth. If I lost Simon I would want to die.'

'No, you bloody wouldn't!' Ginny raised her voice. 'You are a beautiful girl. Yes, you are. And you've got all your life in front of you.' She ran her fingers through her short curly hair. 'You wouldn't . . .? She looked frantically round the kitchen as if searching for a lethal weapon. 'You haven't got any tablets upstairs or anything, have you? Because if you have then I am going up to get them.' She stood up, poised for action. 'It's your unstable background, that is what it is. Your mother going off and everything, and your father being sent to prison. You won't accept happiness. It scares the pants off you. That is what it is. You *are* depressed,' she finished triumphantly.

'Okay, you win.' Emma managed a smile, and sensing her change of mood, Ginny changed the subject and showed Emma the leaflets she had brought with details of the various courses to be had for mature students.

'Now is the time to make a start. Roger says he will come in and have a talk to you. He's really keen. It takes one compulsive student to recognize another. Thank God I never had any academic tendencies. Shitty nappies fulfil my leanings. I could sometimes lick my baby all over.' She clapped a hand to her mouth. 'Oh, God! I always say the wrong thing.'

'You are the nicest friend I have ever had.'

Ginny whipped round at Emma's words, pity welling up in her and spilling out into her expression. For a moment they stood and stared at each other, with the width of the kitchen floor between them.

Why, Ginny was wondering, why can't two women put their arms round each other and just hug the pain away without being thought abnormal? Why couldn't she take that small girl into her arms and pat her sorrow away? Why was she so conditioned that the very thought was taboo?

'What *you* need is a mother,' was all she could manage to say, and as she ran back to her own house through the gap in the privet hedge she was swearing at herself for once again putting her big foot into it.

'Oh, Mum,' she said, as her mother looked up from stirring something at the cooker. Then she scooped up her baby from the floor and buried her flushed face in the downy softness of his fluff of hair. 'Oh, Mum.'

*   *   *

When Emma went up to the bedroom the first thing she did was to take the slip of paper with her own mother's address on it from the drawer in the dressing-table.

She smoothed it out and read the neat writing over again so that the words were imprinted on her mind. But the words she was hearing in her head were the words Ginny had tactlessly thrown out as she left the house: 'What *you* need is a mother.'

The ache that was in Emma's chest dissolved as the tears filled her eyes. She walked over to the bed and sat down on the green spread, hunched over like an invalid with her hands hanging loose between her knees.

You could not mourn a mother you had never known. Okay, she accepted that. A child identified with the woman who brought her up. Right? And that woman had been Mam. So far so good. Emma drew her eyebrows together, then rubbed the place with her finger as an ache like a thousand hammers beat rhythmically.

Her mother was an unknown quantity. Emma knew nothing at all about her, because every time she had asked, out of what was surely a normal curiosity, John Sparrow had clammed up tight.

'When was my mother's birthday? I mean, what month was she born in?'

'Why do you want to know?'

She did not know why, but somehow it mattered. Like wanting to know the colour of her mother' eyes, or whether she had a sense of humour. Whether she read a lot, or whether she was musical. Whether she had wanted her baby and, most important of all, why she had walked away?

It was the sense of rejection her daughter could not come to terms with, even though she knew there must have been two sides to the argument, because anyone knew that there were *always* two sides. Mam must have come on the scene *before* Emma's own mother went off. She must have. And yet how did a man like John Sparrow have two women at one and the same time?

The questions were now part of the hammering in Emma's head, as she saw in her memory Mrs Collins sitting on the settee, as close to her father as if they were actually touching.

And what of him? Was John Sparrow a lady's man? That

221

small, shrivelled, coughing man – did he possess some magnetism that enslaved women? Sexually? Was it his infidelity that had driven her mother away? And why had she not taken Emma with her?

'Your mother has married and has children of her own.' John Sparrow had shouted that in angry frustration when Emma had rebelled against Mam's strict discipline, and cried for her own mother.

'But *I* was her baby first!' Emma had yelled back.

And now because of her deep unhappiness, because of Simon's attitude of uncaring solicitude, she wanted her mother so desperately that her whole body ached with the wanting. She wanted loving arms around her; she wanted a comforting shoulder to cry on; she wanted to sob and wail her sadness away.

She wanted her mother.

Getting up from the bed and walking over to the long cupboard, she took out a short jacket and slipped a silk square from the rail on the door. .

The house was closing in on her. She felt ill, but not too ill to get out. She was still losing blood from the miscarriage, and even as she stood there she felt a warm trickle between her legs.

It would be better outside. There would be the cold clear Lancashire air on her face, and more than that, she would be away from the house so filled with Chloe's choice of furniture, Chloe's choice of curtains. Green, always green. The colour of jealousy.

Taking her leather shoulder-bag from the hall table, Emma went out and shut the door with a final-sounding click behind her.

Then, shivering a little, she tied the scarf round her head and began to walk away in the direction of the bus stop.

In the glass-fronted office of Delta Dresses, Simon Martin glanced at his watch and reached for the telephone. There was just time before the meeting with the shop steward to ring Emma. He nodded as Mrs Kelly switched off her electric typewriter, gathered her handbag and a magazine together and, right to the minute, went out of the office en route for the canteen and her morning coffee.

Harry Gordon was out in the yard talking to the van drivers. If Simon turned and looked down through the high window he could see him standing there, a squat black beetle silhouette, writing busily on a clipboard.

He had been right about Harry. He had the common touch, human relations they called it, and the men, although they laughed at him, respected him and knew he always knew what he was talking about. Simon dialled. Yes, Harry Gordon would keep the flag flying over Delta Dresses, and once the mail order side was tidied up Simon could really begin to think in terms of moving back down south. His parents, before leaving for their cruise, had hinted that their house might be too big for them and declared their intention of looking round for a smaller place. A bungalow maybe to ease the strain on Bernard Martin's tired heart.

That meant that Simon could move into their house with Emma. That meant there would be no trauma of searching for the right place, with hours off to drive Emma round, because since the accident she had cancelled her driving lessons and showed no signs of ever wanting to take the wheel again.

Simon listened to the ringing tone, scribbling a list of figures with his free hand.

'Come on. Come on, love.' His voice was sharp with impatience which changed to anxiety as there was no reply.

As he faced the shop steward across his desk he forced himself to moderate his growing irritation. Where the devil *was* she? He had left her that morning looking so pale and diminished that his instinct had been to turn back and take her in his arms.

Women sometimes got queer notions in their heads when they lost a baby. He must have read or heard that somewhere. But it had not been a full-term baby. It had not been much bigger that the one Chloe had deliberately 'gotten rid of ' – to use her own phraseology.

He stared into the red face of the protesting man jabbing with a pencil at a sheaf of papers, and tried to smooth his own expression into one of co-operation. A strike was all they needed at this time: an all-out strike would finish Delta

Dresses, and the stupid, bigoted sod couldn't realize that. Simon nodded, agreed and went into what Chloe would have called his charm routine.

'I am sure that between us we can work out a compromise.' His voice was smooth and his manner filled with reassurance, but all the time his mind was telling him that whilst Chloe had apparently shrugged off losing a baby, Emma could not.

Chloe was Chloe, and Emma was Emma.

'You were saying?' He raised an inquiring eyebrow at the calmer face of the man facing him acoss the cluttered desk.

'I was saying my members won't stand for it,' the man said, pushing his already jutting chin forward to challenge Simon. Eyeball to eyeball.

When Simon went into the house that evening it was just like the last time, with empty rooms and everything neat and clean, like a house built specially for the Ideal Homes exhibition. He called upstairs, then getting no reply went into the kitchen and stood there, still holding his brief-case, a tall, bewildered man with shoulders already beginning to stoop a little from the weight of too much responsibility.

It was strange, but he had never really felt at home in this house. It was as if Chloe had left too much of herself in every corner, while Emma had left no imprint at all.

It was cold too, now that the harsh bleak winter was coming. Lonely, cold and about as cosy as an army barracks. He went into the living-room and threw the brief-case on to the velvet sofa.

Was this how it was for Emma when he was away or out all day? Simon walked over to the sideboard and reached for the decanter. She had never said. Not once had she ever complained of being lonely, not even that time she had flared up at him, and he had drunk too much and been sick upstairs.

There was a sad soft sighing in the trees outside, and the darkness was already inky black. Simon put his glass down untouched and ran upstairs, taking them two at a time. Where the devil *was* she?

Chloe, he decided, must have been thinking of the warmth of the sun back in the States when she had chosen the colour scheme for this bedroom. This cool sharp green needed blue skies outside, not an infrequent sun which, because of the northern outlook, did no more that touch the outer wall first thing in the mornings.

Emma, he felt sure, would have chosen pink, or a soft pale yellow. He knew that instinctively, and yet he had brought her here and expected her to like it; expected her to be overwhelmed by the contrast with the house she had left in Litchfield Avenue. Expected her to be *grateful*.

Oh, God, what an unfeeling, patronizing, insensitive dope he had been!

He turned to go back downstairs and as he turned saw the slip of paper on the dressing-table.

The name and address meant nothing to him. Birmingham? He frowned. He had stayed overnight in Birmingham once or twice on business, stopping at a hotel in the centre, all black plastic, vivid carpets and ultra-modern light fittings. He tried to think. . . . As far as he remembered, Emma had never mentioned knowing anyone there. Picking up the piece of paper he held it in his hand, trying to reason why it was there in the first place. With any significance? With intent?

Outside the wind sighed and rain lashed the window. He left the room to walk slowly downstairs, to stand for a while staring at the telephone on the hall table.

He was uneasy without knowing why he should be so uneasy. The last thing he wanted to do was to ring Litchfield Avenue and have that woman with the biting tongue answer the phone, but he had to know. There was no way he could decide what to do, not without finding out first if Emma was there. Not without knowing she was safe.

He braced himself for the sound of Mrs Collins's strident voice. He had only spoken on the telephone to her once before, but she had yelled at the top of her voice as if she thought she was speaking to someone in Outer Mongolia.

'Hello? Yes? Who is it?'

John Sparrow answered the telephone only when he was forced to. To him a ringing telephone spelled bad news, or at least something unpleasant. He shifted the cigarette from one side of his mouth to the other, narrowing his eyes against the upcurling smoke.

'Who?'

'It's Simon Martin. Simon.' He wished he hadn't rung now.

If Emma had been there she was sure to have answered the telephone herself. Simon drummed with impatient fingers on the polished half-moon table. 'I was wondering. Is Emma there?'

John Sparrow's hacking cough exploded in Simon's ear like nails rattling in a tin can. 'No, she's not here. She'll be at home likely as not on a night like this. It's pissing down.'

'I *am* ringing from home.' Simon bit his lips hard. 'Thanks, anyway. She's probably next door. Thanks a lot.'

'Mrs Collins has gone to bingo.'

'Oh, yes.' Simon glanced down at the slip of paper, frowning. 'How is she?'

'Fair to middling. Our Joe's off school with a cold.'

'Do you know anyone . . .?' Simon had made his mind up. 'Do you know anyone called. . . .' He read the name and address from the paper, waited, then held the receiver away from his ear and sighed. They had been cut off, or the phone was out of order. Damn, that was all he needed.

'Say that again.' John Sparrow's hoarse croak of a voice crackled into life again. '*What* did you say?'

Slowly, pronouncing every syllable, Simon read the name and address again. 'I've just come across it and, well, I wondered if it meant anything to you?'

He seemed to wait an interminable time for his father-in-law to stop coughing, then his reply caused Simon's eyes to narrow and his heartbeats to quicken.

'Mean anything to me, did you say? Oh, aye, well, it doesn't *mean* nothing to me, but I know who it is all right.'

'Then who is it?' Simon tried to curb his irritation. 'Is it somebody you know?'

'It's only Emma's bloody mother, isn't it?' John Sparrow began to cough, and was still coughing when Simon slowly replaced the receiver.

Seventeen

Getting there had been almost too much. Emma had waited at bus stops, walked in the rain with head bent and finally, when she reached her destination, wondered why she had come.

There had been a need to talk; she had known that much. A powerful ache somewhere deep inside her, and a desperate urge to get out of the house. But when Patty Bamford opened the door to her she knew she had been right to come.

Here was sincerity. Here was caring, and here was a girl who because of her own deep unhappiness understood.

Patty, in the short time since her hospital visit, had come to terms. She would be coming to terms perhaps for the rest of her life, making the best and accepting the inevitable. Her face was as rouged as if she were made up for the stage, blue eyes ringed with black, and cheeks shaded into hollows with a blusher of a strange coppery tinge. She had just been on the point of going out to see about a full-time job as a cleaner-cum-usherette at one of the town's smaller cinemas, but as she stared in surprise at Emma's face she recognized heartbreak, and acted accordingly.

'Come on in, love. I'll put the kettle on. Our Ben's shaping up grand. He'll be out in a couple of weeks on crutches for a bit, but knowing him he'll be shut of them before long. He's the life and soul of the ward he's in, and every time I go he asks about you. I reckon he'll always fancy you, but knowing Ben he'll never say.'

Emma glanced round the room and, coming straight from her own comfortable house, was struck afresh with its shabby neglect. All Tracy's things had disappeared, the broken push-cart she had used to get around with, the dummy rolled to a corner of the room, the little cardigan draped over the back of a chair.

'I wish I could think of something to say,' she said, sitting down gratefully and leaning her head back against the greasy upholstery of the small upright settee. 'That time in the hospital. I never got a chance to say much, I seem to have been so full of my own problems; yet when I think what you have faced, mine are nothing.'

'You mean us both losing our babies?' Patty was like Ginny Boland. No beating about the bush. And though their backgrounds were completely different Emma realized how very alike they were. It was she, Emma, who was mixed up.

She shook her head from side to side as if trying to compose her thinking into some kind of normality. 'No, Patty. You are quite wrong. I told you when you came in to see me at the hospital: you can't possibly compare what has happened to me and what happened to you.'

'I'll make us a cup of tea; you look awful,' Patty said, just as Ginny had said. 'You shouldn't be out if you ask me. It's the shock coming out. Shock can do funny things.'

Emma watched her light the gas and bend down, putting her plucked eyebrows into jeopardy as she lit a cigarette before putting the kettle over the flame. She shivered and wondered why she had come out on an afternoon like this wearing only a short jacket. She considered quite calmly the possibility that she might be going mad. Making a determined effort to pull herself together, she spoke quietly.

'No, Patty. What you lost was a child. What *I* lost was a hardly-accepted *idea* of a child. There's a big difference.'

Patty smiled. 'Ben always said you talked lovely, and you do.' She put the milk bottle on the table beside two cups. 'I expect it is because you were clever at school. I know I wasn't. My teachers all gave me up, but then I was hardly ever there, and when I was I didn't listen. I was just waiting for the day when I could leave.'

She was deliberately biding her time. As far as she could make out, Emma Sparrow, or whatever her name was now, was on the verge of cracking up. She had turned up here, for what reason Patty hadn't fathomed yet, but she guessed it was because there was simply nowhere else for her to go. If she had

Emma's gift for putting her thoughts into words she would say that the anguished girl sitting so still was like a lost soul. Patty screwed up her face with the effort of her thinking. Maybe biding time wasn't what was needed in this case. Just maybe a straight out-with-it talk was called for. She half turned away, telling herself she was proper flummoxed.

Emma *needed* to open her heart, that much was certain. Not necessarily to a close friend, so Patty Bamford might be just the job. The kettle came to the boil and Patty poured the boiling water into a brown teapot. Now, if she was clever, she would know what to say. Her eyebrows drew together in a deep frown. She remembered the time she had run out in the night with her lip cut and bruised after a bashing. She had run out in her nightie and met a policeman down the street, and had told him her whole life story. And he had said bloody nowt; just walked her home and said nowt.

But his hand on her arm had been caring and she had felt a lot better.

'Here y'are, love.' She passed a cup of tea over to Emma. 'I hope you don't want a biscuit 'cos I haven't got none.'

Emma's mouth curved upwards slightly into a stiff semblance of a smile.

'It's funny how everybody puts the kettle on at times like this, isn't it?'

Patty sat down and waited. Any minute now and she'd be out with it. It wasn't about the baby, she could stake her life on that. Maybe, just maybe, a nudge in the right direction wouldn't come amiss.

'Having trouble with your fella, love? They are all shits, so you can tell me.'

But suddenly, sipping the hot strong tea, Emma knew she could not talk about Simon to Patty Bamford. It must be her natural reticence or something. Her eyes softened with the threat of tears. Some women could sit opposite a marriage guidance counsellor and stumble through the debris of their relationship with their husband. And maybe it acted as a catharsis. Some women could criticize their husbands, comparing notes, describing their man's filthy habits, or lack of feeling, then agreeing that all men were the same, with not a good one among them. She had often heard women in the avenue doing just that.

But it wasn't for her.

Simon wasn't a monster. It wasn't his fault that he could not feel the same way as she did about him. Simon was so special that just remembering how special he was made her weak with love. She liked and admired Patty, but discussing her marriage with her would be as disloyal as being unfaithful. Because, oh, dear God, what she felt for Simon was precious. His indifference was *her* problem – just one more problem Emma had to work out for herself. An' if she did not feel so ill, so diminished, she was sure she could think it through. Maybe it would have helped if she had been forced to sit at the buttonhole machine hour by hour with her mind transcending the mechanical movements of her fingers. She wasn't sure. She wasn't really sure of anything any more.

Patty was waiting. The weather was closing in so that soon darkness would fall. It was time she was getting back, but the effort of making a move was at the moment beyond her. Two nights almost entirely without sleep had left her dazed with a longing to close her eyes that was overwhelming. Emma reached out and put the cup on the table before it slipped from her nerveless fingers.

Why was she here? She could hardly remember getting here. All she had known was that she had to get away, out of the house where Chloe, dressed always in green to match the cushions and the curtains, laughed at her from every corner.

Green, the colour of jealousy. But whose jealousy? Her own?

'That's right, love.' Patty's voice seemed to be coming from a long, long way away. 'Just you lie back and put your feet up and have a bit of a sleep. C'mon, shift over and I'll put this cushion behind your head.'

She stood looking down at the girl with a face as white as bleached linen. So it *was* fella trouble! An' if Emma didn't want to say, then she didn't want to say. But one thing was sure. She would have to get herself sorted out somehow, or she would end up where Patty's own mother had ended up, an' that was tearing out her hair in handfuls in a loony bin.

Tenderly Patty covered Emma's legs with the ironing blanket, the nearest thing to hand. She shook her head from side to side and sighed.

Men! She could shoot the lot of them. But just now there was something more practical she had to do. Emma was not, in Patty's forthright opinion, fit to go back home on two buses. An' if the telephone box at the corner of the street hadn't been vandalized, she would ring that husband up and ask – no, *tell* him to come and fetch her. Patty tightened her mouth as she remembered the tall dark man chatting her up over the bar counter at the pub. He had seemed nice enough, but then with bloody men, who could tell? Posh he might be, but he wasn't good enough for Emma, an' that was telling him!

Boy, could she write a book about men!

An' now she was going to go over the street and ask the fella who worked a taxi round if he was free to run Emma home when she woke up. The cab was outside the house – she had seen it when she let Emma in.

Caring nothing that she was wearing down-trodden bedroom slippers and her pinny, Patty let herself out of the house, leaving the door wide open and, cursing the rain wetting her elaborate hairdo, ran flat-footed across the street.

Simon Martin, after an uncharacteristically long period of indecision, had rung directory enquiries, only to be told that the Birmingham address was not on their list of subscribers. He had picked up the glass of whisky, looked at it, then put it down again. That was no way round a problem.

He was used to acting quickly, making snap decisions. He could act or talk his way out of any dilemma, but now, faced with Emma's disappearance, he quite literally did not know what to do. For once in his life he was at the mercy of his own emotions, and they were swirling round his blood-stream so that his heart thumped against his ribs and his legs buckled beneath him as he ran upstairs.

It was quite dark outside the house, and now the rain was sweeping down. Simon stood irresolute in the middle of the bedroom, a fist clenched against his forehead.

'Emma!' Had he cried her name aloud, or was it a moan coming from somewhere inside him? He tried to remember how she had been when he left the house that morning, and all he could see was her little white face and her soft brown eyes gazing mutely at him, as if she were pleading with him.

Hardly knowing what he was doing, he opened a drawer and threw a shirt into an overnight bag, then went into the bathroom to collect his shaving things. If Emma had gone to find her mother, then he was going to find her, and when he found her . . . if he found her . . . oh, God, he *had* to find her.

He clicked the locks of the bag shut, and took a last look round the bedroom. He stopped and rubbed his hand in a circular motion round his chin. *Would* she have gone off just like that, without telling him? Because if she had, then she had needed love so desperately that she had been driven to find a woman, a stranger, who just happened to be her mother, in her search for it.

Stumbling downstairs he stood once more by the telephone. Ought he to call the police? He picked up the receiver, then put it down again, biting his lips. Single-handed almost, he had, over the past weeks, steered the business into what seemed to be calmer waters, and yet now he was as indecisive, as jittery as an adolescent schoolboy.

He was standing there, the case on the floor by his side, tears of frustration stinging behind his eyes, when the front door opened.

And Emma was there . . . pale and bedraggled in her short jacket and still damp skirt, her brown hair wisping round her face. For a moment neither of them spoke, then almost without volition he stretched out his arms to hold her close, straining her to him.

He found the words would not come. His throat had closed; he could only keep her there, safe in his arms, his heartbeats jerking painfully.

'I thought you had left me,' he managed to whisper at last. 'I thought you had gone away. I didn't know what to do.' He raised his head and she saw the anguish etched deep on his thin face.

Then he showed her the Birmingham address written on the slip of paper, and saw the emotion drift across her expression like a shadow creeping into sunlight and back again.

She was so small that her head came only to his chin, but as she reached up and held his face between her hands he grew calm and still. And now for the first time in their turbulent relationship she was master. When she took him by the hand and led him upstairs, he followed her like a child.

On the landing she turned to him. 'I've been to Patty Bamford's house, and I didn't get wet coming back because she sent me home in a taxi. I got wet going there.'

She took him into the bedroom, shrugged off her jacket and began to unzip her skirt. But he would not let her. He wanted to do everything for her, to show her that his caring went so deep it was a physical ache inside him.

So she stood quietly and allowed him to undress her, and his hands were the gentle hands of both lover and friend as he took her nightdress from beneath her pillow and lowered it over her head.

He brought her housecoat and tied the ribbons clumsily, but she made no move to help him, knowing that this was what he needed to do, although her hands ached to touch his thick hair and pull him close to her.

Then he led her downstairs, past the cold and cheerless sitting-room into the warmth of the kitchen.

'You must sit there,' he told her, pulling a chair out. Then he broke four eggs into a bowl and took the hand-whisk down from its rack on the wall.

'I am a wizard with omelettes,' he told her gravely. 'Which shall it be? Cheese or herbs?'

'Herbs, please.'

Emma watched him with love, aching with love as he stood by the cooker in his dark business suit, tipping the pan so that the beaten eggs ran evenly. And still she made no move to help, knowing that this was the way it had to be.

'There!' he said at last, cutting the omelette carefully into two pieces. He set a plate in front of her and placed a fork in her hand. 'Now we must eat. *You* must eat it all up, love, and then we can talk.'

She smiled. 'It's lovely, Simon.' Then she put her fork down. 'I wasn't going to Birmingham. I am just not made like that.' She tried to eat again, but the food stuck in her throat. 'Oh, yes, my mother does live there. You found that out?'

He nodded, his own meal untouched.

'I realized that she is only my mother because she gave birth to me. I am too . . . too sensible, too much a product of Mam's upbringing to make a dramatic gesture like that. Anyway, she would probably have had a pink fit if her long-lost daughter had turned up on the doorstep without warning. It would have been an embarrassment for both of us, don't you see?'

Simon pushed his plate away. There was so much that he *did* see, so much he should have seen long ago, and it was important that he said the right words. Far more important than giving in to the overwhelming urge to take this small girl in his arms.

'But you *needed* her. You needed the thought of her. Your mother symbolized all that need, didn't she?' He ran his fingers through his hair and his eyebrows drew together in a puzzled frown. 'Then why Patty Bamford, Emma? Why on earth, out of all the world, Patty Bamford?'

What he desperately wanted to say was 'Why not *me*?', but he knew he was afraid of what the answer might have been.

Emma pushed her own plate away and clasped her hands together. She too realized the enormity of what she was going to say, but being the way she was could only tell the honest unvarnished truth.

'Patty Bamford knows what it feels like to be lonely. Oh, she has had men, lots of them I should imagine, but she is still about the loneliest person I know. So I thought if I went there she might say something, something I could identify with that would help.'

'And did she?'

Emma shook her head. 'When I tried to tell her how I felt the words weren't there.' She stared straight into his troubled face. 'I just wanted to come home. To you,' she added softly.

Simon took a deep breath. 'And I had failed you. No, don't say anything. Let me finish. Whenever you needed me I wasn't there. I was so wrapped up in the business, so engrossed in making it tick over that I couldn't see that I was neglecting you, shutting you out.'

Emma sighed. He was trying so hard, and still he hadn't said the words she wanted to hear.

'But every woman married to a man like you has that to put up with.' She was achingly serious. 'I understood, Simon. No, maybe it's been, as Mam would have said, six of one and half a dozen of the other.' Then her brown eyes widened with

234

indignation. 'But remember one thing, Simon Martin! I am not another Chloe, nor am I another Ellen. You mustn't use either one of them as a yardstick when you're measuring *me* up!'

Suddenly, without warning, Simon banged his fist down so that Emma blinked in surprise.

'Don't say that! Don't ever *think* that! No, you are not Chloe, little sweetheart. Nor are you Ellen.' His whole expression softened. 'You are, and always will be, the love of my life. The love I have wanted and been waiting for. . . . You are beautiful and kind, and sweet, and unselfish, and I wish I could change into the kind of man you deserve.' He held out his hand, and she saw the sparkle of tears in his eyes. 'And I can't promise to change all that much. I will always be dashing off to some meeting; often doing sums in my mind when I should be listening to you.' His voice broke so that what he said next came out in a hoarse whisper. 'But I will always love you, Emma. Always. And I will cherish you to the best of my cherishing. So now you know.'

It was Emma who moved first. She moved quickly and put her arms round this proud, clever, often thoughtless man she loved with all her being.

'Oh, dear God, how I love you,' he whispered into the satin ribbons of her housecoat.

And he could not see the blinding joy on her face as she pressed his head close, tangling her fingers in his hair.

'Keep on doing just that,' she said softly. The joy was there in her voice and, hearing it, he sighed, and was at peace.

MAGGIE CRAIG

Marie Joseph

From the natural successor to Catherine Cookson

At the turn of the century, the north of England was a hard, bleak world. A world where the only things in plenty were work and poverty – where joy and love were words in someone else's book. A world where men were resigned and women oppressed. It was here that Maggie Craig was born.

Strong-willed and spirited, as rebellious as she was beautiful, Maggie Craig flew in the face of the harshness of her life – and found a man she truly loved. But that passion was to cost her dearly all her life . . .

A LEAF IN THE WIND

Marie Joseph

She was hardship's child – born to struggle and to serve.

He was fortune's favourite – born to flourish and be served.

They lived worlds apart. Jenny was the girl from the cat-meat shop, born into squalor and defeat. Paul Tunstall was a soldier and a gentleman, arrogant and charming, with his silver-light eyes and boyish smile. And yet from the moment they met there was a spark between them – and their separate lives of pain and loneliness seemed to beckon to each other.

But should she succumb to that plea in his eyes, to that longing in herself? Should she cross the line of class, the boundaries of propriety? Dare Jenny risk all to lose herself to love?

Emma Blair

WHERE NO MAN CRIES

Glasgow between the wars. It was a town divided, taut with violence and steeped in hardship – a town with no time for dreams.

Angus McBain knew that better than anyone. Being poor in Glasgow had killed his father, aged his mother before her time, and crushed with fear and frustration everyone he knew. But Angus was different. He would never be content to stay where they had put him, doing the job the bosses allowed him, wanting only a woman of his own kind. Angus McBain wanted to be his own man, to make his own place – and to share all he had and was with the woman he so passionately loved...

MARIE JOSEPH

Marie Joseph is one of Britain's top-selling authors and her books are available from Arrow. You can buy them from your local bookshop or newsagent, or you can order them direct through the post. Just tick the titles you require and complete the form below.

☐	EMMA SPARROW	£1.50
☐	FOOTSTEPS IN THE PARK	£1.50
☐	GEMINI GIRLS	£1.60
☐	A LEAF IN THE WIND	£1.75
☐	MAGGIE CRAIG	£1.75
	Non-fiction	
☐	ONE STEP AT A TIME	£1.50

Postage _____

Total _____

☐ Please tick this box if you would like to receive a free sheet of biographical information about Marie Joseph.

ARROW BOOKS, BOOKSERVICE BY POST, PO BOX 29, DOUGLAS, ISLE OF MAN, BRITISH ISLES

Please enclose a cheque or postal order made out to Arrow Books Limited for the amount due including 10p per book for postage and packing for orders within the UK and 12p for overseas orders.

Please print clearly

NAME ....

ADDRESS ....

....

Whilst every effort is made to keep prices down and to keep popular books in print, Arrow Books cannot guarantee that prices will be the same as those advertised here or that the books will be available.